The Devil's Doorbell

A woman's pleasure is a dangerous thing. A primal appetite that, once awakened, can never be sated. A secret that gives power to those who know it. A magic that, once unleashed, can never be contained.

Some say the clitoris is the devil's doorbell, set to summon him forth at the merest touch…

It's time to ring the bell.

Here are seven tales of sexual empowerment and erotic defiance, featuring the hottest storytellers of erotic fiction.

The Devil's Doorbell

AN EROTIC ANTHOLOGY

Anne Calhoun, Jeffe Kennedy

Delphine Dryden, Megan Hart

Christine d'Abo, Megan Mulry

M. O'Keefe

Copyright © 2016 by ANNE CALHOUN, MEGAN HART, M. O'KEEFE, CHRISTINE D'ABO, JEFFE KENNEDY, MEGAN MULRY, DELPHINE DRYDEN
Print Edition

All rights reserved.

No part of this book may be reproduced in any form or by any electronic or mechanical means, including information storage and retrieval systems, without written permission from the author, except for the use of brief quotations in a book review.

Contents

In the Garden	ANNE CALHOUN	1
Exact Warm Unholy	JEFFE KENNEDY	47
Red Leather	DELPHINE DRYDEN	105
Drowning on Dry Land	MEGAN HART	137
Devil in the Dark	CHRISTINE D'ABO	197
London Calling	MEGAN MULRY	227
We Are All Found Things	M. O'KEEFE	283

In the Garden

Anne Calhoun

Forbidden fruit is the most delicious…

A wedding in the bucolic English countryside offers Kelsey ripe temptation in the form of a hot groomsman, Julian. Will the illicit attraction satisfy an old craving or stoke a new desire?

Chapter 1

Mr. and Mrs. John Sewell
request the pleasure of
your company at the marriage
of their daughter
Sophia Helen
to
Mr. Martin Fairfax
at Fairfax House, Wiltshire
on Saturday, August 27, 2016

THE PUB IS a solid wall of noise and people by the time I arrive. I shoulder my way into the bar, weaving between tables, past the big screen television broadcasting the rugby, to the patio overlooking the fields rolling down to the river. Sophie's text says they've staked out a big table and two of the dartboards.

"Kelsey," Sophie calls. She hugs me and kisses both of my cheeks. "Hello, my darling girl."

"Hello, my happy girl," I say, laughing. Her cheeks are flushed, her eyes bright, and no wonder. In two days she's marrying one of the few really good men I've ever met.

"How was your trip? No baggage?" Still holding my shoulders, she checks beside and behind me. Sophie's a toucher, even more so when she's a little plastered.

"Fine, and I left it with the bartender."

"Copenhagen?"

"Glorious in the summer, as always." I'm technically on a business trip from New York City, efficiently bookending the long weekend of Sophie's wedding with meetings in Copenhagen, then in London. Fortunately it's the kind of work trip that involves lots of business dinners at charming restaurants with sidewalk seating, sharing bottles of wine. The Europeans are so…European.

"Well, you've got a lovely weekend here. The weather looks fabulous. I'll take you out for a walk tomorrow and show you the estate. In the meantime, come and say hello to everyone. Then we'll get you a drink."

"Everyone" includes Martin's friends from uni, Sophie's older sister, and miscellaneous family who have descended on the charming little village of Dockery Norton for the wedding. Sophie's been my best friend since my exchange year in college; when I moved back to the US we started trading summer holidays at my family's farm in Pennsylvania and her family's house on Cornwall's coast. I'm two glasses of wine into the evening and have just started putting names to faces of extended family members when one appears, both familiar and impossible, that makes me stop mid-sentence.

Dirty blond hair, longish and swept back from his face. Brown eyes shot with gold. The build is right, broad through the shoulders, slender through the hips. The stance is right, casual, knowing, confident. The attitude is right, radiating roguish charm. My heart is pounding, and a hot thrill ignites in my belly before my brain catches up.

Can't be. Not here, my brain shouts, but my body isn't listening. Instead it's dumping all manner of endorphins and hormones into my system, setting off a haze of desire.

"Have you met Julian before?" Sophie's tone is curious. "He's Martin's favorite cousin—best man, of course, but went to school at St Andrews."

Of course it's not *him*. Just his double, right down to his full, distinctive, mesmerizing lips. They promise a debauchery that's familiar, and dangerous. I allow myself one more second to gape while Julian focuses, brow furrowed and plush lips firmly set, on a conversation between Martin and Sophie's sister, Cathy. Then I tear my gaze back to Sophie's face. "No. I've not had the pleasure."

Sophie draws my arm through hers. "Let's introduce you, then."

JULIAN RANDALL SHAKES my hand, kisses my cheek. It's all very proper, but the fleeting touch sends sparks flying over my nerves. He flirts, checks me out in that automatic way of bad boys the world over, cataloging, admiring, but not showing his hand; the night is young, the weekend even younger. He's wearing fitted jeans the color of the wheat bending in the summer breeze, a white button-down shirt, and his hair has furrows in it where he's raked it back from his face.

Martin draws Julian back into a running argument about the events of a long-ago summer, the outcome of which seems to involve a highly desirable girl. They make a big deal out of relating the details in stage whispers designed to reach Sophie's ears; she rolls her eyes and ignores them. Martin, for all his short height and amiable demeanor, cut a wide swath through the girls in our year at uni. I'm relieved to leave that conversation and get swept up in the bridal party's comparisons of their dresses.

I try not to stare at Julian.

I try rather hard, and succeed most of the time. Through the darts games and the walk along the footpath back to Fairfax House, and the next day, through the brunch and rehearsal and more walks through the sun-drenched summer air to the garden and round the estate, I try to think not about him, but about landscape, architecture, history. The sixteenth-century, gray stone house sits adjacent to a large, walled garden, where the wedding and reception will be held. A flagstone walk bisects the lawn from the front door to the wrought iron garden gate. A twelve-foot-high brick wall smudged with yellow and white lichen encloses the grass and lower level of flower beds, while a second level is reached by rounded stone steps set into the back of the green swath.

It's all straight out of a Jane Austen novel. I half expect to see Lizzie and Jane emerge from the house, pulling on their gloves while they wait for the carriage to take them to Meryton. Even when we're clustered around the large pine table in the kitchen, sharing the meals Martin's mum makes for us, I don't stare. Much. The house is crammed full of people. I focus intently on aunts and uncles, cousins and family friends, force my brain to branch through the family tree I've pieced together after years of knowing Sophie and Martin, call up names of children, details about home improvement projects, career changes, exotic trips. I limit myself to what I think are quick glances between conversations.

Until he catches me doing it. One minute he's across the parlor, losing rather loudly and badly at chess to Martin's twelve-year-old nephew, and the next minute he's behind me, leaning over the back of the settee to pick up my empty wineglass.

"You should take a picture. It would last longer."

My face heats in a rush, and I look away, overcome by a dark throb of hurt feelings blending with the lust that got me into trouble in the first place.

"More wine?" he asks the group in general. A chorus of *yes, please* rises. All I can do is nod. To distract myself from what's rapidly growing into an obsession, while he's gone, I rehearse a comment about the final book in the Maria Ferrante series, and strategically time the delivery to coincide with his return bearing glasses.

Getting caught should stop me. It doesn't, because whether by accident or design, he braces a forearm on the mantel and joins a conversation with Martin, placing him directly in my line of sight. Backlit by the fire, I can see the silhouette of his arm and chest through the fine cotton of his shirt. This time he catches me straight away, and this time, there's a challenge in those tiger eyes.

I lift my chin and look away. Sophie's sister Cathy draws me aside for a conversation about the flowers. I feel the weight of his gaze even after we leave the sitting room.

EVERY TWENTY-SOMETHING WOMAN has an ex-boyfriend story. There's nothing original about mine. Good girl, the kind who's prioritized school and work over sex and dating, meets bad boy. Good girl falls for bad boy. Bad boy, who prefers freedom to fidelity, breaks her heart by changing his relationship status on Facebook and posting pictures of the other woman.

"Stop being so melodramatic," I say to my face reflected in a gilt-framed mirror hanging in one of Fairfax House's several bathrooms. I am, after all, a project manager for a global corporation. I make my living nailing down deliverables and deadlines. Melodrama doesn't get the job done. "He didn't break your heart. He...bruised it."

There's nothing like discovering via social media you're not worth a conversation, or even a text, to bruise to the bone.

I run my finger along one of the marks, feeling the raised edge. The gilt is dull, scratched in places. Left by a careless maid, or was the mirror a hasty replacement purchased from a jumble sale? No matter. I sweep my hair back from my face, cup my hands under the tap, and swallow a few handfuls of water to cool my heated body.

So what if the bruise still throbs if I so much as think about it? So what if seeing Julian, my ex's doppelgänger, is like pressing down, hard? I've learned my lesson. I'll hide my risky preoccupation, protect my heart. We're in the middle of a wedding. No one has to know.

Especially Julian.

THE WEDDING BEGINS without a hitch, easy enough to do when the vicar is an old family friend included in the lunch party, and starts the ceremony by rising to his feet and saying, "Shall we?"

Sunlight pours through the tall windows as we bridesmaids adjourn with Sophie to the dining room to fuss over bouquets and check our lipstick. When we're ready, Sophie's sister Cathy leans out the front door and gives the okay sign to the musicians, Martin's teenage cousins on the harp and the cello. They play the Happy Birthday song until Martin turns around and shouts *Oy!* at them. Everyone laughs; the musicians compose themselves and start in on "The Swan" by Saint Saëns. The notes linger in the air, rich and evocative.

The groomsmen are arranged alongside Martin, something I

see as we bridesmaids precede Sophie to the white arbor arch. During the mercifully short service I'm thinking about not wobbling on my heels in the grass, not the orders of bridesmaids to groomsmen, so I pause slightly when Julian offers me his arm to escort me back down the aisle. He flashes a little grin, impish and dangerous all at once. I slide my hand to the crook of his elbow, feel muscles flex minutely as we walk toward the garden gate. I stare straight ahead, a smile plastered to my face, so Sophie's photographer doesn't record for all time an image of me mooning at Julian.

While everyone congratulates the newly married couple and poses for pictures, the discreet, efficient caterer arranges clusters of tables and chairs, then sets up the buffet and bar. Giggling children scamper among their relatives. Julian leans his body close to mine for a casual shot of the wedding party. The sun sets in the cloudless sky behind Fairfax House, bathing the garden in shimmering red-gold warmth that settles low in my belly.

Chapter 2

OKAY. THAT'S OVER. All I have to do now is avoid him until everyone leaves tomorrow afternoon. Not a problem. I'll do what Jane and Lizzie would have done and take a turn in the garden.

I climb the steps to the second level and meander along. Below me, guests laugh, drink and dine; above me, the silent summer sunset gilds the treetops, all I can see of the parkland surrounding the estate. In the farthest corner of the garden I find a pear tree tamed to grow flat against the wall, branches spreading away from the trunk. In the bed in front of the tree, flowers and ornamental shrubs grow in profuse sprays of color and greenery, probably to set off what likely took a gardener hours of patient tying and trimming during the tree's early years. Laden with early fall fruit, the poor thing looks constrained, heavy, contorted.

Or maybe I'm projecting. It's possible. I've had several glasses of champagne, so I'm tipsy enough to be super-pissed that this poor tree has been restrained as it has. I can smell the ripe fruit, imagine the skin giving under my teeth, the juice spreading over my tongue as I bite into the flesh, but something about the trunk pinned to the bricks stops me from stepping between the asters and the lavender to twist a pear free from its spur.

Behind me the party's in full swing. I think the Fairfaxs fall into the impoverished English gentry category; without a steady income from the land, maintaining a house like this costs more than the family has. Over the last few years, Martin's family has sold off most of the estate, leaving only Fairfax House and the garden. A hundred years ago he would have married an American heiress for an infusion of funds. What remains in their family is falling apart around them, in the most beautiful, shabby chic way possible.

Martin married for love. I'm glad of it, because Sophie deserves him.

I can't be gone too long. I'm not the maid of honor so I don't have to make a speech, but I do need to be present. Sophie held my hand through more bad breakups than I can count. I'm happy for her, even if Julian reminds me I'm a bit worse for wear at the moment.

"Espalier."

I startle and swing around, sloshing champagne over my wrist. Julian stands in front of me, carrying two glasses of champagne.

"Sorry about that," he says, nodding at my wet wrist. "Good thing I brought you another glass."

I shift my nearly empty glass to my left hand, hold out my right arm, and try to shake my hand dry. It's a futile gesture. I can feel the liquid drying on my skin, leaving a sticky residue. "It's not your fault."

"I don't have a napkin. Or a handkerchief."

I glance at his pocket square, a gorgeous shade of red peeping perfectly out of his breast pocket.

"Of course. Silly of me." He looks at the glasses in his hand, then at me. He straightens up and angles his left shoulder forward just a little, subtly offering.

"I couldn't," I say. It's definitely not polyester or cheap cotton, probably silk, and taking anything from him is not a good idea.

"Please do."

I've got three options. Relieve him of his pocket square, which means touching him and therefore feels intimate enough to be dangerous. The second option is to wipe my hand on my bridesmaid dress, but Sophie was kind enough to let us choose our own dresses, as long as they were in a range of blue that didn't clash horribly. I'm wearing raw silk the color of cornflowers with rather sexy crisscrossing straps, a fitted bodice, and a swirling skirt that stops just above my knees. It cost half my monthly rent. I'll wear it over and over again, and I'm not wiping champagne on it.

Which leaves option three: licking the champagne off my wrist.

"No, thank you, that's very kind, but I couldn't possibly." I didn't pick up an English accent while I lived here—the affectation felt ridiculous given my totally American, totally salt-of-the-earth upbringing—but I did pick up the speech patterns. Extra words, lots of apologizing and deferring and demurring. When it comes to who walks through an open door first, Chip and Dale have nothing on the English. "I'll dry quite quickly."

Amusement flickers in his eyes and he settles his shoulders back to a more relaxed state. "Be a love and take one of these glasses," he says. Like he would owe me the biggest possible favor when he's the one doing a kindness.

I shouldn't…I really shouldn't…. I set my empty glass on the grass in front of the pear tree and take the less-full flute from his hand. "Thanks so much."

"Cheers," he says.

We clink glasses and I take a sip. It's Veuve Clicquot but the dry flavor and bubbles can't explain all the heat rising in my face. I look around the garden, hoping the deepening twilight will cover my blush.

"Espalier," he says again with a nod at the pear tree. "It's a technique for producing more fruit. That wall faces west, so it gets more sunlight, and the bricks retain the heat. Extends the growing season."

"Oh, I didn't know that. Are you interested in gardening?"

"Not even remotely, but Aunt Molly does go on about it," he says with a smile. "Enjoying yourself?"

From my vantage point the rich blue of the bridesmaids' dresses stands out against the white chairs and tablecloths. Down below Sophie and Martin are making the rounds of the tables. "Very much."

Julian follows my look. "Do you think they'll be happy together?"

They're obviously, gloriously in love, starry-eyed and smiling and touching each other at every possible moment. Their fingers are woven together in a loose, comfortable way, not the tight grip of people who are afraid they'll lose what they have, or want everyone to know they're paired off. On this perfect late summer evening I can't imagine a future for them that doesn't include laughter, two or three bright-eyed children, and a seventieth anniversary celebration, probably in this very garden, if they can keep up with the taxes.

The confident intimacy slays me.

"Very," I say, still watching them. When I tear my gaze away from the bride and groom, I see Julian standing with his legs braced, sipping his champagne. Once again, I can't stop looking at him. The resemblance is more than skin deep, down to the bone structure, almost eerie. My insides can't decide what to do.

My heart skips a beat, my breathing quickens, my stomach lurches.

Amusement glimmers in Julian's eyes. "You're doing it again."

"Doing what?" I say, a hint of challenge in my voice. I'm counting on his good English manners to not point out exactly what we both know I've been doing.

"Staring. Well, not exactly staring. More like looking, then looking away. Glancing. Furtively."

So much for manners. His accent, "glahncing," throws me for a moment, but only a moment. I shouldn't do this. I really, really shouldn't do this, but I just can't help myself. "You've thrown a few heated glances of your own," I say. He has. He's mastered the art of looking at a woman through his stupidly thick lashes.

One corner of his mouth lifts. "You might as well get a good long look. Maybe that will help."

It won't. I'm tempted, though. Very tempted. To cover my indecision I make a soft, noncommittal sound and turn my attention to the famous English landscape. The stately trees dip and sway in a soft evening breeze. The lawn is green, lush, and riddled with clover, tiny white flowers occasionally peeping shyly from the grass. Hedge-edged fields, some fallow, some deep green and fertile, fold down into the valley and rise again on the other side. The rolling hills are dotted with black-faced sheep, and the fields look small until you realize the trees growing in the middle of them are hundreds of years old, and immense. On our walk the day before, we girls couldn't encircle one massive oak. There were dozens of these trees, solidly rooted in the countryside, individually and in clusters along streams.

The gardens around Fairfax House look equally spontaneous, which probably means they've spent quite a lot of money hiring a gardener who knows what they're doing. I grew up in the suburbs, a place prone to matchy-matchy, the prairie grasses and wood chips and bushes exactly the same from house to house. There's a space and size here that unlocks something inside me. It's all very earthy, nonchalant and perfect. Even the sun seems to linger for bride and groom.

Or perhaps it lingers for Julian, standing close enough for me to feel the heat radiating from his chest to my bare arm. He hasn't moved. Julian wears easily the label "rake" or "rogue", so he knows indecision when he hears it, knows to wait until the warning voice in my head trails off to silence.

I turn. Meet his gaze. Lose my breath. Dozens of moments of eye contact, the flirty lash-diluted glances like little jabs—saucy, seductive jabs—coalesce into the full impact of his direct stare. For a moment I can't breathe because desire, pure and demanding, swells in my chest, paralyzing my diaphragm.

"Is it helping?" His voice is a low, sandy murmur, rough in all the right ways on my skin. He's back to the sidelong looks, this fabulous bit of trouble. The delicate hairs on my exposed shoulders and arms lift and settle, like he nipped at my nape.

What drags me back from the edge is the knowledge that it would be wrong. "No," I say, pleased I've managed a regretful little smile. Time to change the subject. "You're Martin's cousin?"

He shifts from seductive bruiser to responsible host in the blink of an eye. "Yes. If this were an Austen novel, Martin would be the conscientious landowner, steward of the ground beneath his feet. He actually visits people in the village when he's here, to check on family members who used to work for the estate. I'd play the role of the wastrel cousin. I'd gamble the family's money away or lose it all on a highly romantic but tragically unsuccessful stud farm, then go abroad to spend the rest of my life frittering away my allowance on cards and loose women, and living in shabby foreign hotels."

I have to laugh. "I don't doubt it." There's a word for men like this, and that word is *louche*. He's appealingly disreputable, or disreputably appealing, his hair brushed back from his face, his lips pouty and full, the startling white crooked teeth in his smile. His brown-gold tiger eyes are even more entrancing as the late afternoon light gilds the white tablecloths, the tips of the flowers, and I can't, I can't, even though I want to.

"Why are the windows bricked up?" I say desperately.

"Taxes," Julian says, seemingly willing to take a conversational back road. "King William III needed money. An income tax was very unpopular, so he taxed windows instead, which led to people bricking up their windows in order to reduce the tax. That's Fairfax House, formerly the dower house," he adds. "Fairfax Abbey, the main house, is that way." He turns, points over his shoulder in the opposite direction of Fairfax House.

"I know. We've been on several walks. I saw the abbey then." Only from the outside. It's been sold to a tech billionaire, or maybe someone in the Saudi royal family.

"It's a monstrosity," Julian says irreverently.

I try to smile. I should be making an effort. He and Sophie are family now, and Sophie's one of my best friends. Our paths will cross again, I'm sure of it. Setting the wrong tone tonight will make things awkward down the road. But my animal body is responding not to stern logic and rational thinking, but to Julian. The summer light and heat are seeping through my skin to pool in my sex. It's not a fire. It's a thick, hot weight that collects in my nipples and collarbones, in my lips and—I'm very, very sure of this part—in my eyes.

In the Garden

The sense of teetering on a precipice, or at least on the very edge of a flight of stairs, surges again. "Well, the garden is lovely."

He clasps my elbow, sending a frisson along my nerves, guiding me away from the reception. The beds are a riot of color, pink roses far more fragrant than any I've smelled in the States, purples and fuchsias and lavender and pink. I'm drowning in color, in scent, in Julian.

"I'd show you round, but it sounds like Sophie already gave you the grand tour."

There's my out. My excuse. I should agree that I've seen everything, and take a step back toward the reception to make his hand drop from my arm. "We mostly walked by the main house, and past the stables to the fields," I say.

"Ah," he says, conspiratorially, leaning even closer, thumb stroking bare skin. "Did she show you the ruined church? It's the best bit of the estate."

Martin's rake of a cousin knows exactly what he's up to. "No, it's on the grounds that belong to the new owner. We aren't supposed to walk there."

He arched an eyebrow at me. I can see where this is leading, and I'm torn. On one hand, I want nothing more than to sneak off with Julian; on the other hand, I really shouldn't. *Yesnoyesnoyesnoyes...*

I tip over, into empty space. "Show me?"

Chapter 3

Julian's not put off by my mixed messages. He draws me into a nearby grotto, with its stone floor and a white-painted wrought iron table and two chairs. It's the kind of place you'd take tea, except these days you'd carry your own tray and pour your own cuppa. Hidden off to one side in the twining branches is a small wooden door I've not seen before. "Go out that way," he says. "I'll get more champagne."

I turn the thick iron handle, tug the door open, and duck through to the expanse of lawn on the other side. Julian reappears in a couple of minutes, an unopened bottle of champagne in one fist.

"You swiped an entire bottle of Veuve Clicquot?"

He looks at the bottle with mock surprise. "Appears so, yes." When I arch an eyebrow, he leans in and murmurs in my ear, "We're about to trespass on private property. Nicking a bottle of champagne is the least of our concerns."

I expect him to open it so we can drink as we walk, but he just sets off up the slope, into a stretch of mature trees too sparse to be a forest but dense enough that the safety of the walled-in garden quickly disappears from view. He's wearing a dark suit that blends into the shade, but my dress glimmers when it catches the odd ray of sunlight. I feel like a woodland creature, a fairy made flesh. We've set off into a golden gloaming, another word I love to turn over in my mouth.

He turns to check on me, his gaze taking in my flushed face, the strands of sunstreaked blond hair escaping from my loose French braid, and my strappy sandals.

"Very poor planning," he chides, looking me up and down.

"Sophie's timetable didn't include a forced march through the woods."

He grins at me, pure delight in the smile, then turns around so he's walking backward. It slows him down, keeps him just out of my reach. I find myself thinking far less about the uneven footing and far more about the way his hips shift as he walks, the flash of white shirt, belt buckle, and blue silk tie caught by his buttoned jacket.

When my gaze reaches his face, he's no longer smiling. He's looking at me like he knows exactly what I'm thinking, and it's not amusing. It's arousing.

Sweat blooms at my temples and between my breasts, even though we're walking through sun-dappled shade, the leaves shifting and dancing overhead and under our feet and on our skin all at once. I stumble, because I'm not looking where I'm going but at him. Without changing pace or position, he reaches out, offering me his hand. I take it and let him draw me deeper into the wood. He's got the champagne bottle in one hand and my fingers in the other, moving with a dancer's grace, or an actor's, or an athlete's. For a moment my brain chases after the memory of what the wastrel cousin does for a living, but the thought disappears into the heady pressure of his fingers around mine.

Through the trees I can see flashes of gray stone arches, empty spaces where stained glass windows should be. The trees grow more thickly just before we reach the church. He draws me all the way in, then drops my hand. The walls and floor are intact. Someone has hacked away exterior sections of stone, perhaps when they carted off the windows, and some of the finials and bits of decorative carving now litter the floor. Through the empty windows I can see an apple tree, branches bent with the weight of the first fruit. The sweet smell lingers in the air, clings to my nostrils and skin.

"It's hardly in ruins." Visions of a country vicar saying Evensong in this lovely little building flit through my head. "Some windows, a sturdy door, get some pews in here and you have a working church. Why isn't it in use?"

He sets the bottle of champagne on what's probably the base for the altar, leans a hip on a chunk of broken column, and peers up at the rib vaults supporting the roof "The Church refused to consecrate it. One can't worship in an unconsecrated space."

"Oh. Back home we have churches in strip malls and repurposed box stores," I say, waving my hand. "'Wherever two or three are gathered—'"

"'—there I am in the midst of them,'" he finishes, surprising me. "Not according to the C of E. Two or three can gather only where the Archbishop says they can."

"So the family just let it fall apart?"

"It's a folly. Pleasing to the eye. In the winter you can see it from both Fairfax Abbey and Fairfax House."

"Ah. Very thrifty of them."

Conversation halts for a moment, the silence taking on some of the late summer afternoon heat and light. There's a density to it, a weight that seeps through my skin as I stroll around the small building, pretending fascination with the lichen growing on the stone, the vines tendriling freely up the wall, the view through the windowless arches to the path leading into a head-high thicket of laurel bushes.

"Where does that go?" I ask idly.

In the Garden

Showing a fine disregard for what is obviously a very expensive suit, he joins me at the window, bracing his elbow on the window's edge to peer out. It's obviously a ruse. He knows the grounds like the back of his hand. "To the fields Sophie showed you."

He's close, not quite touching but near enough that I can feel the damp heat of his skin through his shirt and suit jacket, smell his sweat so deeply I can taste the salt on my tongue. I'm getting slick. I can feel it as I shift my weight from one foot to the other, the better to turn my body into his. I'm no longer the pretty picture of a bridesmaid. My silk underwear is stuck to my hips and ass, and tendrils of hair cling to my neck and cheek.

I shouldn't do this. I know I shouldn't do it, but I'm going to do it anyway. What's another bruise, another scrape? Maybe a wedding fling will erase the memories of my ex for good.

I reach out and curl my fingers into the waistband of his trousers. I can feel the button and hook-and-eye holding the fly closed, and more importantly feel the muscles in his abdomen tense when I do this. There's no give in his abs, and I'm showing off a little. I've spent time at the gym to look good in this dress; my shoulders and arms are curvy with muscle. Looking up into his eyes, I pull him toward me, lift my mouth to those gorgeous full lips, and kiss him.

This close he smells very faintly of cologne and some kind of product in his hair to stop the fine, thick strands from sliding over his forehead. His mouth feels so good against mine, his lips hot and obliging. He's got the confidence of a man whose looks are far too unusual to trade on but who compensates with the things that really matter.

Like kissing.

He kisses really, really well. His tongue darts out for a very brief second to touch my lower lip but retreats before I open my mouth in response, leaving me with a bubbly, light hint of champagne and a whole lot of dark desperation. We kiss for a few moments longer, the pressure of his mouth increasing to draw me toward him, then backing off again when I follow. With no more contact than my hand at his belt and our mouths together, he seduces me into pressing full length against his body.

Oh God, I *want* this. I can feel his cock hardening in his trousers, blood pumping into the shaft, the heat and thickness just beyond my grasping fingers. I fist my hand around his waistband and pull him with me as I turn so my bare back thuds against the stone window frame and his hard body slams against my front.

He doesn't stop, bending at the knees and hitching forward to grind his cock into my belly. I let out a little gasp, because stopping my momentum with my spine against the curved edge of the window wasn't my smartest option. He licks the gasp from my mouth like the pained edge of it tastes good. One hand pushes on my hip to pin me to the stone while the other slides along my nape, strong fingers weaving into my loosening braid and not-quite-gently tugging.

It's so good. So right. Exactly what I want, but I'll never be able to live with myself if it happens like this. "Wait, wait," I say, pushing at his hip, his shoulder.

He looks at me with eyes drugged with lust. "What?" he asks, visibly dragging himself back from what promised to be a headlong plunge into hot, slippery sex.

"It's just…"

My voice trails off. This is why I should have walked away from the offered glass of champagne, or turned back when he reached for me as we were walking here.

I screw up my courage. "It's just…you remind me of someone. That's all."

He studies me for a second, obviously gathering his functioning neurons to understand what I said. "Who?"

I refuse to look away, not with his body so close I can feel his pulse in his cock. "An ex. It didn't end well."

Then the light dawns. The furtive glances I can't help. The mixed messages. He smiles, amused and a little intrigued. "We're having that fuck, are we? The *you remind me enough of someone who hurt me for me to feel like I'm getting revenge* fuck? I've had that fuck before. Never played this particular role in it, though."

His thumb is stroking my throat, slow, possessive, right over the bump-bump of my pulse. My ears are growing hot. "Well. I wanted you to know."

Julian hasn't moved back so much as an inch. He's still got his hand in my hair, his body pushed against mine. His gaze is far too astute and far too compelling to look away, no matter how much I might want to. "I remind you of the bit of rough that got away."

He's smarter than he seems, observing everything, putting together pieces based not only on what I just said but also on what my body is saying. I open my mouth but no words come out. The good girl in me wishes I could say it was only a superficial resemblance, that I could see a quiet sensitivity in his eyes, or a kindness in his mouth, but the truth is, there's an edge to Julian that's setting off every pleasure receptor in my body.

He doesn't move. He's waiting, going to make me claim it. A delicate shiver runs through my sex. I lift my chin and own it. "Arrogant smirk, cocky eyebrow raise, lifting an entire bottle of expensive champagne? Down to the very marrow of your bones."

The words are barely out of my mouth before his hand shifts

from my nape to my throat. His thumb presses under the hinge of my jaw, and my mouth drops open. "And you fucking love it."

My pleading little gasp confirms his bold statement. He tilts his head down and bites my lower lip, hard enough to sting, followed by my upper lip, just as hard. Then he turns my head and scrapes the sharp edge of his five o'clock shadow over the sensitive corner of my mouth.

"Is this what you want?" he murmurs. The words blend into the air, liquid, humid, the molecules vibrating at his voice.

"Yes," I say, dizzy.

This time he actually kisses me. No biting, no scraping, no waiting. He keeps his hand on my throat to hold my face where he wants it, and kisses me like he's a ruthless lord choosing from the village girls. I've got one hand still clutching his waistband and the other straining to hold onto his upper arm through his slippery wool suit coat.

"Well, then," he says between kisses. "I know exactly how this should start."

He doesn't move his hand. Instead he changes the pressure from closing around my throat to pushing down until I get with the program and get on my knees. We have to step away from the window to accomplish this, and all I can think is that if someone had told me an hour earlier that I'd be on my knees in the gritty stone dust of a ruined church, about to suck Julian Randall's cock, I would have told them they had to stop being on crack.

My dress billows around me. The few functioning brain cells that remain wonder how hard it will be to get the dust out of the skirt, but then reality kicks in. Champagne and body fluids are in play. The dress is a goner.

Julian stares down at me. He unbuttons the front of his suit coat and pauses. The rest is my responsibility.

Chapter 4

I STARE AT his trousers. Quality fabric and tailoring hides so much; there's nothing so gauche as a bulge in the front of his pants, rather a hint of heat and hardness that my animal brain translates into power. Belt, unbuckled and opened. Fly, unbuttoned, unhooked, unzipped. The scent of him is stronger here, musky and hot and thick. I part the fronts of his shirt, pull down his cotton boxer briefs, and his cock springs out to bob in the air in front of me. My mouth floods with saliva as I look at it. It's not especially long, but it's deliciously thick, his foreskin furling back to expose the head. It's going to stretch me in ways I'll feel long past tomorrow.

I've gone molten. Absolutely, utterly molten. The silk of my dress rubs against my nipples. Between my legs, my body grows slick and hot and swollen. I reach out, toy with the foreskin, slide my hand down to the base, look up at him, lick my lips and dip forward to take the head in my mouth.

The sound he makes is quiet and sandy-rough, like a cat's tongue on my heated nerves. I lick around the head, diluting the precome collected there, then take him a little deeper. It's been a while since I gave head to an uncircumcised man, but the little tricks, the sensitivity around the foreskin, pulling it up over the head when I hollow my cheeks, all come back to me in a hot rush. He feels good in my mouth, really good. Solid and demanding in the best possible way. When he moves his hips, thrusting with a hot restraint ever so slightly into my mouth, the demand increases. I want to meet it, want to test myself against his strength.

And against his sexuality. He—and the man he reminds me of—is a brand of man that always made me curious. Can I meet that challenge?

I'm about to find out.

The sharp edge of a rock digs into my left knee, but I don't care. Desire hurts. The pain blends into the other discomforts of sex, the soreness developing in my jaw, my stretched lips, the delicious ache deepening low in my belly. The bitter almond flavor of precome blooms on my tongue, thick and salty. It's quiet here in the deer park, the slight breeze in the leaves nearly drowned out by the unladylike, slick clicking sound of his cock thrusting in and out of my mouth, the even dirtier choking noise I make when he glides to the back of my throat.

"Sorry, fuck, sorry," he moans.

I hum softly to let him know I'm quite all right. His fingers work into my hair, then sink into my scalp. Without doing anything quite so gauche as fucking my face, he shows me the rhythm he wants.

I give it to him, peeking up at his face. I expect the slack-jaw, dimwitted expression most guys have when they're getting head, but instead he's looking at me, his eyes heavy-lidded, as hot and liquid as I feel. In a moment of clarity I realize I have exactly one chance to get what's on offer. He doesn't know me. I don't have to impress him, be funny or sweet or clever, pretty or sassy or sexy. I don't have to be anything. I get to take. He knows this, is fully engaged, holding space for me to explore, to take exactly what I want, right here, right now. He's thrown himself wholeheartedly into it.

Right now I want to take his cock as deep down my throat as I can get it. I consciously open my throat and grip his hips, giving him more pressure to thrust against. Saliva coats my chin as he sinks deep, again and again. His balls, when I reach down to stroke them with my fingertips, are tight against his body. The hand on my head tightens, then gently pushes back until I slow, then let the tip pop free from my mouth.

"Fuck," he says, breathing hard.

I wipe my mouth with the back of my hand. The taste of champagne spreads over my tongue, unexpected and tart. I make a satisfied little noise and lick my wrist, my fingers, my palm, then the tip of his cock.

He reaches down and grips my arm to haul me to my feet, and walks me back into the wall. For the second time pain shoots down my spine but this time I laugh, the sound shocked and frantic and wild. It cuts off abruptly when he lifts my wrist to his mouth and sucks the tender skin, pressing against the tendons, the delicate bone. I want to feel his tongue against mine, so I lean in and lick next to his. He groans and pushes my wrist against the wall by my head and kisses me.

He'd been holding back before. This kiss is the kiss of a pirate, plundering my mouth. He bends at the knees and whisks up my skirt, then shoves against my body, grinding his spit-slick cock against my bare belly. A new sound joins the muffled grunts and clack of teeth, the rasp of his pubic hair against my lace panties. We're skin to skin and simulating sex, and I want him naked. Now.

I shove his jacket off his shoulders, onto the gritty stone floor, then attack the buttons on his shirt. He reaches behind me and finds my zipper, yanking it down. He mouths at my shoulder, nipping the curves, licking the hollows, until he can curl his fingers into the crisscrossing straps and pull them down. In an ideal world my dress would slide gracefully to my feet; in this dirty, ruined, unconsecrated church, he has to yank a little when the silk sticks to my sweaty skin.

That feels beyond right.

Panting, I lift my chin and stand in nothing but my panties and my strappy heels while I loosen the noose of his tie and lift it over his head. He shoulders out of his shirt, helping me get him half-naked. He looks me over, that possessive glint back in his eyes. I experience a moment of disorientation so profound I wonder where I am.

I want his hands on my body. Instead he reaches for the champagne bottle and opens it. He's deft with the wire and foil, gets a grip on the protruding cork.

"Ready?" he asks.

"Sure." I have no idea what's coming, but I'm as ready as I've ever been in my life.

Gaze firmly locked with mine, he pops it open. Foam spills over his hand, then down his arm as he lifts the bottle. I catch on just in time, tip my head back to catch the champagne in my open mouth. The effervescent liquid spills over my chin and down my throat. I swallow, gasp, laugh.

The sound transforms into a shocked moan when he licks the bubbly froth coating my throat, my collarbone, my breasts and nipples. He retains enough presence of mind to set the bottle down on the floor beside him as he goes to his knees, tongue rapacious and sure on my body. I stare down at him, on his knees, cock out and flushed, trousers sagging on his hips, then I tip my head back and see nothing at all.

He licks my nipples, sets his teeth into each hard bud and flicks his tongue until my knees are trembling. My hands find his sweat-damp hair and tighten in the thick strands as he continues, until my nipples are sensitized to even the humid summer air. When I yank on his hair he stops, considers the state of my torso for a moment, then works my panties down. I'm trembling, on edge, until he picks up the champagne bottle and pours a little over the swell of my belly.

My head thunks back against the stone as he laps at my skin, slow, sure, moving incrementally lower until he sucks the liquid from my soaked curls, then darts his tongue into my folds. He finds my clit easily, using his thumbs to open me slightly so he can slide his tongue against the tight bud. My head rolls on my neck, loosening my hair enough that half of the braid falls down to drape over my shoulder. I'm on the edge when he gets to his feet and kisses me.

I taste champagne, my juices, sweat. He cups my folds, fingers gently petting there, driving me a little wild, and sets his mouth to my ear. "If I get you off now, can you come again?"

Sometimes is the precise answer to that. *Absolutely* is the answer right now, because our chemistry is off the charts. Immolating. I'm not given to dramatics, but I might die if I don't get to fuck him. I reach for him. "Yes, but I want you inside me. Now."

His laugh isn't a laugh, but the sound of a man on the ragged edge of his control. "It's all I can do not to come all over your stomach like a kid."

His fingers weave into mine, lifting my hand up and back as he leans on one elbow, subsequently pinning the back of my hand to the wall. His other hand hasn't left my pussy. His fingers make a slick sound as he parts the folds and, without any warning, pushes two fingers into me. I stop breathing for a moment, then moan out what air is left in my lungs.

"Fuck." His hand adjusts, and his thumb finds my clit. For a long, strange moment the garden and the sacred setting take over my mind, and I remember a friend joking about nicknames for the clitoris. The devil's doorbell. How apropos, given our location.

"Come back," he croons, brushing a finger lightly over the swollen bud. "You just disappeared into your head. Come back or I'll have to ply you with more champagne."

He's watching me closely. I can feel it more than see it because my eyes have gone sightless with the pleasure spiraling inside me, loose and free. It's the opposite of espalier. I'm grounded, roots spreading deep as I arch to the sky.

"I'm here," I gasp, head tipped back, gaze hazily taking in the elegant ribs supporting the stone roof. "I'm definitely here. I want to feel every single second of this."

He trembles a little against me, like he's fighting the impulse to fuck me, right now. My body is tightening around his fingers as I swivel my hips. He leans into me, pinning me so I can lift and grind. His body is a wall of heat at my front. The stone is unyielding and dirty at my back. He's deftly stroking the bundle of nerves inside my sex, and pressing against my clit. His teeth close hard around my ear, and I come, back of my hand shoved to my mouth to stifle my cries.

When I open my eyes, he's still leaning against my body. He's panting, his cock rock hard, the foreskin fully retracted, and glistening at the tip. "You were too worked up. I would have gone off in a second if I'd got inside you like that." A smile flashes over his face, the crooked teeth gleaming in the shadowy light. "I want more than a second."

He's seizing what's on offer, too. I love it, that he's as greedy and hedonistic and amoral as I feel right now. He picks up the bottle of champagne and takes a swallow, then hands it to me. I glug it like we're freshmen chugging beer at a kegger. It should be going to my head, but it isn't. Perhaps the adrenaline and endorphins are burning off the alcohol like a flambé.

"Better now?" Like I'm solicitous. Like I'm not about to demand more from him.

His dark grin tells me he recognizes the irony. "Yes, thanks," he says, just as absurdly.

"Good." I reach out and tug his balls down. "I want to fuck you."

Chapter 5

THIS PART REQUIRES some thought. We've both learned our lesson with the floor, so we end up on one of the larger slabs of stone covered with his jacket. He shoves down his trousers, then sits down and reaches up to hold my hips as I straddle him.

"Condom?" I ask.

He fumbles in his jacket pocket, pulls out his wallet, then flips it open to slip a foil packet from an interior slot. He rolls it down while I watch. It's a bit awkward—I lift my hips and scoot forward, he holds his erect shaft to align us, and all is well until I wince at his size.

"Patience, you little tart," he says, his hands tightening on my hips to hold me.

I laugh, but this is an issue. I'm balanced on my feet, which taxes my thigh muscles. I lean both forearms on his shoulders, forcing him to bear some of my weight while my body adjusts around him, distracting myself from the strain in my legs by kissing him, again and again, rubbing my lips over his, biting, sucking, until my inner walls give way and I slide down with a slow, soft moan.

He throbs once inside me, mutters "fuck" under his breath, and distracts himself by taking my hair all the way down. For a long moment I close my eyes and savor the sensuality of his hands in my hair, unraveling my braid, spreading the strands over my shoulders.

I open my eyes. "How long can you last?"

That startles a real bark of laughter from him. "See, it's questions like that that render men powerless to resist."

I shift a little, watching his muscles flex in response, feeling him stretch me. "*Powerless* isn't the word I'd use here."

His cock presses against the nerves inside me, sending a little zing to my clit. "As long as you want," he says.

I'm alight with power and desire. Nothing like seducing a mysterious, edgy bloke into fucking you in an unconsecrated church to make you feel kicky. I still for a moment to get in touch with my body. An assortment of bruises and tender spots are beginning to make themselves known, but the loudest message popping and fizzing in my veins is that I want to kiss him. So I do.

I drape my arms over his shoulders and let my body go hot and soft around his cock, the better to feel the rigid strength inside me. I brush my lips over his, stroking the already tingling nerves, then add tongue and teeth to the kiss. It's wet, languid, slow, his hands roaming my back as we sink into the push and pull of our mouths. We taste like bubbly and each other; the heated scent of our bodies rising into the summer evening air that smells of hot earth, old stone, green grass, fruit ripening on the vine.

Birds chirp and sing, leaves whisper and gossip to each other. I can hear the dust settling again, faint laughter in the distance, but it all seems very far away. We could be a medieval knight and his lady, stealing a moment out of time. We could be a Roman lord and his slave girl. I don't like that particular adaptation, not today. We could be a Roman lady and her gladiator, because while circumstances have always conspired to lock down a woman's sexuality, in every age and time there have been women capable of ringing their own damn doorbells.

The thought makes me giggle.

He tucks my hair behind my ear, and uses his thumb at the hinge of my jaw. "Are we amusing?" he asks.

"A little." I explain my ridiculous thought process to him, because I am already naked and sitting on his cock. Maintaining dignity went winging into the hedgerows some time ago.

"Of course," he says in his most thoughtful British schoolboy demeanor. "But it's rather more fun to have someone else ring it for you. To your satisfaction."

I'm glad we're on the same page, and confident enough not to say it out loud. Instead, I rise a little bit, so sensitized I imagine that despite the condom I can feel his foreskin drag against my inner walls as I do, then sink back down. It's a tease, a good one, heightened when he slides his hands up my back to close around my shoulders and drive me down on his cock, but it's not long before even that isn't enough. I want his hips in motion, driving deep.

"Fuck me hard," I gasp against his jaw. "Hold me down and fuck me hard and fast."

His breath hitches to a stop in his throat, and his hands tighten reflexively. "I won't last if it's fast."

"Then hard and slow."

"You will kill me," he groans. "Literally. Stone dead."

"Is this a problem?"

He purses his lips at me, feigning a reflective moment. Then the world spins and I'm flat on my back on the gritty floor, Julian braced on his elbows above me. It's a feat of athleticism I wouldn't have suspected him capable of. Lust seizes my throat as he uses his hips to shove my knees apart and plunges back inside.

I struggle a little, push at his shoulders, twist under his hips, but it's impossible to dislodge him. It's fantastic, veering between lust and panic in a way I've never felt before. It's the thing you want, that scares you and delights you at the same time, a roller coaster of sex, totally safe and yet terribly thrilling.

I love it.

"Is this what you want?" he murmurs in my ear.

"God, yes," I say.

He makes another huff that sounds amused to me but quickly turns into the kind of hard-edged, animal grunts, the sounds a man makes when he's fucking somebody hard. His hips pound deep and relentless, driving me inch by inch across the floor. I fetch up against a block of stone that's tumbled to the floor, which is how I feel, like I'm cracking, splitting, falling away. Bracing one arm against the block gives me the leverage to push back into his thrusts. Every muscle in my body tightens, increasing the delicious friction inside me. He's kissing me, his luxurious mouth open over mine, our tongues flirting, slick and hot against each other.

Pain and pleasure, soft and hard, slick and friction all blend together into a sensation that's at once real and devastating and frighteningly intense. I open my eyes and stare up at him, seeing his face, seeing him as I tip over the edge into a freefall. There's a blinding flash of light, then the world goes black.

WHEN I SURFACE from a truly delicious round of aftershocks, he's draped over me, weight on his elbows, hips working lazily through his own aftermath, setting off little quivers inside me. Heat radiates from his cheek to my temple. I turn and touch my tongue to the sweat glistening there.

He pulls out and deals with the condom. Satiated but shaky, I struggle into a sitting position, fold my legs to the side and paw my hair back from my face. Julian pulls up his trousers, sits back on his heels, and reaches for the bottle of champagne, courteously offering it to me first.

Still naked but for my shoes, I take another swig, hand it back, swipe the back of my hand over my mouth. I still can't stop staring at him. I wonder what he's going to say, now that we're done. I wonder if men ever worry about that.

Chest still heaving slightly with exertion, he puts his hands on his hips and considers me. "I've always wanted to be someone's bit of rough," he says.

I laugh. Once I start, I can't stop. Giggles pour out of me until I have to wipe tears of laughter from my face. "Thanks for being okay with this," I say.

"Any time," he says, very sincerely. His moods change lightning fast. Keeping up would be easier if I were sober, but that seems like a silly thing to attempt when the air is the color of champagne and I've just had the best sex of my life.

We stagger to our feet. He snags my dress from the stone block where it landed and offers it to me. In exchange I hand him his shirt, then step into my dress and adjust it while he shoulders into dirty cotton. "You look like you've been through the wars," I say.

"Pot, meet kettle," he retorts. He pauses in the act of yanking on the shirt to get it over his sweaty shoulders to zip up my dress.

"I know. I can't go back to the reception. Not like this." I'm a wreck, and I haven't even seen my face. I swipe under my eyes to clear up the eyeliner, then wipe around my mouth for smeared lipstick. "Have you seen my panties?"

He shakes his jacket, sending dust and my underwear flying

into the air. I snag them, shimmy them up, and smooth down my skirt. A few quick swats to the back and shoulders of his jacket and he looks presentable. Based on the smug, satisfied expression on his face, I look like I've been ridden hard and put away wet.

"I'll go back. You go through here." He points through the side door, open to a tangled tunnel of laurel bushes. "Follow the path. When you get to the fork, turn right, then right again at the lane in the orchard and you'll be at the kitchen entrance."

"Thanks," I say.

"We all ran wild in these woods as children." He stoops to pick up the champagne bottle.

"That's not what I mean."

He looks at me.

"Thank you."

"You're welcome." He reaches for my hand. My fingers tremble a little as he lifts them to his lips, kisses them. It's warm, sweet, enticing. Then it's over.

I crouch and shoulder into the laurel bushes, leaving Julian behind. I'm high enough on endorphins that I welcome the scratches. The branches and twigs catch at my hair, my bared arms and shoulders, but fighting them back and shoving through feels good, right. The path opens into a little orchard, where apple trees bend under the weight of the season's first fruit. The air is sweet, redolent with the juices straining at their skins. I can hear music and laughter. I reach out, pluck a ripe apple, then another, from a branch that bends and snaps back when the fruit comes free, and bite into one. The juice runs down my chin, tart, sticky, delicious.

Chapter 6

I MAKE IT through the kitchen and down the hall to the main staircase without incident, but my luck gives way when Sophie comes out of the downstairs loo. We both freeze with surprise.

Laughter dances in her eyes. "And where have you been?"

My knees are raw. My dress is both dusty and damp. I've got leaves in my hair and scratches on my arms and legs, and the smell of sex, champagne, and Julian's cologne on my skin. I want to crawl into my bed, pull the covers over my head, and breathe in the intoxicating scents until I can think of nothing else.

"In the garden," I say, and take another bite of the apple.

Her laughter follows me up the stairs.

THE NEXT MORNING sunshine absolutely pours through the big windows in the room I'm sharing with Cathy and Louise. I roll over and stifle a shriek when the sheets rasp against the scrapes and bruises ranging the length of my body. It takes a little longer for my head to stop throbbing. Did I have half the bottle of champagne, plus the two or three glasses I drank before I met Julian in the garden? No matter now. My head says I had too much. When the pain and headache subside to a dull swell, I ease out of bed and stagger into the bathroom, clutching the wall for support until the water's warm enough to step into the shower.

Soap stings in the abrasions, tiny reminders of the totally out-of-character encounter the day before. I gulp water straight from the showerhead, and down a full glass with three aspirin after I brush my teeth. Back in the bedroom Cathy and Louise are dead to the world, Louise sprawled half in and half out of the covers, still in her bridesmaid dress. I dress carefully—in a silky long-sleeved deep v-neck shirt (that won't aggravate the scrapes) and a pair of jeans that will hide the state of my knees—then make my way downstairs to the big kitchen. When I reach the door, I hear Julian and Sophie talking. The tone is friendly, although I can't make out the words.

Walk in or walk out? I fish a bottle of water and a pair of sunglasses out of Sophie's bag, which is lying on the floor by the back door, and escape.

The sunshine is brutal, although after a while I can't tell if my eyeballs hurt from the hangover or from trying to focus through Sophie's prescription Ray-Bans. The birds are chirping, the sheep grazing, and the horses come over for a friendly sniff. I walk away into the fields, away from the garden and the church, drink the bottle of water, and try not to think too hard about last night. It's not difficult. My head aches rather murderously.

But eventually the sun is high enough in the sky that I can't legitimately avoid seeing him any longer. When I arrive back at Fairfax House I'm able to follow Louise into the kitchen. "Morning," she says cheerfully. Her eyeliner is smeared into punk rocker, and she's barefoot.

"Morning," I say.

The kitchen is now full of the wedding party and family, with the exception of Cathy. I can hear water running in the pipes, so she's likely in the shower, which explains why Louise is still in her bridesmaid dress and her rat's nest hair. They probably flipped for first chance at the bathroom. In the generalized chaos

I'm able to slip into a chair at the far end of the table. It's a typical post-party late start characterized by green-tinged people holding their heads rather carefully and pouring coffee with intense focus.

Martin's mother stands at the Aga, frying bacon and sausages and tomatoes, a two-for-one morning remedy against both hunger and hangovers. Unexpectedly, Julian is perched on the counter, manning the four-slot toaster. I reach for the teapot covered in a faded, stained cozy and pour myself a cup of milky hot tea.

"So," Martin's mother says cheerfully. "Plans for the day?"

"Not so loud," one of the other groomsmen says. He's got his hand over his eyes even though his back is to the window.

"Not so many plans, Aunt Molly," Julian says from his spot between the dish drainer and the cutting board smeared with tomato juice and seeds. The toast pops up. He collects the slices, adds them to a stack on a plate, and pops in four more. Molly swats at him with her tea towel and sets him to distributing plates of food. Mine comes with a big glass of water. "You're still staring," he murmurs in my ear.

I am. I blush, which makes my scrapes sting and my sex throb. Julian walks away without so much as a wink. The room falls into a companionable silence while we eat, BBC News playing on the radio in the background. When the meal's finished, I wash dishes, collect another cup of tea, go upstairs to grab the second apple from my room, then head for the little table and chairs in the grotto at the back of the garden.

Julian is already there, sprawled in one of the chairs. I stop. "S-sorry, I wasn't expecting—"

"Sit," he says.

I do, because now I see the difference between my ex and Julian: the iron control regulating the powerful charisma suffusing the striated depths of his eyes. I'm also not yet coordinated enough to dart back inside. While I set the cup and fruit on the table, I assess how I feel. I'm not ashamed of myself. I simply hadn't thought there would be a performance review. "Why aren't you hung over?"

He's balanced the chair on the back legs. "Experience," he says, then squints at me. "Lightweight."

"It was a lot of champagne," I protest. "Breakfast and water are doing the trick. I feel almost human."

"The walk probably helped," he says, a hint of challenge in his voice. Like he thought I was avoiding him earlier.

"You and Sophie are family now," I explain. "I wanted to give you some time together."

He adds a raised eyebrow to the sidelong narrow-eyed look.

"All right. Sophie would totally quiz me about last night in front of you. I didn't want to talk about it."

He eases forward until the chair's front legs land with less of a thump than I expect, then reaches across the wrought iron table. "May I?" he asks, waiting for permission.

I nod. He turns over my hand, thumbs back the edge of my sleeve. A faint ring of bruising extends around my wrist, darkening where he held my hand to the wall, the floor. He brushes his thumb over the tender skin. "Sore?"

"A little."

His eyes flick up, questioning, concerned.

"More than a little. I'm not complaining."

"My knees are scraped raw. We're playing tennis today. How am I supposed to explain that?"

"My back is scraped raw," I say, then push up my sleeves to show him my elbows. "We're going shopping in the village, then to see the gardens at Stourhead."

He looks at his watch, then toward the sun. "That's a very ladylike day for someone who pleaded with me for more and harder not eighteen hours ago."

I allow myself the brief pleasure of imagining him in tennis whites, thigh-length shorts showing off the muscled power in his legs. I manage an offhanded delivery when I say, "Tennis sounds equally improbable for someone who was face-deep in pussy eighteen hours ago."

He shouts with laughter. There's an obvious relief in his eyes, quickly subsumed by delight. That's where I find the difference between him and his evil doppelgänger. The Not-Julian wouldn't have blinked an eye at my possible discomfort. Julian went there, willingly flirted with danger and dark desire, but retained enough awareness to wonder, question, care.

"Yes. Tennis," he says, back to squinting. His forehead wrinkles in the most endearing way.

"Gardens," I say.

"I'd like to see you again," he says, rather unexpectedly. "How long is your visit?"

"Only through the weekend. I'm due in London for meetings tomorrow morning."

"I'll give you a ride back to town, shall I?"

It's a question, although I don't get the impression he asks this one often. The party is breaking up after our outings. Sophie and Martin are spending a couple of days here, postponing their honeymoon until the winter, when the weather is ghastly. From the moment she asked me to be a bridesmaid, I've appreciated Sophie's low-key approach to this wedding, but never more so than right now.

I fall back on English reserve. "I couldn't impose."

He tsks his tongue, calling me out as a coward. "I'm giving you the chance to actually kill me. You only came close out there."

"I'm not normally like that—"

"Neither am I—"

"—and it was a one-time thing," I finish.

"The thing about a one-time thing is that sometimes it happens twice. Or several times. Because you liked something far more than you anticipated, and want to do it again. Not necessarily the sex that makes us look like we were in a motorbike accident, although I wouldn't say no to that."

I hesitate.

"Once I realized you were staring at me, I made Joshua switch places with me so I could walk you back down the aisle," he says.

The scent of pears drifts along the garden wall, faint but alluring. The comment is so perfectly Julian—opportunistic and flattering at once—I have to laugh. "How did you get here?" I ask.

"Motorbike," he says, then looks at his legs. "I've had wrecks where I walked away with fewer scrapes."

"My suitcase…"

"Liam can bring it."

With Julian, obstacles are as butter to a hot knife. I pause to pick up the apple and examine it for bruises. "You really don't care that I fucked you because you look like someone else."

His eyes glint. "Yes, I'm disgusted. Appalled. I feel thoroughly used and hastily discarded, you dirty, dirty girl." Then he sobers, his gaze searching mine with an intensity I've not seen before. "Did it work?"

I lean forward, unabashedly staring. He returns my gaze with level calm. No more furtive. No more glancing. No more bruise of hurt feelings. No more second guessing. The past is the past.

I lean one elbow on the table and offer him the apple. He takes it, his grin ripe with promise of a wide open future.

Also by Anne Calhoun

Liberating Lacey
Fighting Fair

Spice Briefs
What She Needs
Under His Hand
Versed in Desire

Cosmo Red Hot Read
Working With Heat
The Uncommon Series

Uncommon Pleasure
Uncommon Passion

The Walkers Ford Series
Unforgiven
Jaded

The Irresistible Series
Breath on Embers
Transcendent
Afternoon Delight
The List
Evening Storm
The Muse

The Alpha Ops Series
The SEAL's Secret Lover
The SEAL's Rebel Librarian
The SEAL's Second Chance
Under The Surface (available May 31, 2016)

Visit Anne's books page on her website for her latest releases!
www.annecalhoun.com/bookshelf

About the Author

Anne Calhoun is the national bestselling author of sexy romantic fiction. Her first novel, *Liberating Lacey*, won the EPIC Award for Best Contemporary Erotic Romance and was chosen as one of NPR's 100 Swoon-worthy Romances. When she's not writing, her hobbies include knitting, reading, yoga, and horseback riding. Anne lives with her family in the Midwest, and has recently overcome her Starbucks addiction.

To be notified when Anne has a new book out, sign up for her (very infrequent) newsletter (http://eepurl.com/1VJ9L).

Exact Warm Unholy

Jeffe Kennedy

Tonight my name is Mary...

Or is it? Sometimes she's Tiffany or Syd or Bobbi. But whatever face she wears, she returns to the same bar, to find a new man and seduce him, safe in the knowledge that no one will recognize her. Until one man does.

Chapter 1

Tonight, my name is Mary.

Mary, Mary, quite contrary. That calls for fiery red, steampunk crimson carved into long, perfect ringlets. Not a corset, though. Not for Circle², a bar that tends toward the conservative, at least so far as cosplay is concerned, unless it's Halloween or something. Instead I choose the black sheath dress with the deep vee neckline to show off the inner curves of my breasts, and advertise that I'm not wearing a bra. Or anything else beneath.

Have to set the bait properly, after all. And Mary can do what I never could.

For makeup, I go with a retro vibe. I have to layer it on thick anyway, to make myself into Mary, so the heavy stuff works best. Theater pancake in the fairest tone to complement the hair. False lashes and black eyeliner, with a cat's eye flair. Bright green contact lenses. Lipstick in screaming scarlet, just shades darker than the wig. Amazing, really, how redrawing the lines of lips and eyes change a face entirely.

No one ever recognizes me, not even me. Maybe G_d does, but we've had a falling out and I don't care.

At the last moment I go for boots instead of stilettos. High heels, black leather, over-the-knee. Maybe I'll let him fuck me in just the boots. Whoever he'll be tonight.

The night air slaps chill on my bare arms, so I hurry the few blocks to Circle². I don't like to wear a coat. They're too expensive to take a different one every time and I'd rather spend the money on wigs. Too bad there's not a wig wear-and-return system, as I never use the same one twice.

I don't mind the coolness either. It helps combat the heat. I'm alive with the anticipation, already wet, primed for the release to come.

Tonight I pick out a stool at the bar. Mary is the sort who'd do that. I cross my legs so my hem rides up to show a strip of skin above my boot, turning sideways to display my cleavage.

Come and get it, gentlemen.

"What'll you have?" the bartender asks. He's a genial sort, always ready with a friendly smile. Never hits on me, no matter who I am that night, which makes me think he doesn't take advantage of the women who come to the bar. That's part of the reason I go to Circle². It sets a tone to the hookups, I think, as the men who frequent the place are generally clean and polite.

He's always working, six nights a week. The bar is closed on Mondays. I suspect he owns it, but we don't have conversations. At least, not connected ones. I'm always a stranger to him. He smiles, asks what I'll have, then leaves me alone.

Tonight it's Prosecco and he gives it to me in a tall flute. He's wearing a shirt that says "The book was better."

"I'll get that for the lady." A tall man, dark skin, pretty brown eyes, makes the offer hopefully. He's wearing a good suit, has nice hands, long fingers. I've never seen him in here before. Yes. Yes, he'll do nicely.

"I'd love that," I purr. I always keep my voice low, though I doubt the bartender would recognize it, above the din of conversation and whatever's playing on the television screens. It's best to keep conversation to a minimum, regardless. I'm not there to talk.

"Do you come here often?" The man asks.

"My first time," I lie.

"Mine, too." He's telling the truth, nice man that he is. He holds out a hand. It's chilled from the ice in the lowball glass he set on the bar. "I'm Tom."

"Mary," I say.

"I'm here on business," he tells me. They usually are, another reason I like Circle². It's next door to a hotel where a lot of those types stay. Frequent traveler points, reasonable rates for client budgets, decent linens. But the hotel rooms are lonely and the front desk recommends Circle² for the good prices and proximity.

I like that, too.

Tom shrugs, a bit self-deprecating. We're doing the dance. He's being careful, feeling his way through. None of them realize that they all say the same things. It's like we all know the code, the order of the invitations. It didn't take me at all long to learn the steps. "Hotel rooms get lonely, you know?"

"Would you like some company?" I finish my Prosecco and set the empty flute next to his lowball. I've left scarlet lip prints on the fine rim.

His pretty brown eyes fire with excitement, but he pauses at the speed of my capitulation. Sometimes they get the wrong idea. Sometimes they try to pay me anyway, or offer to buy me dinner. I don't want food. Food I can get on my own.

"You don't...you're not—"

"Not a prostitute." I smile, slide off the barstool, and take his hand. "Just lonely."

He's relieved, eyes going to my breasts. "Let's go then."

The bartender picks up the glasses. "You don't want another round?" He often asks that, too, if he catches me before I leave.

His way of making sure I'm okay, that I'm going willingly.

I shake my head and wave goodbye.

IN HIS ROOM, Tom offers me a drink from the minibar, but I decline. I simply turn my back to him and hold up my hair. "Would you unzip me?"

He's surprised, but tosses aside his suit jacket and obliges, then runs his hands down the exposed skin of my back and kisses my shoulder. Mmm. Very nice hands.

"You move fast, Mary."

Yes. Mary needs no seduction. She's slick with wanting, aching with it. She drops the dress to the floor and turns to face him, naked except for the thigh-high leather boots. His hands go to her breasts, his mouth to hers and—oh, yes—I lose myself in it. I'm Mary, who can have whatever she wants.

He grunts as she frees his cock, springing up thick and dark between the tails of his white shirt. Knowing her scarlet lips will look good around it, Mary kneels and takes him into her mouth. He groans, hands going to her head and I stop him.

"Not the hair. Never the hair."

He's stupid with desire and blinks at me in confusion, then the meaning penetrates and he drops hands to my shoulders instead. To reward him for being a good boy, she takes him into her mouth again. Mary likes to suck cock. The heft and heat of him in her mouth is almost orgasmic in itself, the flavor of man filling her head. She yanks his suit slacks down his thighs, his neat boxers a white contrast to his lovely skin, and grasps his ass in her hands to control his thrusts.

Mary is powerful as well as contrary. It's fun to be her.

She releases his cock with a pop, stands and slaps it, watching

Tom's face go shocked. Such a nice man. Mary pulls a condom out of her boot and hands it to him. While he puts it on, she clears his things from the desk with the mirror over it, pushing aside the laptop and the many cords. His phone is there, charging, silently scrolling text messages about cost proposals. He'll probably work after they're done. His room no longer so lonely.

She bends over the desk, legs invitingly spread, and I watch her in the mirror. Mary is beautiful, with the dramatic crimson curls falling around her defined cheekbones, her green eyes sultry. Her white breasts hang down like fruit between her braced arms and Tom's hands look good as they come around to squeeze them, rolling her nipples. Mary's scarlet lips part in pleasure. The lipstick is a good one—the lines that created the lush shape still crisp and clean.

He slides his hands down to her waist, smoothing over her hips and then into her folds, murmurs about her beauty, her slick heat. It's all good. He finds her clit, rolling it as he had her nipples, and she shivers. She wants to close her eyes, but I don't let her.

I want to watch. Not him. He doesn't matter.

I watch her, my creation.

Her mouth opens on a cry as she comes, face contorting in that curious way that looks like pain, but isn't. She presses into his hands, demanding he fuck her and fuck her now. He has his fingers in her and she wriggles in abandon, makes her demands again, snarling at the nice man. Mary knows how to deal with his type.

He eases into her, gripping her hips and it's not enough, so she reaches for her clit, rubbing it the way she likes. Tom says something appreciative, accelerating his thrusts. They're both watching Mary in the mirror. She is wanton in her pleasure, completely abandoned. She climaxes twice more before he does.

And it's nearly enough.

Almost exact.

As soon as he pulls out of Mary, she heads to the bathroom, scooping up her dress from the floor. She's not the sort for cuddling in the afterglow. Mary might have work, too, before the evening is done. Perhaps she's a CEO of a major company. No. That's not quite it. I watch her in the mirror as she wipes herself down with a soapy washcloth. Mary is an artist. A painter, maybe, and now she'll go back to her trendy loft and paint on huge canvases. Flowers, in sultry shades, flagrantly sexual.

"You okay in there, Mary?" Tom adds a tentative knock on the door.

She shimmies into the dress and walks out. Tom has another scotch on the rocks poured.

"Want a drink now?" He's unsure of her, which is as it should be. It's when they're sure of you that things get bad. "They don't have Prosecco, but there's some white wine that—"

She stops his words with a kiss. Very nice man. "I have to go. Will you zip me?" She turns around, holding the crimson hair aside, bookending their assignation. He raises the zipper and she gives him one more kiss. "Thanks. That was fun."

"I'm in town for a couple of weeks." He starts to hand her a business card.

She shakes her head. "I'm not."

It's true. Mary will go home to her trendy loft to paint all night. In the morning, she will be gone, as if she never existed.

Too bad. I really liked that wig.

Chapter 2

TONIGHT, MY NAME is Tiffany.

Like the jewelry. Maybe the platinum blond is cliché, but that's my gut instinct and I like how it looks with the dangling crystal earrings. Tiffany would wear diamonds but I don't have any for her. The men who frequent Circle² won't care anyway. They'll like Tiffany's cool, aristocratic manners.

She wears lingerie—all matching—complete with garter belt and stockings, all shades of cream. Her makeup is more difficult as it can't come across as heavy as it is. I try cornflower blue contacts, but trade them out for a darker shade. That's much better. They make her eyes into deep sapphires. Tiffany is all about the jewels. I give her a Martinique tan and a few rhinestones at the corner of one eye. Her lashes are much lighter, her eyes round. For her mouth, I go with hot pink in a piquant bow shape. She wears a business suit. White silk blouse, narrow skirt with a slit to just over the knee. I take the time to apply fake nails. Pink, like her lips.

Circle² is quieter tonight. Tuesday nights can be like that, but I don't want to wait until later in the week. I needed to get out, to find a man, burn off the restless ache. Maybe not a nice man this time.

Tiffany chooses a booth. Long day at the office, stopping in for a quiet drink. The bartender gives her a nod and a smile, calling out that he'll be right over. I peruse the cocktail menu, not something I do often. Usually I have my drink decided ahead of time, but Tiffany isn't much for having the same thing. She likes to try the specials, the signature cocktails.

"What'll you have?" The bartender has a towel draped over his shoulder and he's wearing a Guinness T-shirt. It's amusing because it shows only the glowing yellow bottle cap and has the caption "Guinness by night."

It makes her smile and he grins back. "Not everyone gets the shirt."

Because I really want a Guinness and Tiffany isn't that kind of girl, I break a rule—a minor one—and ask, "What should I have—what's your specialty?"

"I make a mean Cosmopolitan."

"Sounds delicious." Tiffany hands him the cocktail menu as if it shouldn't stay on the table, along with a cool society smile. She's done with the bartender and peruses the pickings, though they are slim, indeed. Several of the men seated at the bar watch only the television. A group of guys in fraternity letters play darts in the corner. A couple are cute, but Tiffany doesn't do college boys.

When the bartender returns with her drink, elegantly prepared, as perfectly pink as her fake nails, he says, "Gentleman at the corner of the bar offered to buy, asks if he can join you."

"Oh?" I have to lean forward to see around him. An older man, silver hair, very distinguished, raises his beer in a salute and question. A nice man and I don't want a nice man tonight. "I don't think so." I open my slim clutch and give the bartender a twenty. "Keep it."

It's a big tip, especially if he is the owner, but I rarely tip him. Because I almost never buy my own drinks, I usually can't see if the men who do buy them leave tips.

"Thanks." He doesn't go right away. "Does that count for all takers tonight? I can tell them to leave you alone." He's never asked me this before and I wonder if it's something about Tiffany that makes him more protective than usual.

"I'll review on a case-by-case basis." She gives him a coy smile, but he doesn't return it. Simply shrugs and goes back to his routine.

The exchange leaves me thinking, though, and I turn it over in my mind as I sip the cocktail, idly watching the college boys, with their exuberance and tight asses in perfectly faded jeans. If I'd known they'd be in here, I would have been someone else. Caitlyn the college cheerleader perhaps. Or Sydney—call me Syd—a first-year grad student.

I know the bartender hasn't recognized me. He showed no sign of that. It only seemed that way because we exchanged more words than ever before. Tiffany, apparently, is a talker. I need to pick a man and leave before she gets me into trouble—or worse, ruins things for us both—so I undo one more button on her blouse and rearrange her on the seat so the slit in her skirt exposes more thigh.

The older man is watching Tiffany, and no one else is. I should have been someone else if I wanted to attract rough. Sheryl, the biker chick. But she would go to a biker bar and I like Circle^2. Tiffany crooks a finger to the man, beckoning him over. She is a fragile creation who won't last long. And he'll do for the night.

He smiles and orders another round. The bartender casts a quizzical look in my direction, but sets to making the drink while my date strolls over.

"What changed your mind?" he asks.

Tiffany shakes her short platinum do. "I decided I was bored.

And lonely. I'm Tiffany. Like the jewelry."

He takes my hand by the fingertips, not a real handshake. Not for a woman like Tiffany. "Daniel Holscomb."

"Won't you sit?" She gestures languidly to the opposite bench and Daniel sits, just as the bartender arrives with our drinks on a tray.

"How was the Cosmopolitan?" he asks, catching and holding Tiffany's gaze. Asking her if she really wants this guy here. She's fine with it. She doesn't hold strong opinions for the most part.

"It's fine," she says. "Not exactly what I wanted, but sometimes we settle." Downright chatty, Tiffany. I have to make her voice throaty, to help disguise it, just in case he recognizes it in the future. I'd hate to stop coming to Circle^2, but I'll have to if it comes to that. The ritual depends upon it.

"Don't settle." The bartender gives Daniel his beer but keeps the cocktail. "Give me another chance."

He doesn't wait for me to reply, but takes the Cosmopolitan away.

"You must come here often," Daniel says.

"No. My first time. I'm a buyer for a New York boutique. Just in town to investigate a tip on some local crafts."

"I'm traveling for business, too." Daniel smiles. "Hotel rooms get lonely, don't they?"

I laugh at the standard ploy and his smile fades. I'm saved from explaining by the bartender's return. He sets a champagne flute in front of Tiffany, which gives me pause, but it's not Prosecco. Curious, I hold the glass up to the light. It's golden on the bottom, deep brown on top.

"A Black Velvet," the bartender explains. "Guinness floated on champagne. Want to give it a try?"

Tiffany rewards him with a flirtatious smile, but I manage to keep her from saying anything by putting the glass to her lips. Delicious. "Much better. Thanks."

With a last glance at Daniel, he goes.

"Where were we?" Daniel is frowning, ever so slightly. I don't think he's aware of it.

"Talking about your hotel room." Tiffany cocks her head and leans on the table so her blouse gapes open enough to show off her lacy bra. "Is it next door?"

He swigs his beer, on firmer footing, and puts his hand on Tiffany's knee under the table. She doesn't love that, but I keep her there and don't move to stop him. If I let them chicken out, we'll never get laid. "Or we could go to your room."

"I'm not staying nearby. Yours will do."

Tiffany finishes her drink. Too fast, because I really wanted to savor it, but time is running short. The pink lipstick barely shows on the glass. Tiffany is ephemeral.

We get up to go. "Don't you have a coat?" Daniel asks.

"Can you believe I left it in the cab this morning?" Tiffany laughs, sounding drunker than she is, and loops Daniel's arm around her shoulders. "You'll have to keep me warm."

"I can do that," he assures her.

As we go, I wave at the bartender, a carefree, Tiffany wave, more a flutter of fingers. He nods, taps his finger to his temple in a sort of salute, then turns back to the man chatting him up.

DANIEL'S ROOM IS immaculate, his clothes put away and no suitcase in sight. His laptop sits neatly on the desk, the cords arranged just so. I stop to review Tiffany's appearance in the mirror. She still has her perfect shine. Daniel hands her a vodka rocks, no doubt still thinking of the Cosmopolitan, and I set it aside, even though Tiffany wouldn't.

He kisses me, politely, a brush of lips to test, then deepening. I usually love this moment, the first taste of a man. There's nothing like that first kiss, the first unveiling of the body I wear to another. Despite the sameness of the act, each man's approach to sex is as different as the capillary map of his retina. As each man sees me, I'm patterned upon his eye in a new way. Always someone I've never been before. When I come for him, I lose a little more of who I used to be, purified in the *mikvah* of carnal lust.

Daniel is careful with Tiffany, which is only what she deserves. He undresses her and she lets him, making little sighs like butterfly wings on ice. He tells her she's beautiful, but he doesn't mean it because he barely looks at her. His phone rings, a song from the seventies, and he hitches before ignoring it. He helps Tiffany sit on the bed, watching her as she stretches out, languid, passive.

He undresses, hanging up his suit. He has his own condom. Tiffany doesn't offer to suck his cock as she doesn't really like to. She'll do it if they insist, but grudgingly. She never swallows and they don't much like her gagging.

Daniel works her clit deftly enough and she comes for him, light as a breeze, and then again when he's inside her. She clings to him, breathing in the expensive aftershave, lifting her pelvis so he goes deeper. But that's me. Tiffany doesn't know to ask for that. I learned it from some of the others, the ones I love best.

In the end, it's not exact, but warm enough.

When I wash Daniel from Tiffany's body, I study her in the mirror. She's abashed and vaguely guilty, though not certain why. When she gets back to her hotel, she'll stop at the pantry by the front desk and buy a pint of ice cream, then eat all of it while watching a pay-per-view movie she treats herself to.

Both will be better than sex with diffident Daniel.

I won't miss Tiffany. She's maybe a little too familiar.

As I walk home, I pass Circle^2. The lights glow golden and welcoming. The bartender is laughing at something before glancing out at the street. He can't see me on the other side of it. Still, I'm tempted to go in and order another Black Velvet.

But Tiffany is already dying and I can't go as myself, so I go home.

The wig itches and I can't wait to take it off.

Chapter 3

TONIGHT, MY NAME is Sydney.

Call me Syd. She's easy to dress as she doesn't worry much about clothes. Plain cotton bra—no underwire because they pinch—and her panties have colorful unicorns on them farting rainbows. Syd isn't all about the books, she has her whimsical side, too.

Her hair is dark brown, a simple square cut with heavy bangs. She wears glasses with thick black rims and a hint of a cat's eye horn at the edge. All of these things are important because I can't put too much obvious makeup on her. Syd's getting her master's in comparative religious studies and she's particularly interested in the question of vanity and mortification of the flesh to purify the spirit, New Testament style. I can't go near the Torah anymore.

I go with darker foundation for her skin, not so much that it will look funny when she's naked, but enough to distort her mouth and cover the putty on her nose—the only features that really show. I go with a matte lipstick for her, the kind that looks like none at all, and add a cherry ChapStick overcoat, then stick the tube in her jeans pocket. Dark brown contact lenses for her eyes, which look intense even behind the unfashionably thick lenses of her glasses.

Even without the underwire, Syd's tits look pretty good in the tight sweater. Enticing enough to reel in a college boy, anyway. They're always hard up.

The college guys aren't there, however, though it's a Tuesday again. Disappointing as the thin crowd doesn't promise much. Maybe Syd will sit at the bar, read a book and nurse her drink. A girl like Syd might go home alone. She doesn't *have* to get laid.

But I do. After Disappointing Daniel, I need to get off. Badly. I'm restless with it, edgy. Probably I should have been someone else for tonight, to score the really good bang. I nearly went for Caitlyn and couldn't. Too soon after Tiffany. I still miss Mary. I'd had to force myself to burn that wig, lest I break down and wear it a second time. It never works to be the same woman twice. Too much like my life before, the forever trying to be the right person and forever failing. I want to be Mary again, but that way lies disappointment and more of that might break me forever.

The only other disguise that appealed was Sydney's dark wig and obscuring glasses, so that's what I did. I've learned to go with instinct.

Syd chooses a stool at the darker end of the bar, as far from the televisions as she can get, and puts her book on the glossy golden wood.

"Be right with you," the bartender calls out, and Syd nods, opens her book, clips on the little reading light. A guy down the bar a bit raises a glass to her. She smiles. A bit shy, but she'll warm up. He's her type, academic-looking, not a suit. I've had enough of the business travelers for a while.

"What'll you have?" the bartender asks. He tosses the towel over his shoulder. Tonight his T-shirt says, in faded white letters on soft black, "There are 10 kinds of people in the world. Those who understand binary and those who don't."

"Ha! Love the shirt," Syd says before I can stop her. What

happened to shy?

"It's always interesting who gets it," he replies, with that grin I like. He peers at my text. *"Confessions of St. Augustine?"*

"The saint who gave up wealth, wine, women, and excesses of all kinds to purify the spirit."

"Yeah—but at the end of his life. I'm not sure it counts when you indulge for sixty years and then go all holy when you can't get it up anymore."

"How do you know he couldn't?"

"Who gives up sex when they can still do it?"

I grin back at him. There's the zing, the spark I'm craving. The bartender is better looking than I thought. The kind of guy who grows on you. He has nicely muscled shoulders and the T-shirt looks old and touchable. I'd like to run my hands over his chest and then slide them up beneath.

But I shouldn't do that because then I'd have to stop coming here. The ritual is both precise and delicate. So Syd pulls out her ChapStick and layers on another coat, to give herself time to think. He doesn't recognize me, but talking this much—and with a man about sex even—is fun for me. I've never had this experience. Before, we never discussed it, never used any of the words, as if sex didn't exist outside the bed where he penetrated my body in the dark of halakhic obligation. With the men since, we talk only enough to get to the sex.

It's never occurred to me that talking about sex could be a kind of foreplay. I'm wanting to take over the conversation, which makes it harder to let Syd exist. The bartender has cocked his head, waiting for an answer, to at least the drink question.

"I'm pretty sure he was more like thirty," I finally say, letting it go there and handing the reins to Syd. "I'll have a Harp," she says, though she really wants a Black Velvet. Another Irish beer is close enough. He nods and moves away to get it. Something happens on the television and people cheer. Academic guy dips his chin at the bottle and pint glass the bartender sets down.

"Let me get that for you."

The bartender raises a brow at Syd. She digs a crumpled ten out of her jeans pocket and gives academic guy a reproving shake of her head. "I can buy my own drinks, thanks."

"I was trying to be nice, not make a statement on feminism."

"You heard the lady," the bartender inserts. "Ah, woman, I mean." He winks at me. Academic guy mutters something in a disgusted tone and gets up like he wants to check out something on another television. Oh well, he didn't ring my bell anyway.

"So," the bartender says, lingering while keeping an eye on the other patrons. There aren't many. I really shouldn't come in on a Tuesday again, even at the prospect of hot college boy sex. "Are you Catholic?"

"Not so much," Syd answers. "But it's interesting. I'm doing grad work on a comparison of how Christians interpret the Old Testament compared to the same texts that make up the Torah. You?"

"Lapsed." He shrugs. Nice Irish Catholic boy, I'm guessing. Maybe a crucifix under that T-shirt, gleaming silver against his chest, which is a more erotic image than it ought to be. Just a little hair on it, dark and wiry like on his forearms, which flex as he dries a glass with long fingers. I'm mesmerized enough that I realize he's asking a question and I'm not listening. "What's your hypothesis?"

"The field doesn't work like that so much." Syd should stop there. Hell, she should have stopped a long time ago, but she doesn't. This is more than I've talked to anyone not work-related in…months. It's easy to lose track of time. The bartender has good eyes, on the hazel side, maybe even mossy green in daylight. I take a pull on the Harp, surprised to hit bottom. The bartender takes the empty and moves to grab me another when I nod. What the hell.

"Okay, this is my idea. Did you know that people call the clitoris the devil's doorbell?"

He cracks up. "You're kidding! What people? I don't know those people."

Syd waves a hand. "There are Internet sites you wouldn't believe. Female pleasure is wicked is the idea, leads to sinfulness."

"Not in my book." He's not flirting, exactly, but he's talking to Syd more than he has with any of the others. Maybe she's more his type. Or maybe because she's talking to him and it's a slow night. He's studying me, eyes locked on mine.

"It's more a Christian idea, that women lead men into sinfulness with their bodies. Judaism embraces female sexuality. Did you know a husband is obligated to divorce his wife if he doesn't give her pleasure? The Talmud specifies both the quantity and quality of sex that a man must give his wife."

"See, now there's a holy obligation I could get behind." He's leaning folded arms on the bar now, eyes glinting with mischief. "Where do you come out on the debate?"

A dangerous path I'm treading so I decline to answer directly. "You know how people always say that it's Eve's fault that she and Adam got kicked out of Eden?"

"Because she handed him the apple of knowledge and invited him to eat it."

"Or told him to, or tricked him, depending on who you ask. Anyway, what if the real meaning of that story is that woman recognized they'd never grow in paradise. If they stayed there they'd just be God's little goody-two-shoes pets forever. Maybe Eve deliberately handed Adam the opportunity to wake the fuck up and see they could have more out of life than being kept."

"Some people want to be kept," the bartender points out. "It's comfortable."

"No, that's complete and utter bullshit." I say it too strongly. I've shocked him, so I take a moment. Syd pushes up her glasses. For her it's all theory. She hasn't lived through what I have. "They make you think that, that you're comfortable, that you're happy and cared for. But it's all lies. Just like Eden. Dressed up to look like paradise—look at all the pretty fruit! And animals for you to name!—but it was prison. Eve was goddamned thrilled to meet Satan."

The bartender looks thoughtful. I haven't offended him. But hey, he's a bartender. He's heard worse than my rant. "But when they ate of knowledge, they knew shame and tried to clothe their nakedness."

That makes me think of Tiffany, which only depresses me. I take a deep swig of the beer. "Yeah, well, it's a theory in process. I'm working on it."

The bartender considers, polishing a glass. He's contemplating his reply and I'm no longer angry. I'm...curious as to what he'll say. Me, not Syd. For a moment I'm confused, forgetting who I am and what point I'd argued for.

"Hi." A guy in a black leather jacket sits beside me, straddling the stool with lanky legs, and holds out a hand for me to shake. "I'm Alan."

He's got an attractive scruff and eyes that are just a little hard. Not a nice man. Syd wants him to mortify her flesh in a big way. This is what she came her for. Real sex, not the conversational variety. She takes his hand. It's callused from some kind of manual labor. There won't be a laptop in his hotel room, no high school sweetheart wife calling to check up on him. He'll be rough, maybe a little mean, and Syd needs that. Her pussy clenches with heat.

"Sydney. Call me Syd."

He points at my nearly empty. "Can I buy you another?"

"Sure."

"I haven't seen you in here before."

"My first time."

The bartender sets down a fresh bottle, flicks a glance at me, and moves a short distance away, turning to watch the game on the screen above the bar. I drink deeply and Alan puts a hand on the back of my neck, under my hair.

"Don't touch my hair," I say.

"Why not?" His fingers stroke my neck and the heat grows, blessed distraction.

"I don't like it," I tell him, and his lips twitch, eyes on mine like he's thinking about kissing me.

"What do you like?" The question is a caress.

"Everything else."

"I can do that." He picks up my beer and finishes it for me. "Let's get out of here."

"Next round is on the house," the bartender says, catching my eye. "Hang a while."

He's never tried to get me to stay before. All that conversation has changed up the ritual, just as I've feared.

"Hey, thanks, dude." Alan snugs an arm around my waist and pulls me tight against him, taking the decision out of my hands. "But I've got someone to do, if you know what I mean."

I go with him, not waving goodbye to the bartender this time.

ALAN ISN'T CRUEL, but he treats Syd harshly in the back seat of his extended-cab pickup. I'm happy it's not a hotel room, but I can't watch her the way I like to. With the dark, though, it doesn't matter when he takes off her glasses, or that he mushes her nose out of shape while kissing her hard before stripping her out of her clothes.

"Such fucking honeypot under here, aren't you?" he mutters, touching me everywhere at once, then shoving two fingers into my slick heat. I cry out and he smiles, teeth white in the dark. "A hot little cunt."

Syd comes, pleasing him even more. He starts to climb onto her, but I need to see. I clamber up and bend over the back of the seat to the front. Suddenly I'm face to face with her naked brown eyes in the rearview mirror. Alan cackles and smacks her ass. Her eyes dampen with incipient tears.

"You like that, huh?" Alan spanks her again and again, anchoring her there with a rough hand in the small of her back. She's crying now, her mouth open in sobs. "I heard you spouting that Catholic shit. You pious girls are all the same." He drags moisture from her cunt up to her asshole, thrusting in. "You all prefer anal so you can pretend you're virgins. Isn't that right?"

Syd is crying too hard to answer, so he spanks her several more times. "Answer me, little virgin angel. You want me up your ass don't you? Dirty girl."

"Yes!" Syd gasps out the admission. "Do it."

Even with the high ceiling, he's forced to bend over her, his harsh breath hot on her neck. It hurts and Syd's face blurs in the mirror. The contortions I can make out, however, are of genuine pain and look just the same as orgasm. When she comes, it's wrenchingly hard.

Convulsive.

Unholy.

Chapter 4

TONIGHT, MY NAME is Bobbi.

As in Bobbi Socks. For her I dye a wig bright blue with magenta tips, then scrape it into spikes with paste. I go with Kiss-style makeup, but of Bobbi's flavor—black and white greasepaint, scattered with Day of the Dead rose petals. She wears buckled biker boots, torn fishnet stockings, a barely there skirt, and a net midriff-baring top over a black lace bra. There's a retro-punk band at Circle² tonight, so I can get away with the outfit.

That's what gets me to go there again, though I've stayed away for nearly a month this time. Circle² should be crowded and full of different people. No chance of being tempted into risky conversation with the bartender. I'll blend into the crowd. All of this is an excuse, because I really want to go. The flyer flapping in the October wind blazed a fluorescent omen, an answer to the grinding question of whether I dared go back.

Sometimes I feel like a serial killer, the way they supposedly go dormant for a while, like snakes do, digesting their infrequent, large meals. Then the need begins pricking, the hunger rising again, a little bit more every day, until I know I have no choice. I have to leave the sterile silence of the condo and go find flesh. Nothing but a man's hands on me, his cock in me, will do. Only that fills the hole rent in my life where family and belief once sustained me.

I suppose it is a kind of hunting, though I leave my prey alive, with the illusion that they bagged me.

No more car sex, though. I didn't like that Syd had to walk home with Alan on her skin. Blood leaking out of her, too, which ruined those funny panties. I burned them along with Syd's wig, and the washcloth I bathed her with in my own bathroom mirror. Letting Syd die wasn't easy. She'd been interesting. She'd gotten me into the conversation with the bartender that led to a different kind of sex. A session intense enough to sate me all this time. Quite the meal.

Which is good because I don't want to repeat it. Despite her intelligence, Syd hadn't been too smart about that one. Alan could have hurt her much worse than he did.

Bobbi will lay out the rules for her encounter, though she doesn't know what she wants yet. She likes to be spontaneous, go with the flow, love the one you're with.

Circle^2 is gratifyingly packed and Bobbi spots several candidates right off the bat. More locals than usual, though, and I'm not sure about going to anyone's actual home. I might have to lift the ban on car sex. Maybe judge by the car? I'd cross that bridge. I'd broken other rules, though I'm not sure I should have. Things aren't as black and white as they used to be.

No more conversations with the bartender though. That much is clear. Not that it's likely with the din of the band and people shouting over it.

Bobbi wedges her way through the press of standers and sitters at the bar. With the crowd, they have a couple more bartenders working and she angles herself to the gal with the blond ponytail serving drinks at the far end. But just as the guy in front of Bobbi gets his drinks, the blonde moves down five people to take another order, and Mr. Irish Catholic Guy moves into the void.

"What'll you have?" he shouts over the music to Bobbi, giving a distracted nod to another man who calls out an order. His shirt tonight says "Carpe Cerveza."

It doesn't count as conversation. But, to be safe, I point at the bottle of beer in the hand of the guy next to me. A lite American beer that will be cheap and tasteless. Bobbi can pound a lot of those and not feel it.

"Get me another, too, and I'll get hers," says the guy, giving me a once-over, gaze lingering on the cleavage revealed by the black net top. "I'm Mike."

"Bobbi," I tell him, "like bobby socks."

The bartender checks with me, and I nod. Why the hell not? He shrugs, holding my gaze a moment longer. Bobbi's eyes are a lightish brown, unremarkable as the beer, nothing to snag such attention. All of her sizzle is layered on top. Not unlike the real me. Regardless, I'm not sure why he's giving me that look. Protective, maybe. Bobbi looks young.

"You got ID, *Bobbi*?" he asks, confirming it. I mentally stumble. He's never carded me before. Something I should have thought about, with the band and all. I haven't been asked for ID in years, but with the all-ages band night he's probably being careful.

"Left it at home," I mumble. Maybe that fluorescent flyer had been a warning, not an invitation. I turn to go.

"I'll be her guardian." Mike slings an arm around my shoulder, hugs me to him. "I'm of age and can supervise." He manages to make it sound dirty and I smirk, though mainly it's funny because he's probably ten years younger than I am.

The bartender isn't amused and holds out a hand. I stare at it, momentarily dumbfounded. He says something I can't hear, so I have to lean in.

"You need a wristband." He dangles it, pulling it back when I reach for it. "I have to put it on you myself," he says, very seriously. "It's the law."

I'm quite certain the law specifies no such thing, but arguing the point would just suck up time and—not incidentally—make me violate the no-conversation rule. Bobbi puts on her best anti-establishment sneer and sticks out her arm, stiff, fingers in a fist. Mr. Irish Catholic makes a production of it, like he's putting a diamond bracelet on me instead of a cheap paper wristband the same obnoxious orange as that flyer. He makes sure it's secure, fingers brushing the underside of my wrist, a shockingly erotic contact for something so chaste.

It's because I went so long, let the hunger grow teeth. Bobbi nearly climbs onto the bar to seize his face in her hands and kiss his gorgeous mouth that smiles so easily and speaks so frankly of sex. The sudden lust must show on my face, because his hands are still on mine, his friendly eyes darkening with an answer. The band goes silent, the hoots of appreciation fading as they go on break.

"What'll you have?" the bartender asks me in the relative quiet, for the second time, and I feel like he's asking me something else.

"Hey, do you two know each other or something?" Mike is little whiny. No surprise as I've forgotten about him, even though he still has an arm around my shoulders.

"No," I say.

"Yes," Mr. Irish Catholic says at the same time, giving me a slight smile, still holding my hand. "How about a Shirley Temple?"

"Club soda," I snap, yanking my hand away. "Twist of lime."

He grins, easily ignoring the patrons trying to get his attention, and pours it into a flute. "On the house," he says and moves off.

"Hey," Mike complains. "He forgot my beer."

Except I know he's forgotten nothing. My bartender is making a statement.

I don't know how, but he's recognized me.

Chapter 5

TONIGHT, MY NAME is Eris.

The goddess of discord and strife. It's only two nights since Bobbi fled Circle² in unseemly haste. Notably without getting laid, and the hunger is that much worse for being denied. I'm still pissed about it.

Or I'm something about it that I haven't yet defined.

I don't much care about missing out on Mike. He was okay but that's all. I can't even bring up his face in my mind. I keep thinking about Mr. Irish Catholic, about the brush of his fingers. Even if he hadn't tipped that he recognized me—though I don't know how he possibly could have—I would have been thinking about *his* hands on my body, not Mike's.

I'm still thinking about them. And so I'm going back to Circle², even though I know I shouldn't. I am the serial killer pushed past all discretion. I can't stop myself.

I've spent the past two days scouring Yelp for potential new bars because I can't go back to Circle².

I can't make myself go anywhere else.

It's Halloween, so I justify that this makes all the difference. Everyone will be in costume. I can go to the extreme and not stand out. This is how the bartender recognized me, I've decided. Even in dim bar light, heavy makeup shows. So he somehow connected Bobbi and Tiffany. And maybe Syd, too.

He won't know me tonight. If he does, it won't matter because this is my last excursion to Circle². I repeat that resolve, my own personal kaddish of mourning before the fact.

I dress Eris according to an illustration I like on Etsy. Any of several wigs with long black hair will do, but I pick the rattiest one. I pile her hair into tiers of ropy pony tails, decorated with gold bands. Her lips are full, pointed and a deep magenta. I make her eyes so smoky, with deep shadows and a double layer of false lashes, that they look like bruises in her white face. The contact lenses make her eyes look black and are so dark the room dims.

This is how Eris sees the world. Through a glass, darkly.

I dress her in a black silk nightgown with nothing beneath, risqué, even for the wildest of my personalities. But there will be women out tonight wearing much less, stretching the boundaries to breaking. People like to bitch about the costume companies pandering with all the sexy female outfits. It's not them, I think, but us. What woman gets to go out in public as the decadently sexual person she fantasizes she could be?

I do, but I pay a price for it. Or, rather, I paid up front and now scrape to gather whatever rewards my pain bought me.

Halloween lets us all be that slut, without censure.

Of course, I am not the poster child for healthy sexuality.

I add black fingerless gloves and night-dark feathered wings from the temporary costume shop down the block, and a half mask of ebony beads on dark velveteen. Carrying a golden apple, I walk to Circle², ready to sow some discord.

The place is busy. Nothing like when the band played, but more packed than usual. I study the room, picking my spot. Eris would simply force someone to move from the seat she fancied, through guile or outright aggression. She'd likely steal someone else's man. I won't let her do that, I think. Even I have my lines in the sand and I won't do that to someone else. Not right in front of them, anyway.

Besides, I have my target in mind. For my last visit to Circle².

I'm having some Irish tonight, and then I'm never coming back.

Never taunt the goddess of discord and strife.

The blonde is working the bar, along with another guy. My bartender is nowhere in sight. Unusual, but not disastrous. Not yet. I circle the room, the place looking like the Mos Eisley Cantina with the array of costumes. He doesn't appear. He must be in the back. That's it. Grabbing a fresh keg or some such.

He's always here. He can't not be here.

Unless, with the finely honed instincts of any prey animal, he'd known to keep clear. The hairs prickling on the back of his neck, a chill passing over him as if someone stepped on his grave. A smart man to avoid making a pact with this particular demon. My heart thuds with disappointment. I try to make Eris look around for someone else, but she's stubborn. She has one man in mind and a goddess doesn't easily give up her target.

"Can I buy you a drink?"

I bite down on the automatic no. I'm bitter that Mr. Irish Catholic isn't here, but I will get laid regardless. Who it will be doesn't matter. It's never mattered. I can't let that change now.

I force a smile onto Eris's magenta mouth and turn. And catch my breath. He's got his dark hair in a side part, sleekly combed over, and heavy rimmed glasses dominate his face, mossy green eyes looking larger with the thick lenses. An old-style trench coat hangs open over his gray suit, a too-wide red necktie askew on his crisp white collared shirt. One of the buttons is undone, giving a glimpse of scarlet and yellow beneath.

"Clark Kent." He holds out a hand to shake. "Reporter for the

Daily Planet."

"Eris," I say, taking his hand. "Goddess of—"

"Discord and strife," he finishes, pumping my hand and then pushing up his glasses with one finger. "Started the Trojan war by tossing that golden apple into the feast of the gods."

"I like an educated man."

"Good." He smiles easily. "I was hoping you'd be here tonight. *Eris*. What'll you have?"

I hesitate only briefly. He knows it's me, but I take the plunge. I want what he has to offer. "Black Velvet."

His smile widens. "A house specialty. Come with me."

Keeping my hand, he pulls me to the bar, lifts the pass-through and parks me in a corner where my wings won't be in the way. It's far less crowded inside the circle than out. With a shimmer of growing anticipation I watch him build my cocktail. Those lovely, competent hands of his work with brisk yet careful skill. I want them on me. I set the apple on the bar.

He uses Dom Perignon for the champagne portion and I raise a brow. "Expensive."

He gives me a half-smile, a bit of self-effacing shyness in it. "It's my place, so I get it at cost. Besides, it's a special occasion."

"Why did you name it Circle^2?" I've wanted to ask this for a long time, but none of the women I'd been had cared.

The half-smile spreads into a grin. "Two reasons. The second circle of hell."

"For those overcome by lust?"

"Why I could never become the priest my sainted mother hoped I'd be." He leaks a bit of an aggrieved Irish accent into the words.

"And the other reason?"

"You can't square a circle, no matter how hard you try." He's made two of the cocktails, the separation perfect, with effervescent gold below, capped by impenetrable darkness.

"To you." He taps his glass against mine. "Let's find a booth."

I smile, not moving. "Let's finish our drinks and get out of here."

That arrests him. He pushes up his glasses, the gesture completely in character and yet so natural to him that I think he's worn glasses in his life. Maybe he normally wears contact lenses, too, and these are actually his prescription glasses. The insight gives me a thrill, like I've glimpsed something illicit that he meant to hide.

He doesn't argue, though he seems to want to. I sip my drink—heavenly!—and wait for him to accept the invitation. He can't refuse. Eris won't let him. I'm depending on her for this. She slips her free hand inside the open placket of his shirt, caressing the spandex beneath, and leans in to breathe in his ear.

"I know who you are."

I mean Superman, all part of the game, but the words electrify him and me both, our gazes clashing like amplifier feedback, then holding. I'm wet. Eris would fuck him right on the bar, in front of everyone. But he wouldn't. "Where's a phone booth when we need one?" I add, and the joke alleviates the unbearable tension.

He wraps strong fingers around my wrist, not pushing me away, but holding me there. "I live upstairs."

My turn to hesitate. I don't want to be in his place, to see the photographs of family or past girlfriends, the dirty underwear on his bathroom floor, crusty dishes in the sink. I want Clark Kent on the bar or Superman in the phone booth.

He reads it in my face, Eris letting me down. She's an imperfect mask. Or maybe it's him, somehow seeing into me every time, no matter who I wear.

"Or your place is good, too," he says softly. Trying to reassure me. "You must live nearby."

I bite the corner of his jaw to punish him, and his eyes widen in surprise behind the thick lenses. A magenta lip print stains his skin. I want to cover his body with my marks. "Mt. Olympus is far away from here."

"Then upstairs it is. You can even bring your drink."

I nearly suggest the hotel instead, but he'd have to pay for the room and that feels unfair. Eris shouldn't care. She, however, is not helping as much as she should. Once we get there, once I find her reflection, she'll take over. I won't notice anything else.

He takes my hand in that way of his and we exit via the pass-through. Only dropping my hand long enough to unlock the deadbolt on a door at the back of the bar, he leads me up a narrow stairway with boards that creak underfoot, audible even over the muffled din of the bar. It's an old building, smelling of brick dust, worn wood and the passage of many footsteps.

There's another door at the top of the stairs and once that's closed, there's remarkably little sound. If I don't listen for it, I can't hear the bar at all.

He starts to say something, but I don't want to risk looking around, seeing something I can't unsee, so I take his drink and put it with mine on the closest surface and stop his words with a kiss. He returns it in kind and I drink him in. The taste of champagne and stout overlaying another flavor, something essentially him. His hands encircle my hips, moving up my back under the wings, caressing me with gentlemanly care. With something that feels like affection.

It kind of breaks me, that tenderness. Suddenly, I'm not sure I can do this.

Where has the driving hunger gone? It hasn't vanished, but it's…metastasized in some insidious way. I want him to fuck me, yes, and I also want—something I can't have. I've been down this road. I know better.

Then, his tongue touches mine, he murmurs something sweet against my mouth, and I nearly weep.

So I pull away and begin to tug the slim straps of my gown through the elastic bands of the wings. I want to keep them on, keep Eris on, even though she's not doing her job. Maybe it's too hard to be a goddess. I don't know what she's like, what she does when she can't sleep at night and the glowing numbers of her cell phone glare at her, ticking her life away.

He stops me, hands on my wrists again. "What's your hurry?" He kisses my throat, making me hum and arch against him. "We have all night."

We don't, but I don't say so. I like that he's taking over. That always makes it easier because I can let go and drift on the tide of sensation. Let the physical wash away everything else. He draws my hands around his neck, kissing his way down my throat, tracing my collarbones with his clever mouth. He's humming, swaying with me in his arms, and I realize we're almost dancing, moving to the nearly subliminal throb of a song from below.

It would be our song, if this were a romance. The fact that I can't quite identify the melody is perfectly apt. Such things always slip away, just outside my grasp.

Unable to contain my impatience, I pull at his buttons, blindly pushing the ridiculous tie aside and yanking open his shirt. He groans, mouth finding mine again. His hair is mussed and his glasses are askew.

Underneath, he is Superman.

I get his belt undone and his dorky pants open. He is old-style

Superman, and the yellow-belted red groin-covering should be silly, but it's not. It's strangely erotic, especially with his generous cock upthrust inside. I stroke him over the sleek spandex, swallowing his hum of pleasure.

"The bedroom," he says into my mouth.

"No. Here is good."

I risk a glance around to spy a mirror, but I don't see one immediately. I get an impression of gleaming wood floors, thick throw rugs and vivid paintings on the walls before I close my mind to them.

"The bedroom," he insists and puts me away from him. He picks up our drinks and walks off, turning into a dark hallway that brightens as he elbows on a switch. I stand there, annoyed now that he's taken the upper hand. Eris could show him by leaving. She could find someone else, take refuge in the anonymity of the hotel.

But we don't want anyone else.

I make sure the door is locked, then follow him down the hall.

Chapter 6

IN HIS BEDROOM, he's lighting candles, of all things. And he has the bed turned down, scattered with bloodred rose petals. He sees me looking and gives me a serious smile. "I told you—I hoped you'd come tonight."

My heart thuds, beating against my ribs in a last-ditch escape attempt. I have to leave. Leave now before I crack open. I turn around, and his hands are around my waist before I take two steps. His mouth is against my cheekbone, the wings rustling between us. I cannot fly.

"Don't run," he murmurs, coaxing. "You like dim light, yes? This way we can turn off the lights. And you like red. I meant all this to...ease the way."

It rattles my skull that he planned it out, that he expected me at Circle^2 and that he'd predicted I'd come upstairs with him, observed what I'd like. Of course, if he'd been recognizing me all along, he knew my patterns. I'm too exposed.

"I can't do this," I whisper, not at all sure who I'm talking to.

"Okay," he replies easily. "No pressure. Let's sit, have our drinks and talk. Or go back downstairs and talk. Or dance. Whatever you like."

I spin, and he ducks the stiff wing, his smile fading immediately at the look on my face. "What do you think this is?" I hiss the words through my teeth. "Do you think this is about talking and dancing and... and rose petals?" I fling a hand at the bed, my fingers tight in a fist.

He takes off the glasses and tosses them aside, rubbing the bridge of his nose. "I don't know, do I? I don't know anything about you, not even your name."

"I am Eris, goddess of—"

He seizes me by the upper arms, the grip arousingly tight. "Not whoever you're pretending to be. Mary, Tiffany, Syd, Bobbi—all of them. I think you're all of them and none of them. I think you're in *my* bedroom for a reason. I want to know more about you. I want *you*. Don't go."

I watch his lips move. They're smeared with my lipstick and he still sports the magenta stain on the corner of his jaw. I want him with searing intensity.

"Help me out of these wings," I say.

He relaxes his grip, sliding hands up and down my arms, as if comforting me. "Are you sure? We don't have to have sex."

"I have to. I need this." I shrug off his hands, then the wings. I strip off the straps and let the black silk puddle at my feet. I've covered Eris's skin with honey dust, so she gleams naked in the candlelight, her nipples rouged as dark magenta as her mouth. I've waxed her clean, so none of my natural hair shows. He stares at me, transfixed. Eris is beautiful, full of the allure of chaos, those destructive acts that are too compelling to resist. "Here are the rules. You can do whatever you like to me. Do the romance thing. I don't care. But this is only fucking and only for tonight. After this you'll never see me again."

He hesitates. "What if I want more than tonight?"

"Not on the table. You'll never see me again either way. So either you fuck me before we say goodbye forever or not. Your call."

He's frustrated, his jaw tight, but he bites it back. "Will you take off the mask and the wig?"

"The mask, yes, the hair, no. Never the hair."

"Why do you do this? What drives you so hard?" His eyes are back on mine, staring into them, as if he might read my secrets there. Eris is naked and available, and he wants to talk psychology.

In reply, I take his hand and put it between my legs so he cups my bare mons, the liquid heat there making his fingers slide. "For this," I say and move in closer, pushing his shirt from his shoulders and rocking my hips on his hand. He strokes me and it's so good that I moan. "Always this."

"Take off the mask." He's watching my face. "I want to see you."

I oblige, untying the ribbons and tossing it aside. He can't really see me anyway, behind the bruised makeup and my dark glass. I try to kiss him, but he leans his head back. "No—I want to watch you."

His other hand slides up my spine, supporting me as his fingers work their magic. He crafts my orgasm with meticulous care, building sensation upon sensation, finding a rhythm that drives me hard, then backing off, leaving me panting, begging, just short of the climax I so desperately need.

"Enough already," I growl, digging my nails into his neck. They're long and gold and he hisses at the pain but sets his jaw, holding me in place with an insistent grip. "If I only get one night, then I get to have you my way."

"You're having me."

"Yes." He pushes a finger inside me finally, but still not enough for me to come. "You're so beautiful, coming and going like a dream. An enigma. Playing those guys. Every night I watch for you, wondering if you'll come in. And I watch you go home with those other men. None of them mean anything to you."

"I went home with you tonight." I finish the words on a gasp.

"And I mean nothing to you."

I don't answer. Partly because I can't and…because this once I don't want to lie. Or because I don't know what the truth is. He's slowed again, two fingers curling inside me, the heel of his hand constant pressure on my clit, driving me wild.

"Are you playing me?" he asks in an academic tone, as if I'm not nearly frantic, pumping on his exquisitely competent fingers.

I laugh, the sound feral, almost unhinged. "Of course," I say, and I barely get the words out before he presses hard on my lower back, forcing my hips into his hand, ripping me into orgasm so I scream.

It tears from my throat as I throw my head back. *This.* This is what I need from him. I ride his hand, clinging to his shoulders, all the while aware that he's watching me, studying my face. Finding my equilibrium, I reach for his cock, but he takes my wrists, his one hand slick from being inside me.

"Not yet," he says, and backs me to the bed. He is Clark Kent in the phone booth, pants and shirt gaping ragged over the electric blues, reds and yellows of Kal-el. I whisper that name and he smiles, laying me back and spreading my knees. Then his mouth is on me, hot, wet, devastating. No deft manipulation this time. He makes me come, over and over, his hands pinning my wrists by my hips and his dark head between my straining thighs until my voice is ragged and my body limp as the bruised rose petals staining the sheets. More magenta smears, as if I'm a virgin who's given up her sacred blood again and again.

Not the goddess, but the sacrifice. I am laid open on the altar of his bed, split apart by ecstasy.

Shattering an infinite number of times.

Chapter 7

FINALLY HE LETS me go.

He crawls up my languid body, kissing and stroking. I can barely move, much less assemble thought. I curl against him like a cat and he kisses my damp temple, careful not to disturb the wig. Every capillary in my body sings with the effort of pumping blood, every tissue throbbing, wrung to inertia.

In a moment, I'll catch my second wind. I can't believe we haven't fucked yet, that I haven't even seen his cock. Already I've spent more time with him than I have with any man since…well, since before. Any second now, I'll resurrect.

But I like being held. He smells nice, like good beer, expensive champagne and hot sex. And his arms around me are warmly soothing, as are his lips at my temple, pressed in an unending kiss, a message penetrating the depths of my mind, past conscious thought, to the part of me who lies buried in ice.

WHEN I OPEN my eyes, the candles have burned down considerably. We're in the same position, but hours have passed. I'm still naked and he's still in his layers of costume. It should be absurd, but it's not. I move, and his eyes open, slits of moss green behind feathery dark ferns of lashes.

"Hi, lovely," he says and my throat tightens.

In answer—the only reply I have anymore—I put my hand

on his cock. It hardens from semi-erect, leaping to my touch. He puts his hand over mine. "Not yet."

I have to smile, stroking him harder. That gets to him and he shudders. He might have tremendous control, but he's not superhuman. "Then when?" I murmur, finding the glans beneath the tight material and pinching.

He groans and takes my face in his hands, kissing me. It's both tender and ferocious, communicating a different kind of fierce need than the one his hips thrust through my fingers.

"I don't want this to end," he says, and he sounds on edge, a little desperate.

"All things come to an end," I tell him, tugging on the tight spandex. "Take this off. Don't you want my mouth on you?"

His eyes glint with wild desire even as his jaw sets in obstinate refusal. I think he's going to say no, but he sighs out a ragged breath and pulls away from me, briskly shucking off the cheap suit and the costume beneath. He's naked, slim-hipped and sprinkled with dark hair, his cock perfectly shaped and enticingly thrust toward me.

I'm back in my hard-won element.

I crawl up onto my hands and knees, slinking over to him, and taking him in hand. He's transfixed, so hopefully I still look more like Eris than Medusa. I'd have gone to check, but once I enter the bathroom, things are over and I don't want them to be done yet.

He and I are alike that way. The difference is that I know the end is inevitable.

The sound he makes when I take him in my mouth is everything. As is the hot throb of him. I drink his salt, his desire, the way his hands run over the bones of my face and the length of my throat. Feeding me with his touch.

I've been starving for this and take him deeper, though he's murmuring something, then speaking louder.

"No," he gasps, prying me off of him. "Not like this."

I smile up at him, the cat with cream in her mouth. "It can be."

"Not the first time." He pushes on my shoulders, still gentle but resolved, laying me back and following to straddle me, showering me with kisses.

"Our only time," I remind him.

He leans on an elbow and traces my cheekbone, following it with his gaze. "It doesn't have to be."

"It does."

"Why?" His cock is hard and urgent against my splayed thighs, but he looks as if he could wait forever. "Are you married?"

"No." *Not anymore and never again.*

"Won't you explain?"

My heart cracks a little and words spill out of it, but they never reach my lips. I turn my head so I don't have to look at him. "There is no why. There is only this."

"I don't understand."

He sounds distressed enough that I look at him, then lay a finger over his sensual lips, shushing and stroking him. "There's nothing to understand. You wanted me. You have me. Take what's yours."

I slide my hand down his lean body, taking his cock in my hand. He loses the argument he was about to make, groaning and dropping his forehead to mine. His lips search out my mouth and I welcome him in.

This he can have.

This I can give.

He stops my hand and grabs a condom from under the pillow. I love how he's planned this. It no longer frightens me, which should be a warning, but I'm not interested in running now. Not when I'm about to get what I need. I'm weeping for him and undulate to show it, as he strokes firm hands down my sides to part my legs.

Poised at my entrance, he holds himself there. "Tell me your name."

"Eris."

"Your real name."

"That's as real as any, Clark."

"Peter," he says. "My name is Peter."

He enters me and I sigh out the unbearable bliss of it, digging my fingers into his muscled shoulders. I've broken off three of the fake nails along the way. A holy trinity of self-destruction. "'Upon this rock I will build my church.'"

In that moment, I believe it. He could be my rock. Is that for at least these fleeting hours.

"'And the gates of the netherworld shall not prevail against it.'" Peter chants the lines with his thrusts, the silver crucifix swings from a chain like a censer, glinting. "'I will give you the keys to the kingdom of heaven. Whatever you bind on earth shall be bound in heaven; and whatever you loose on earth shall be loosed in heaven.'"

I am both bound and loosed. Pinned under him, trapped between the twin possession of his relentless cock on one end and his ravenous mouth on the other, I give myself up. With only the mirror of his mesmerizing gaze, I give him everything.

We sync, moving together in a mindless rhythm. Rising. Falling. Ascending to that moment of sheer, shimmering gold, where all is perfect, without shame or sorrow.

Exact. Warm. Unholy.

And gone.

HE KNOCKS ON the bathroom door.

"Are you okay?" When he says it, it sounds real. Like he truly wants to know.

I, however, can't come up with an answer.

I am a mess. There's no sign of Eris, only me, a shattered crush of blue, black and magenta. I'm trying to wash, but I need makeup remover, for my face and for the nipples that look obscenely huge now, with the rouging smeared by Peter's mouth and hands.

Peter.

I don't want to know his name. The others, their names didn't matter, but his... I don't want it. *Peter.*

He knocks again, louder. "Hey. Talk to me."

"I'm fine." I manage to make my voice be smooth and unconcerned. Not quite Eris. She's already vanished. Really, she never quite came into being. I practically hear Peter hesitating, thinking through.

"Can I get you anything?" he finally asks.

"I'd love another Black Velvet," I say, scrubbing at the mascara on my cheeks. It looks like I've been on a crying jag, but I haven't done that in forever. I never finished the first drink, which is a waste.

"Okay." There's a soft thunk and I imagine him leaning his forehead on the door. "Promise you won't leave."

I will leave, of course, but I promise not to anyway. Promises are easily broken, with no consequences for those who make them. I've learned to do likewise.

"Look," he says, still right there. I'm tempted to open the door, but that would—as open doors tend to do—only let things in. I can't let him in. I'm too afraid. Instead, I lay my hand against the door, as close as I can come to touching him again. "How about this," he continues slowly, thinking as he speaks, "If you won't stay, if you—if Eris can't be with me, with Clark again—come back as someone else. I can be someone else, too."

I'm quiet. He can't be anyone else. He's Peter, now and forever. In all truth, he was always Peter. My rock. A steady foundation. Owner of a bar he works six nights a week, lover of geek jokes and classic Superman.

"Say you'll think about it." He's insistent again. He won't leave until I say so.

"I'll think about it," I lie.

BUT IT'S NOT entirely a lie, because I can't stop thinking about it.

I'm ragged inside. A curious sensation because I'm also sated. For days afterward I'm very nearly happy. As happy as I'm capable of being when I'm only myself. I do my work, quietly, anonymously, to the usual lack of praise or criticism, but I'm glad to do it well.

I think about Peter a lot.

I think about a lot of things. About endings and broken promises. I am not the serial killer anymore. I'm only myself. Lonely in my lifeless condo, owner of far too many wigs. I think about the alpha and the omega and how endings lead inevitably to beginnings. Unless you're dead.

I think I'm maybe not dead.

Chapter 8

TONIGHT MY NAME is Rachel.

Did you know it means "ewe"? Jacob's favorite wife was a sheep. I fix Rachel's hair to the best of my ability. It's short. Has been ever since she chopped it all off in her grief, shame and fury, burning the long locks in the fancy fireplace. The first of many rituals, consigning her hair to ash. Her eyes are not-blue, not-green, not-gray. Not distinctive.

She is not beautiful. Not remarkable in any way. This has always been a problem.

Rachel doesn't wear makeup or paint her nails. Her clothes are as nondescript as her face. She's good at her job, which isn't interesting, and lives alone, which is lonely. She reads a lot and has no friends or family in this city. For a while she thought about moving away again, back to where she came from, but the effort seemed staggering. Even if they forgave her failures. If nothing else, she got the condo. A forever place to live and all she had to pay was everything she believed to be good about herself.

The windows overlooking the city give her a kind of perspective, most days.

Because she can, she wears a coat to Circle². It's cashmere, another expensive thing she sold herself to have. She still has on her suit from the day, along with the conservative low-heeled boots.

It's a Tuesday, so it's quiet in the bar. Only Peter is working.

He's at the far end, chatting with a businessman as he builds a beer. He gives me a half wave as I enter. "Be right with you."

I take a deep breath and a seat at the bar.

"What'll you have?" he asks with no special emphasis. He's wearing a T-shirt that has "-shit" inside a square root sign, then squared and the caption "shit just got real." He doesn't seem to recognize me. I'm not sure if I'm relieved or disappointed. Maybe equal measures of each, both desperately felt.

"Red wine," I say.

"Any particular kind?"

I shrug. "House red. Whatever." Rachel hasn't had opinions about much in a very long time. She barely had any to begin with, which was also a problem.

He brings it back and I hand him a credit card. "I'll run a tab." No one ever offers to buy Rachel a drink. She's not that kind of girl.

Peter studies the card. "Rachel Smith, huh?"

"Cliché and yet—that's my name." My maiden name. He took his name with him.

"Rachel is pretty."

"It means a sheep. A ewe."

"She was Jacob's favorite wife." Peter is still holding my credit card, still standing there, waiting for more.

"Do you ever think about that—what that means for a man to have a *favorite* wife? That implies that someone else is the least favorite. The one he'd kick to the curb if he could."

Peter leans forearms on the bar, my card braced between upright fingers like a text he's studying. "He never loved his other wife, Leah. He was tricked into marrying her."

"And put her on the front lines, in hopes Esau would kill her."

"But that's not you. You're the beloved. Rachel."

"No, I'm definitely the roadkill one." I hold his gaze a moment longer, not sure if he's gotten my message. Unable to stand it, I snatch the credit card back, slip it into my billfold and pull out a ten. "Actually, I've changed my mind. I'm not in the mood for this."

"The drink is on the house anyway. I owe you one."

I pause in the middle of sliding off the stool. Peter is watching me with a solemn expression. "Don't go," he says. "Rachel."

"Okay." I take another deep breath and slide back onto the stool. This is the hardest thing I've done in forever. Much more difficult than I dreaded, talking to him as myself. I pick up the wine and he takes it from me before I can sip.

"Not this," he says, tossing it out. He keeps an eye on me while he makes me another drink. But I won't let myself run. Not this time. Not yet.

I'm not surprised when he sets a beautifully separated Black Velvet in front of me. I sip it, savoring the blend of flavors and textures. Dark and bright together. "I hope it's not Dom again."

"Only the best for you."

"I'm sorry you wasted so much on me the other night."

"Nothing is ever wasted, particularly where you're concerned." Peter waves goodbye to the businessman, who leaves without looking at me twice.

I take a few more sips, gathering my liquid courage. "How did you know it was me?"

Peter thinks about it, washing the businessman's glass. "I think it's the way you move. You have this grace to even the smallest gesture, this sensuality. Like you could be Salome, seductive and mysterious."

"I'm not any of those things."

He cocks his head, frowning slightly. "But you are."

"No. Maybe those other women were, but they're not me. I tried them on like fancy dresses I can't afford to keep."

He considers this. "I didn't expect you to come back as yourself."

"But you expected me to come back?"

"I hoped."

"I'm sorry I broke my promise," I say quietly, studying how the stout and champagne begin to filter one into the other, first with tendrils, dark infiltrating the light. Or maybe it could be the other way around and I can't see it as well. "That I said I wouldn't leave when I was waiting for you to leave me alone long enough so I could."

"I wasn't surprised."

"I'm sorry for that, too."

"Don't be. You were honest with me. At least as far as your rules are concerned. Though I still don't understand."

"Don't you? Even seeing me now?"

His brows draw together and he looks me over, as if puzzling out a riddle. "No."

His pretense throws me, though I am the Queen of Deception, and I take a gulp of my cocktail, too fast, sending myself into a coughing fit that surely makes me red-faced. He ducks under the pass-through to edge a hip onto the stool beside me, taking my hands.

"Just breathe," he says. "Nice and easy. It's only me. You know I won't hurt you."

To my shock, I discover that I might believe that.

Another customer leaves and Peter nods goodbye, then gets up to follow him, locking the door and flipping off the "Open" sign.

"Come on." Peter takes my hand, tugging me off the stool and zipping off the televisions with a remote. "Bring your drink. Let's go upstairs."

"You can't just close early," I protest.

"It's good to be boss." He gives me that same easy grin he did the other night.

"You were supposed to be a priest," I say, foolishly, because of course that's wrong, that's only what his mother wanted him to be and we are never what our families imagine for us. Or maybe that's just me.

"I'm very good at hearing confession. Bartenders and priests have that in common." He keeps my hand as he flips off the lights and unlocks the door to upstairs, as if I might run.

I still might.

He seats me on the couch, taking both of my hands in his again when I set my drink on the low coffee table. It has books piled on it, but I can't take in their titles and covers. I feel naked, exposed in some profound way. Peter lifts my hands and kisses my knuckles, a sprinkling of casual affection. "Lovely Rachel," he murmurs. "I'm so glad you came back."

"Don't lie to me," I grit out. "Please don't."

He gives me a long look. "It's not a lie. I've never lied to you."

I can't say the same and he knows it. All those lies I've spoken, the deceptions large and small, they weigh on me. For a time they freed me, those other women, the many disguises. After a while though, they bound me tighter. *Whatever you bind on earth shall be bound in heaven; and whatever you loose on earth shall be loosed in heaven.*

"Won't you tell me your story, trust me with it?"

"It's boring and stupid." *Like me.* I laugh and it comes out ragged. I'm no good at this.

"Indulge me." He's still holding my hands, stroking the backs with his thumbs.

"I'm not married, but I was." I manage to say it like other women do. Tra la, tra lay. *Oh, my ex*, they breezily dismiss with a wave of their hand, as if they hadn't gone into it expecting forever, hadn't believed that being good meant having it.

"I'm sorry," Peter says and sounds like he means it. "I've got friends who've gone through that and it's devastating, no matter the reason. You must have gotten married young."

"Younger than I knew I was," I agree. "I married the man my family and my temple picked out for me, who I believed was meant to be mine. I believed in all those words, that we'd keep promises and grow old together. I was stupid."

"That's not stupid. If you don't think that going in, why get married?"

Why indeed? "I was stupid because I was Leah and didn't know it. I believed I was *bashert* and what kind of idiot believes in that?"

"What does it mean?"

"Like soul mates." I fumble, embarrassed to articulate it. "Forty days before a male child is conceived, a voice from heaven announces whose daughter he is going to marry."

"A match made in heaven, destined for happily ever after," Peter says, looking thoughtful. "A powerful idea."

"Yes. Until your husband leaves you for someone else, because you aren't soulmates after all." I impress myself, that I get it out so cleanly, barely a wobble in my voice. "He'd been having an affair with her all along and said he'd decided to marry me instead of her, but he realized he'd made the wrong choice. Because I…" I falter completely there.

Peter waits, while I swallow against the confession. Finally he says, "You know it's not real, right? Whatever he told you was the reason was a lie. Because the reason was him, not you."

"I don't know that. Neither can you."

"Yes, I do, and so do you. He lied to you from the beginning, didn't he?"

"He did." All those promises. None of them real. "But I was the problem. Our marriage bed was cold. I was frigid."

Peter laughs. A huge laugh, which startles me. I yank my hands away and stand. "Don't you laugh at me!" I clench my fists at my sides. It's not Peter I want to punch.

"I'm not." He holds up his palms, choking back the laughter, but he's still grinning. "It's just that it's so absurd. You're the least frigid woman I've ever met and, besides, who says that anymore? Did he accuse you of hysteria and penis envy, too?"

I snatch up my cocktail and take a long drink. Not the latter, but he'd definitely wielded the former. I sit again. "I'm such a fucking cliché."

"Were you a virgin when you got married?" Peter asks, brushing my knee, a fleeting touch.

I nod. "Good little Orthodox Jewish girl. I just trusted everything would be wonderful."

"But it wasn't."

"No. The wedding night..." I can't get it out, not this way. "Rachel was a good girl and she didn't know what it would be like. No one told her. She had these ideas..." Much as I hate that girl's ignorance, I want to weep for her. "Ideas that it would be all floaty, with hearts and flowers and...rose petals." My voice finally breaks.

"But it wasn't."

"No. It was pain. And the blood frightened her." I locked

myself in the bathroom for hours, cleaning it off of her, long after it was gone. "I've learned since that not everyone bleeds like that, but I didn't know it then. I thought I was dying." I flush, chagrined at the memory. In a way, the girl I was *had* died that night.

"That's why you do it," Peter says. "Become someone else."

I close my eyes, letting out a long breath. I'm still holding the cocktail. "It's the only way I can do it. Can enjoy it. If I'm not...her. *Rachel.*"

Rachel who'd lost her husband, disappointed her family, disgraced her temple. Frigid, stupid, panicked Rachel. "It was a bad omen, you see?"

"Because a man is obligated to divorce his wife if he doesn't give her pleasure"

He did see. More, he listened. Something in me let go at having told the tale.

"Yes. So, he did. Divorce her. And after a long time, she got tired of being ignorant. I locked Rachel in a closet and found other women to be."

"Have you ever had sex as yourself?" Peter takes my glass away, sets it aside, and cups my face in his hands. His beautiful hands, like an angel's.

"Yes," I say. "With my—"

Peter kisses me. "Not him."

"I can't."

"You can." He kisses me again, fingers feathering through my short hair, and the gold infiltrates the dark. "You have been. All along. Every one of them is you."

"You saw me," I say, our breath mingling with the words. "All along."

"I see you now. Lovely Rachel. I want to be with you, get to know you, inside and out. In the light and in the dark. Can we try that?"

I want to try. "I might not be any good at it. I don't know who I am anymore."

"I know who you are. You're smart and brave. Beloved." He takes me by the hand and leads me to his bedroom. There he'll touch me and I'll close my eyes and simply feel. Afterward, we'll sleep curled together like cats, and it will be only us. I won't vanish with the dawn.

Tonight, my name is Rachel. I suppose it always has been.

Also by Jeffe Kennedy

<u>*Contemporary BDSM Romances*</u>

Facets of Passion
Sapphire
Platinum
Ruby
Five Golden Rings

Falling Under
Going Under
Under His Touch
Under Contract

<u>*Erotic Paranomal*</u>

Master of the Opera E-Serial
Master of the Opera, Act 1: Passionate Overture
Master of the Opera, Act 2: Ghost Aria
Master of the Opera, Act 3: Phantom Serenade
Master of the Opera, Act 4: Dark Interlude
Master of the Opera, Act 5: A Haunting Duet
Master of the Opera, Act 6: Crescendo
Master of the Opera

Blood Currency
Feeding the Vampire
Hunting the Siren

BDSM Fairytale Romance

Petals and Thorns

Fantasy Romance

A Covenant of Thorns
Rogue's Pawn
Rogue's Possession
Rogue's Paradise

The Twelve Kingdoms
Negotiation
The Mark of the Tala
The Tears of the Rose
The Talon of the Hawk
Heart's Blood
For Crown and Kingdom (Coming May 2016)

The Uncharted Realms
The Pages of the Mind (Coming May 2016)
The Edge of the Blade (Coming January 2017)

Other Works

Birdwoman

About the Author

Jeffe Kennedy is an award-winning author whose works include non-fiction, poetry, short fiction, and novels. She has been a Ucross Foundation Fellow, received the Wyoming Arts Council Fellowship for Poetry, and was awarded a Frank Nelson Doubleday Memorial Award. Her essays have appeared in many publications, including Redbook.

Her most recent works include a number of fiction series: the fantasy romance novels of *A Covenant of Thorns*; the contemporary BDSM novellas of the *Facets of Passion*, and an erotic contemporary serial novel, *Master of the Opera*. A fourth series, the fantasy trilogy *The Twelve Kingdoms*, hit the shelves starting in May 2014 and book 1, *The Mark of the Tala*, received a starred Library Journal review and has been nominated for the RT Book of the Year while the sequels, *The Tears of the Rose* and The Talon of the Hawk, have been nominated for The RT Reviewers' Choice Best Fantasy Romance of the year in 2014 and 2015, respectively. Two more books will follow in this world, beginning with The Pages of the Mind in Summer 2016. A fifth series, the erotic romance trilogy, *Falling Under*, started with *Going Under*, followed by *Under His Touch* and *Under Contract*.

She lives in Santa Fe, New Mexico, with two Maine coon cats, plentiful free-range lizards and a very handsome Doctor of Oriental Medicine.

Jeffe can be found online at her website: JeffeKennedy.com, every Sunday at the popular Word Whores blog, on Facebook, on Goodreads and pretty much constantly on Twitter @jeffekennedy. She is represented by Connor Goldsmith of Fuse Literary.

Red Leather

Delphine Dryden

Some activities are definitely not safe for work.

Maggie's sadness over being dumped quickly turns to relief and excitement when she discovers a new freedom…a new Maggie she could have never been with her ex. Combine New Maggie with Tim the Hot Mailroom Guy and an unexpected vibrator…and the office supply room door becomes the portal to a world of devilish fun.

Chapter 1

From the moment Maggie smoothed the suede over her knee and pulled up the zipper, she knew she *needed* the boots in her life.

They were expensive. They were impractical. They went with nothing in her wardrobe.

She walked unevenly to the low mirror, one foot in the boot, the other in a dull white ankle sock. Admired the turn of her calf, the way the gold zipper drew a line through the plush matte garnet. The snug leather hugged her leg above the knee, sending a sensual thrill up her inner thigh.

Jesse's voice whispered in her mind, echoing so many other voices she'd heard through the years: *Not your best look. Your legs probably aren't something you want to draw attention to. Is that really what you're wearing? Not suitable for the occasion. Maybe something less…showy? I don't think that's your style. Why would you want to leave the light on?*

She angled her foot, pressing down on the heel, imagining Jesse's bare foot under it as she twisted. The skin would break; tiny bones would crack under the pressure of her "few extra pounds," a weight that for once could work to her advantage. Alarmed by the clarity of the vision, the sense of power it gave her, she straightened and focused on the mirror again.

The mall was crowded for a Saturday morning. The noise and commotion were taxing on her mild hangover, but at least the salespeople were too busy with other customers to pressure her. She took her time, shifting her weight, wiggling her toes. The boot was more comfortable than it looked. She could easily wear these all day at work. So...not entirely impractical. And with the right dress—

Maggie didn't have the right dress. She pictured her closet, with its ranks of solid pastels and dull neutrals. An impressionist blur of colors that lost clarity and interest the closer you got to it. Nothing that stood out. Nothing that made her happy. Nothing that she'd actively wanted *for herself* and nobody else. So much pale pink, because everyone had always said it was "her" color.

The idea of going home and putting on yet another pink top...

I have always hated pink.

The notion floated up like a cartoon thought bubble, alarmingly clear and sharp. Nothing tempered or softened about it. It wasn't "dislike" or "prefer not to wear" or "don't care for," it was *hate*.

Pressure built behind her eyes, forcing her to blink back tears as her throat tightened. Jesse had reassured her over and over that he didn't hate her. That it wasn't about her. That he still cared. That they could always be friends. How his brand-new fiancée felt about that, Maggie wasn't sure. She suspected Kaitlyn wouldn't appreciate Jesse maintaining a "friendship" with the woman he'd dated for six years, the woman everybody had expected him to marry.

"I thought I knew what love was before, but now I realize what I felt for you was never quite what I needed. I can't apologize for falling in love," he'd said, holding both her hands in his. He'd clasped them at the beginning of his speech, the speech Maggie had assumed would finally be the proposal she'd been waiting for since their sophomore year of college. A fancy Friday dinner date at "their" restaurant, on the anniversary of the day they'd met. Candlelight and wine. Jesse in an odd mood, restless and preoccupied from the moment he picked her up. What else was she supposed to assume?

Certainly not that he was dumping her for somebody he'd met at a fundraiser six months earlier. Nor that he'd been seeing Kaitlyn behind Maggie's back during those six months. Sleeping with her. "I felt so bad for not telling you, but I hated the thought of leaving you alone after so much time. I had to work through that sense of obligation. It's been tearing me apart."

You can shove your goddam man pain straight up your ass, you slimy, cheating motherfucker.

She let the new, wicked thoughts roll around in her consciousness, savoring their tang. She did not hate Jesse, but neither was she going to remain his friend, and she had somehow managed to tell him that in as many words.

"We aren't friends. We aren't going to be friends. Friends don't treat each other the way you've treated me. Don't ever speak to me again." Because if he wasn't her boyfriend, and wasn't her friend, why should she waste another minute on him?

She barely remembered standing, pulling her purse from the back of the chair, making her way out of the restaurant and down the street. Around the corner was a bar, a place she must have passed a thousand times and never entered. She'd gone in and ordered a shot of tequila, because that was the first thing that popped into her mind after *I need a drink.* By the time her Uber arrived twelve minutes later, she'd downed a second shot, and the bartender had given her some side-eye.

Maggie tried to see herself as the bartender must have seen her. A shortish, plumpish woman with her hair pulled back, too young to already look so matronly, wearing a lilac twinset and watercolor pastel scarf, perched on the barstool with a serviceable handbag on her lap. A refugee from a Wednesday night prayer meeting, perhaps, or a small-town schoolteacher running amok in the city. A fish out of water.

If she'd been wearing the red boots, and the outfit to go with them, would the bartender have given her that same slightly bemused glance? What if her date-night purse hadn't looked like a mommy bag? What if she'd finally gotten up the nerve to abandon her mother's hairdresser and gone to one who would give her a style from the current century?

Maggie unzipped the boot reluctantly and placed it back in its large box, folding it carefully over its mate. She replaced the lid, then tapped her fingers against the cardboard a few times, considering her budget. Her wardrobe. Her life. The possibility that she didn't need a team of experts, "What Not to Wear" style, to make her over. She just needed, for once, to believe that her own approval was enough. That she didn't need to court anyone's favor but her own.

She bought the boots, and a dress to go with them. And then she went home and began to stuff clothes into garbage bags to take to the women's shelter. Somebody else could get the use of them, but it wouldn't be Maggie. Not anymore.

"YOU COULD BOUNCE a quarter off that thing." Maggie's cube-mate Delilah craned her neck to watch Tim, the shy-but-hot mailroom guy, bend over to grab a box from the bottom of his cart. "I just want to grab that butt in both hands and squeeze."

Maggie stifled a laugh and kept entering figures into a spreadsheet. "Shhhh."

"Rat me out to HR, I don't even care. I'm thirsty and I don't have your willpower, or your—uh, professionalism."

"Were you going to say *boyfriend?*" Her fingers flew over her keyboard as her eyes scanned the printed columns. She would be working late again today, she suspected, or taking some projects home for the weekend. Another Friday night sacrificed to the work gods.

Delilah coughed and turned back to her computer. "Sorry. Old habits."

"Don't worry about it."

"I'm not. Getting rid of that asshole was the best thing that ever happened to you, girl. I *know* you aren't wasting time on missing that."

She wasn't wrong. Maggie had been shocked to the bone by Jesse's betrayal, and she'd expected to suffer a long period of grief over the loss of the relationship she'd thought she had. Instead, a month after the dumping, she mostly felt a lightness, a relief that she no longer had to speak to Jesse every day. She didn't have to hear his doubt, his negativity, his insecurities transferred to her. The none-too-subtle hints about her weight, the way he would ask her opinion then explain why his was better, the lie at the root of it all: *I'm only saying it because I love you. I love you, I want you to be healthy. I love you, I want us to be on the same page.* Always *his* page. And before Jesse, it had been her mother's page.

Now it was her own. Her choices, her colors, her style. As she saved the spreadsheet, Maggie flipped her hair back from her shoulder and relished the brush of layers across her shoulder and cheek; she could see a hint of the oversaturated merlot color that was revealed through the brown whenever she moved. Delilah had crowed upon first seeing the new 'do, and declared the red underlayer Maggie's "wild streak" finally showing.

But it wasn't just about hair or clothes. Since her transformation, people seemed to smile at her more. Take her more seriously. Ask for her opinion about things as if she were someone whose opinion mattered. And she also got *looks*. Apparently not everybody shared Jesse's opinion about her weight—quite the opposite. She shouldn't like that awareness; she wanted to scorn the male gaze on principle, but she couldn't stifle the thrill in her heart every time she caught some payroll accountant staring at her ass, or the financial records clerk blinking down at her bust. She wore a lot of pencil skirts now, and often showed a half-inch or so of cleavage, and her new wardrobe included a lot of black and red and jewel tones. Colors that were meant to catch the eye, not fade into the background.

"Delilah, you just said a mouthful."

"Mmm-hmm. Speaking of mouthfuls…"

The squeak of wheels announced the arrival of the mail cart outside their cube. Try as Maggie might to keep her eyes trained on her work, she couldn't resist swiveling her chair and greeting Tim with a smile. It was one of her new things, smiling at people and making eye contact and thinking, *I'm going to do what I want because I like myself*—instead of *How can I find out what this person wants so they'll like me*. In the case of Tim, she'd never worried about making him like her. He always had a smile for her.

Delilah had insisted forever that Tim had a crush on Maggie. Until recently, Maggie had ignored the possibility. Tim was shy, yes, but he was nice to *everyone*. Lately, she saw him with new eyes and thought Delilah might have a valid point. She saw that she could have a certain power over him, if she wanted to. She could flirt and make him stammer, or tease him with glances to see him blush.

She didn't do those things. She didn't especially want power, but what she *did* want was definitely not work-appropriate. With her new look had come a new level of imagination, it seemed; she wanted to explore that wild streak in more ways than one, and Tim had starred in more than one lurid fantasy recently.

When she smiled at him, Tim smiled back and blushed to the roots of his auburn hair as if he knew exactly what she was thinking. "I have a package for you."

Delilah coughed again, pointedly typing harder. From the corner of her eye, Maggie could see her coworker's shoulders shaking with the effort not to laugh. Poor Tim closed his eyes and bit his lip, clearly mortified at his accidental double entendre.

He held the box out with a return receipt on top. "You need to sign for it."

Maggie started clearing a spot on her desk. "Wow. It's big."

Delilah slapped a hand on her desk. "*Girl.*"

"The box, Delilah. It's large. I got a big box. Oh, for the love of—here, Tim, just set it down." She shook her head and reached for one of the whimsical pens in the flower pot on her top shelf. Her niece had made it for her—a pot full of beans to hold a bouquet of red silk hibiscus flowers carefully florist-taped onto ballpoints. She'd taken down the framed picture of herself and Jesse and replaced it with a whole scene inspired by the hibiscus pens: a Hawaiian sunset backdrop cut from an old calendar, an inflatable novelty palm tree from the dollar store, and even a tiny "beach" of sand borrowed from a mini Zen garden kit. One foot of shelf space turned into the world's smallest resort. Best of all, nobody ever accidentally forgot to return her pens after borrowing them—people tended to notice a big red flower stuck to the end of their writing implement.

She didn't look at the return address as she signed. She was expecting something mundane—a shipment of forms, some office equipment. So when she yanked open the box and pulled the wad of packing paper from the top, she was caught off guard.

A few items of lounge clothing, neatly folded. A stack of CDs, half a dozen books. A tin of her favorite tea. A note on top, on a sheet of notebook paper, in a feminine hand she didn't recognize. When she picked it up to read it, she found the pièce de résistance: her missing vibrator, its lurid iridescent purple gleaming unmistakably against the soft flannel pants beneath it.

She must have gasped, because Tim straightened from his cart and looked over at the box. His jaw dropped, and his gaze flew to her face, then back to the box, then back to her face. When he clicked his jaw shut, Maggie's mind finally kicked back into gear, and she slapped the box flaps shut.

She stared at Tim, watching his blush deepen, silently daring him to say something. He cleared his throat and ran his hands over the mail in the top of the cart, a quick ruffling motion that looked automatic. His fingers were long, slender, nimble—he had the hands of an artist or a poet. Fine freckles dotted his wrists. She imagined him holding the vibrator, pushing it into her with the same expression of earnest concern he wore right then, and she had to lean against the desk to support herself against the wave of need that nearly swamped her.

"Um." He cleared his throat again, glancing over at Delilah, who was packing up her messenger bag and fortunately seemed oblivious to the proceedings. "What does it say?"

Of all the questions she might have expected about the vibrator, that wasn't among them. "What? It…doesn't say anything, it just—"

He pointed to the note Maggie still clutched in one hand. "That. I meant that."

"Oh. Oh! Right." *Because people don't talk about surprise vibra-*

tors at work, Maggie. He's throwing you a rope here, fucking grab it. She lifted the page, pretending her hand wasn't shaking. "It says, *You left a few of your things. I thought you might want them back.* I guess it's some stuff I'd forgotten at my ex's apartment."

And Kaitlyn had shipped them to her work address, return receipt requested. Kind of her.

Tim nodded and bit his lip again, then gripped the handle of his mail cart hard enough that his knuckles whitened. He was studiously avoiding her eyes now. "Welp. I'm just gonna…yeah."

"Finish your last round of the day, or whatever."

"Mmhmm. You have a nice"—his focus flicked over to the box—"weekend."

"Yes. Thanks. You too."

Delilah stood up, swinging her bag over her shoulder. She already had her coat on and her keys in hand. "Anything good in there?"

As one, Maggie and Tim answered, "Nope."

After a moment of silence, Tim wheeled the mail cart away as Maggie smiled awkwardly at Delilah.

When he'd turned the corner and was out of sight, Delilah shifted her bag and crossed her arms, nodding toward the box. "Do I want to know?"

"Yeah, probably." A handful of coworkers walked by, waving as they passed, barely interrupting their chat about where to go for drinks. Maggie waited for them to disappear before she cracked the box open and let Delilah take a peek.

"Oh my."

"Yep."

"Definitely not work-appropriate."

"Nope."

"And Tim saw—"

"He did." Maggie refolded the box flaps to interweave so it would stay shut. "I think the note was from Jesse's new fiancée. I'm trying to decide if a thank-you card is called for."

"Oh, that's one of those tricky etiquette questions. You can't ask your mama about that one."

"I don't think my mama even knows what that thing is, and if she does, she believes it's a tool of the devil."

Delilah snorted. "Not if you're using it right."

"Stop."

"You're ringing the devil's doorbell, but the only answer you're gonna get is, *oh, Jesus! Oh, yes, God!* You know the Lord loves the sexytimes because they're all about Him."

Maggie covered her mouth to stifle a cackle. "I just wish I knew who found it and what the conversation was."

"Found it? Wouldn't he know where it was?"

"Who, Jesse? God, no. No, that would've been a total threat to his manhood. I'd hidden it in his bathroom for, um, emergencies? There was this sort of…like a space behind the doorjamb in the linen closet, on the top shelf. I got tired of trying to hide it in my overnight bag, and his bathroom was usually where I used it, so… Anyway, after the breakup, I never went back to his place. So I figured I'd lost it forever." And she had a much better one now, so she hadn't really missed it. She was happier about getting the books and sleep pants back.

Delilah shook her head. "So much better off. Well, like Tim said, enjoy your weekend. Don't stay here too late."

"I won't. Promise."

The boss and his admin assistant had already gone for the day. The idea of being the last one out of the office yet again was too depressing. After Delilah left, Maggie made sure the coast was clear, then quickly stuffed the contents of the box into her oversized tote bag. It was a tight fit, but at least it would be easier than trying to wrangle the box, her purse and coat, *and* all the paperwork she needed to take home.

It meant, however, that she no longer had a place to put the paperwork. Slinging the tote and purse over one arm, her coat over the other, she snatched up the stack of files and headed for the supply room to grab an accordion folder on her way out.

The supply room door was still propped open, to her relief; usually the admin closed it at night, and the key lived in her desk so anyone who wanted late-night supplies was kind of screwed.

But when Maggie pushed the door, it didn't complete its usual swing; something clanked, blocking its progress, and somebody cursed in surprise. She peered around the door to see the mail cart, with Tim standing next to it, a look of panic on his face. His blue eyes looked almost turquoise in the fluorescent light.

"Shit." He backed up a step, straight into a shelf. "Ow. Um, hi? Can I help you?"

"Sorry, I just—" *What the hell's he doing in here, embezzling Post-its?* She had to stop staring at his eyes. She let her gaze drop, and…oh. That's what he was doing in there. A thrill shot through her, not unlike a supercharged version of the way she'd felt when she bought what she had since dubbed her Boots of Epiphany.

Tim shifted his weight awkwardly, waving his hands. "It's not what it looks like."

He was adorable, and she didn't want to torture him, though it was tempting. Might as well be honest, since he'd already seen her vibrator. She edged around the door, knocking the rubber doorstop out of place, and let it shut behind her. "It looks like you came in here to wait out an accidental workplace boner."

"Uh…" He lowered his hands. "Okay, yeah, exactly what it

looks like, then."

No wonder he wasn't blushing. Not enough blood volume to power a blush along with…that. She had to restrain herself from asking what they were feeding them down in the mailroom. She also had to stop staring at it, so she scanned the shelves instead, dumping her bags and coat next to the copy machine.

"I just came in for an accordion file."

"Okay."

"You're standing in front of them."

"Oh. Of course. Of course I am." He scooted to the side a few feet, into the corner.

"Thanks."

He stood there, looking miserable and obviously at a loss for what to do with his hands, while she opened the box and retrieved the file. Maggie didn't expect him to converse, so she was startled when he spoke.

"I know it may be hard to believe right now, but I want you to know that I really do respect you as a person. And I am *so* sorry about this. It's not like me. I think it was just because of seeing…the thing in the box, and then you're always so…but usually this doesn't happen, obviously. I mean it has never happened before. Well, not at work."

Her knees wobbled again, and a pulse thrummed between her legs as she thought of when and where it *had* happened before. But part of her mind was still caught in the middle of his speech. She put the folder down and turned toward him.

"I'm always so what?"

"You're—" He started to put his hands in his pockets, then yanked them out and grabbed the shelves to either side of him. "You're always so *nice* to me. Like your smile has extra smile in it or something. It makes me happy. And you used to smell like roses, kind of? And I liked that, but now you smell like some kinda spices and it's even better. Not like I'm trying to secretly smell you or anything, that makes me sound like a stalker and I'm totally not. You just smell really good."

It was the sweetest thing anyone had ever said to her. She opened her mouth to tell him so, but Tim was on a roll.

"The finance department is the best part of my day. They're about to move me into HR—which, that's kind of ironic, right, because oh my God, obviously I've blown the whole workplace harassment thing already—and I've been kind of bummed out about it because . . . yeah, I know it's a promotion. And it's finally sort of using my degree. Not really, my degree is in English, but having one at all made me eligible for the HR job. But that job will mean no more visiting the finance floor two or three times a day, and I never got up the nerve to ask you out because I'm an idiot. And also, you were always really cute. Like, *really* cute. But now you basically look like a pinup girl, but tasteful, and it drives me *fucking insane.*"

"Tim—" She had to stop him or she was going to start humping his leg.

"Can you edit this part out when you do the harassment complaint? I know I'm rambling."

"It's definitely more words than I've ever heard you say in a year of working together." A year of him thinking she was cute, even before the magic boots. Of him noticing her perfume and liking her smile. She'd made him happier that whole year, and not even known. "But I'm not planning to make a harassment complaint. I walked in on you. And it was my vibrator. If anything you'd be the one with a claim."

He blinked a few times at that, apparently stunned. Then a smile broke through and he shrugged. "What does it *say?*" He started to laugh as he slapped a hand to his forehead.

Maggie giggled. "It says, *Oh God, oh God*, because that's all it ever hears." The giggle turned to a laugh, then to near-tears, until she was leaning over and gasping alongside an equally hysterical Tim. She put a hand on his chest for support, and he covered it with his, and their eyes met.

The laughter petered out slowly and the eye contact became a thing in itself, a connection. A conversation.

She had no idea who moved first, only that they were kissing as if they had been doing it all along. Her knee knocked against a shelf as she wrapped one leg around his. His artist's hands pressed her closer, cradling her head, curving into the dip at her waist.

Maggie stretched up, pushing herself against him, tilting her hips until she felt his erection against her pelvis. In her heels, she was just tall enough. A fresh wash of tingling anticipation hit her pussy, making her whimper into his mouth. Tim groaned and lowered a hand to her ass—he squeezed, countering her motion. Shifted his mouth to her jawline, her ear, her neck, nipping and sucking as much as kissing.

"Spices," he mumbled into her hair. Maggie shivered and tilted her head to give him more access. His lips were waking up nerve endings she hadn't thought about in months—years. Jesse was fine in bed, but they'd fallen into a routine after a year or so together. She didn't know if it was the novelty or the danger or something about Tim himself that made this better, only that it was. That she wanted more. That she didn't want to stop.

She ran her hands down his sides, reaching for the fabled ass, grabbing it and digging her fingers in until Tim squeaked a protest.

"Sorry." *Calm down, Maggie. Don't frighten him away.*

He nudged her collar aside with his nose, and nipped the muscle between her neck and shoulder. "I didn't mean you had to stop."

"Oh."

So she dug back in and circled her hips, angling to get the maximum pressure against her clit. It wasn't enough. She needed skin-to-skin contact, needed to really *feel* him. It was the work of seconds to yank his starched blue oxford shirt from his khakis, to run her hands under the warm fabric and wrap them around his bare waist.

He exhaled a shaky breath against her ear, making her wet—wetter. "Can I do that too?"

"Go for it." *Thank God I wore fancy underwear today.*

Tim pulled gently, and her silk blouse slithered free from her skirt and wide belt. He rested his hands on her hips and put a few inches between them, stroking her ass before raising his fingers to her top button and giving her a questioning look. She nodded, sick with need, torn between the sweet delight of his unwrapping her and the desire to rip the shirt off herself.

He made quick work of it, seeming as frantic as she felt, and when he'd undone about four buttons he spotted her lacy deep purple bra and lolled his head back for a few seconds. "Fuck me."

Maggie laughed, covering her mouth, trying to remember to be quiet. "I think that's a given but we probably need to be quick about it."

Tim tried to meet her eyes, but his gaze drifted down to her breasts and she lost him there for a while as he pushed her shirt open and ran reverent fingertips over the lace and net. Circled her nipples through the sheer fabric until they hardened. She pushed her hips against him, trying to find the magic contact point she'd hit earlier.

"I don't have a condom," he finally said, with such evident regret that she wanted to hug him and buy him an ice cream. But she had something infinitely more rewarding to offer.

"I have an IUD. And I don't have any diseases. I, um, went and got that checked after I found out about my ex and his…anyway." The whole office had heard about it. No point getting bogged down in those details right now.

Tim cupped her breasts gently, then pinched her nipples between his thumbs and forefingers. "Was he blind or stupid or what, what was going on there? Never mind, rhetorical question. I am DTF. I mean DDF. I mean—oh God, this is why I don't talk to people, I'm just—"

She leaned in and kissed him. Gently at first, then inevitably harder as the heat between them flared again. She was shaking with it, relying on him for support, and she could feel him trembling too. There was a short stepladder on a hook by the door, and she freed a groping hand long enough to point to it.

"Now," she suggested. But releasing him even long enough to let him retrieve the ladder and unfold it was a hardship. She pushed him down on the broad top step unceremoniously and tugged her skirt up, straddling him with a sigh of need and relief.

"Oh my God, they match." He plucked at the lace of her underwear over one hip. "Is this a thong—oh my God it is. Okay. Yeah. Fast, right? Oh God. This is crazy. Are we actually doing this? We're gonna get so fired if anyone comes in."

"Fast," she reminded him. Then, more soothingly, "The door's locked and the key is in Melissa's desk, and she's gone. We're probably fine if we're quiet, okay?"

Tim nodded, and Maggie noticed that not only were his eyes that unearthly blue, but his well-kissed lips were a gorgeous shade of pink. He was too pretty for words. She was the one who'd been blind, never noticing that he had a special smile for her. Or maybe she wasn't as changed as she'd thought—her assumption still seemed to be that nobody would find her all that compelling.

Except... *Happy. Roses. Spices. Really cute. Pinup girl.* Tim was clearly compelled. And it was intoxicating.

She unbuckled his belt, then stood up long enough for him to shove down his pants and boxer briefs, releasing his cock. It was nice enough, though she didn't have much basis for comparison. His pubic hair was a brighter shade of red than the hair on his head. She caught a whiff of guy-at-the-end-of-a-workday, not an unpleasant smell but an earthy one.

When she started to pull her thong down, Tim stopped her, reaching for her hips and pulling her forward again.

"No, like this." He ran his fingers down the front of her panties, tracing straight down the middle at first and gasping with her when he found her clit. "Like...this." He hooked a finger under the fabric and pulled it to one side, exposing her pussy. Then he stroked her hips again, coaxing her back onto his lap, until her bare slit rubbed against his cock.

It was...too good, too much, for a second. She thought she might pass out from too many feelings. Then they kissed again, and again, and she shifted her weight and reached down and lined him up and...

"Aaaaah." Delight, in unison, as she took him inside her.

"Jesus," Tim whispered.

"Oh, you must've rung the devil's doorbell."

"What?"

"Nothing."

She started to rock, lifting and lowering herself carefully. She was wet, but it had been a while. And it was new, it was all new.

It was all so good. It was probably crazy, but she was so far past caring that the president of the company could have walked through that supply room door and she wouldn't have stopped.

This man, this moment, this action. This choice. It was hers, all of it. And it was *her*, the new Maggie, a person somebody could admire from afar and be too shy to approach.

She sped up and Tim broke the kiss, breathing harshly. "I thought the devil's doorbell was this." He shifted one hand from her ass to the front of her thigh, then felt with his thumb until he found her clit.

A shock of pleasure jolted through her, burning out any remaining rational thought. "It is."

"Oh, wait..."

Wait? No, no waiting, keep going, keep going. She gripped his shoulders hard, digging her fingers in and grinding down harder. "What?"

"Do you want me to use the thing?"

"The th—oh. *Oh.*" She shivered, her lips parting as she gasped. He'd moved his hand away—but his words had hit her hard, the imagery alone almost tipping her over the edge.

He made a noise, not quite a grunt, not quite a hum. His face and chest were pink again, flushing in dappled splotches among the freckles. "I'm sorry. I didn't mean to embarrass you. I thought since you had it, maybe you liked to use it. We don't have to—*ungh.*"

She'd slid up and off him, swinging her leg over his lap so she could take the few steps over to her bag and crouch down to rifle through it. Lounge pants went flying, a CD case cracked as it skittered against the base of the shelving unit, a small pouch of cosmetics bounced by her feet, and then there it was in her hand. Soft, velvety purple silicone, with a single-button control on the base.

A horrible thought occurred to her as she thumbed the switch. "Please let the batteries still be good."

"We're in the supply room," Tim pointed out. "Plenty of batteries right over there."

She stood too fast and whirled around, suddenly conscious of how she must look. Skirt rucked up around her hips, shirt undone, makeup and hair probably a wreck, and her thong still tucked to one side of her labia. With a vibrator in her hand. *Sex Disaster Barbie.* Except not, because her thighs were thicker than Barbie's waist.

The headrush hit, and everything swam for a second. As her head cleared, she remembered the time she'd mentioned to Jesse that she owned a vibrator. His remark about how lucky she was not to need it anymore…his assertion that she was one more sex toy and three cats away from becoming a permanent spinster when he'd "rescued" her. But he didn't like her to touch herself during sex, either. *Don't you understand how bad that makes me feel? You're basically saying I don't satisfy you, Maggie.*

It would have been so simple—so simple, but not easy at all—to say, "You don't." And proceed from there. She had come to realize that she *should* have done that. But instead, at the time, she'd spent several minutes stroking Jesse's bruised ego. She'd learned to welcome the orgasms when they came, and to fake it when they didn't. Jesse had stuck to his few routine moves. And it hadn't been terrible. None of it had been terrible.

But she deserved better than "not terrible." *I like myself. And I can do the things I want to do.* At that moment, she wanted to do Tim. And use a vibrator in front of him. And not be ashamed of anything. Simple. But not easy.

Nervously gripping the vibe tighter, she accidentally pressed on the control, and a buzz filled the tiny room.

Tim's eyes widened. Maggie looked down at the toy, hitting the switch again. Louder buzzing. *Fuck.* A third time turned it off. She held it up, wiggling it from side to side. "I guess the batteries are okay."

"Maggie?" His voice was soft and low—not sultry, but worried. "We really don't have to use it if you don't want to. It was just an idea."

She looked at him again. His eyes were full of concern. His hand was full of cock; he was holding himself, stroking gently and thumbing his tip the same way she was thumbing the end of the vibe. He didn't seem to realize what he was doing. It was a nervous fidgeting action. Self-soothing.

Endearing.

"I don't know what I'm doing here," she admitted. "It's kind of surreal."

"Yeah," he agreed, "I'm pretty sure I fell and hit my head earlier and this is all a coma dream."

"Okay. A good one, though?"

His jaw dropped for a second, a laugh huffing out of him. "Are you kidding?" He tightened his grip on himself and raked his gaze up and down her as if he couldn't believe what he was seeing. "I never want to wake up."

"So we should roll with it." She took a step closer.

"Definitely," he reassured her. "We can, and I'm sure will, analyze it later. Just…later. Because I'm dying here." He started to reach for her, then finally seemed to realize he'd been stroking himself the whole time they'd been talking. The blush deepened.

She took his hand and squeezed it as she straddled him again. "Later."

The fluorescent light picked up the hint of neon in the

smooth purple of the vibrator's surface. The toy almost glowed in Maggie's hand. She swallowed, trying to pick up the thread of insane bravery she'd dropped somewhere between Tim's lap and her tote bag.

He reached between her legs, stroking, tucking a finger inside, then spreading the slickness over her inner lips. She was still so wet, his fingers slipped through her folds, into her body and out again, with no resistance. And they apparently carried the madness she needed to get back into it. She lowered herself, waited for him to angle his cock up, and slid onto him in one deep stroke that made them both groan in approval.

When he murmured something into her neck, she couldn't make out the words at first—she was too busy shivering with delight. His lips below her ear, his cock inside her, his hands exploring her thighs. So many sensations all at once.

"Hmm?"

"You're poking me with the thing," Tim repeated. He didn't sound upset about it.

Reluctantly, Maggie leaned back enough to free the vibrator from between her body and Tim's. "Tit for tat."

"Ha! Oh, tit." He moved his hands up, squeezing her breasts appreciatively. "*God*. I mean. Definitely a coma."

"For sure." She shifted against him, changing the angle of their connection slightly. It...*did* something. Hit a spot. "*Oh*."

"Oh?" He ran a hand down her arm, then wrapped his fingers around hers, turning the tip of the vibe down and bringing it between them again. "How do you...?"

She brushed his thumb aside and pressed the button. A hive of angry bees, that's what it had always sounded like. But she knew it couldn't be as loud as she perceived it, because it had never woken Jesse up.

Between them, they shifted the buzzing vibrator into place. The second it touched Maggie's clit, her legs started to tremble. She whimpered, then pressed her lips together, trying not to make a sound.

Tim stared down for a few seconds, watching their bodies work together, watching her find her rhythm against the vibe. Then he looked back up at her with wonder and delight in his eyes. And then he kissed her. Eager, affectionate. She couldn't remember the last time she'd felt like the person kissing her was actively happy about it, couldn't wait to do it. She kissed him back until neither of them could breathe, until her cunt started to clench out of time with her hips.

When they came up for air and rested their foreheads together, Tim was sweating. "I'm not going to last," he warned.

She didn't have enough brain to form words. The vibe and his cock had already pushed her past the point of no return. She leaned forward and took his bottom lip between her teeth, groaning as the orgasm swept through her, electrifying her, transforming her into the person she'd wanted to become—the person he'd always seen.

He sighed and shuddered and lost his rhythm, pushing up into her in uneven, shaky thrusts.

She pushed harder on the vibe, turned it up to high, and came again, her whole body tightening until she couldn't take it anymore and yanked the toy away.

When they'd ground the last of the pleasure out against one another, they melted into a hug, stroking each other, shushing and petting, as though they needed mutual consolation over the enormity of the cataclysm they'd just survived.

Maggie came to her senses first, or at least spoke first. "We've probably pushed our luck far enough. We should, you know…"

She thumbed the vibrator off and sighed into the sudden silence.

"Yeah. That…was…I probably know words for it? But right now, I, uh…think they're all in your vagina."

Tim. No. The visual struck her, and she giggled, pressing her face into his shoulder and feeling his laugh as she heard it. "It's like a fucking dictionary up there."

"Oh my God. A *fucking* dictionary."

"No!" She smacked her free hand flat against his chest. He wrapped his fingers around hers and brought them up, kissing her knuckles so gently she almost cried.

"But, Maggie. What does it *say?*"

She pushed away from him, failing utterly in her attempt not to snicker. "If you don't know by now…"

"BZZZZZZ. It sounded like a herd of bees. A flock—swarm. *Shit.* See, all the words are—" he stroked the line where their bodies were joined "—yours now. I can't word anymore." He gave a philosophical shrug.

She shrugged back. "We all make choices, Tim. Sometimes they have consequences. My vagina steals language." Some old programming kicked in, and the former Maggie mentally flailed for a moment at the way she'd casually dropped the word "vagina" into a conversation with a guy. But the new Maggie reared up, large and in charge, clad in nothing but thigh-high garnet leather boots and a smile. *He is literally inside your vagina. If you can't say* vagina *when his penis is inside yours, you have a problem. You don't have to be that person anymore. Take a seat with that shit. You are allowed to have nice things.*

Tim nodded but looked thoughtful. "As long as it doesn't steal *tongues.*"

He raised his eyebrows at her, and the thought of his tongue inside her prompted another rush of want. She clenched around him and felt him twitch in response—but they'd already risked enough, and they really did need to get out of there.

"This isn't the place to find out."

He helped her up reluctantly, mock-pouting a bit as he tucked his shirt back in and fastened his pants. "They should make casual Fridays be just…naked time."

She shook her head, reaching up under her skirt to pull her hastily rebuttoned blouse back into place. "You really want to see everyone in this office naked?"

"Good point. How do I look?"

Maggie rubbed a hint of lipstick from his cheek, then stepped back to appraise him. "More rumpled than usual. What about me?"

"Well." He shrugged and carefully wiped what she assumed was another lipstick smear from the corner of her mouth. "Way more rumpled than usual. I'm sorry for rumpling you. Wait, that's a lie. I regret nothing. You look beautiful, you just look really freshly…freshly fucked, and that's a great look on you and I'd like to see more of it and would you like to go to dinner with me? Tonight?"

A date. He was asking her out on a date.

She started to blurt out a yes, then caught herself. He *wanted* her. He had a sense of humor. A little torture…might be safe enough. "Well, gee, Tim. I don't know. I might have to think about that. Get back to you on it. I don't really know you all that well. Don't you think we should talk first? Maybe meet in the supply room a few more times, make sure we're compatible?"

But she was smiling as she said it, and he smiled back, and she thought *my smile makes him happy, even just my smile makes him happy*. It seemed like a great place to start.

He brushed his thumb against the corner of her mouth again,

then cupped his hand around her cheek as if he were holding something precious. "Hey. I did it. I actually did it. I can't believe I finally got up the nerve to ask you out."

The whole year, he'd said. He'd liked her the whole year he'd worked there. She was his coma dream girl. And she'd wasted so much time.

Maggie rubbed her cheek against his hand. "I would love to go out to dinner with you."

Tim did his cute lip-biting thing again and ducked his head, then seemed to recall they weren't quite ready to go yet. He folded the stepstool and hung it back on the hook, and helped Maggie gather her scattered belongings. Then he gestured for her to scoot toward the door so he could angle the mail cart to get it through the opening. She turned the knob slowly and opened the door a crack, peeking through first to make sure the coast was clear before swinging it wide and waving Tim through. He stole a fleeting kiss as he passed, waited for her to pull the door firmly closed, then accompanied her to the elevator.

As the elevator doors slid shut, Maggie glanced up, noting the security cameras with a disappointed sigh. "So. How do you feel about Italian? I'm starving for some reason."

She felt his finger curl around hers. Just the pinky. Out of the camera's view. So circumspect. He would do just fine in HR.

"I'm starving too. And Italian sounds like the best idea in the world."

What happened after that almost didn't matter, whether things went anywhere after dinner or not. Whether they ever fell into another heated illicit tryst, or whether they wound up together, or whether she ended up with somebody else or no one else.

Because she was somebody new now. Somebody new and

possibly a bit unstable, who made unwise choices in the workplace for the sake of getting off. But also somebody who knew what she was willing to risk to get something for herself.

Something nice, something she deserved. Impractical red boots. Tim in the supply room. Pasta for two. Who could say what New Maggie's next adventure might be?

Also by Delphine Dryden

Series Titles:

Escape
The Unicorn
Top to Bottom (July 2016)

Truth and Lies
How to Tell a Lie (Book 1)
Art of the Lie (Book 2)
Naked Truth (Connected Novella)
Tangled Truth (Book 3)
Tell Me No Lies (Book 4)

Science of Temptation
The Theory of Attraction (Book 1)
The Seduction Hypothesis (Book 2)
The Principle of Desire (Book 3)

Tropical Trysts
Mai Tai for Two
Sex on the Beach

Steam and Seduction
Gossamer Wing (Book 1)
Scarlet Devices (Book 2)
Gilded Lily (Book 3)

Single Titles
Toy Box
Love With a Chance of Zombies
Intermezzo
The Lamplighter's Love
Snow Job
Dream

Anthologies
Winter Rain
How We Began

About the Author

Delphine Dryden majored in English at the University of Texas at Austin, and probably should have gone ahead and gone for that MFA and PhD to become an English professor like she planned. Instead, she took a detour through law school, practiced law for a brief time, and wound up working in special education for the next fifteen or so years (first as a teacher, then as an educational diagnostician). Somewhere in there, she also obtained a Master's in Educational Psychology/Special Education.

Delphine has written contemporary and erotic romance for Carina Press, Harlequin, and Kensington, and mainstream steampunk romance for Berkley Publishing. She has also self-published. Her writing has earned an Award of Excellence and Reviewers' Choice Award from Romantic Times Book Reviews, an EPIC Award, and a Colorado Romance Writers' Award of Excellence. When not writing, she can be found editing for various freelance clients and for Riptide Publishing.

Sign up for Delphine's Newsletter of Benign Neglect and follow her online.

Drowning on Dry Land

Megan Hart

Some doors stay open until you close them.

Moving on from a past love, Bette Douglas has discovered a whole new world of satisfaction and contentment with her boy Damian...but when the past comes knocking, Bette's decision to answer it could change everything.

Chapter 1

*H*E KISSED HER *for the first time in Paris.*

On a bench in the shadow of the replicated Eiffel Tower, she'd shivered at the chill she hadn't expected in Las Vegas. The neon lights sent colored bars and shifting shadows over his face as he smiled. She'd made sure there was a space between them even though she wanted desperately to touch him. He kissed her anyway.

Now, of course, put in that same place, she wouldn't hesitate, not even for a second.

She would take him by the front of the shirt and pull him close to get at his mouth. She would linger over the taste of him. Now, she would devour him.

But there was no more now. Only memories that clung to her like wet fabric, heavy and tangling around her so that she felt as though she were suffocating. Drowning on dry land. Loving him had killed her, but she was taking a very long time to die.

Chapter 2

Bette Douglas came home to the smell of something delicious simmering on the stovetop, the light of candles, and a glass of red wine already poured for her. She toed off her shoes by the front door and hung up her coat and bag in the closet, eyeing the elegantly set dining room table through the archway. The candlelight glinted against the crystal wineglass's ruby contents. Her stockinged feet whispered on the hardwood floor as she went into the dining room to take a drink, savoring the rich, earthy flavors.

Her boy was not in the kitchen, though the spoon in the rest next to the stove hinted that he'd been there not so long ago. Bette lifted the lid on the pot to breathe in the mouth-watering scent of homemade tomato sauce, thick with garlic and vegetables. She took a peek into the oven, too, which was warming thick slices of Italian bread soaked with olive oil and spices. She pulled the bread from the oven and covered it with the waiting sheet of aluminum foil to keep it warm while she looked for Damian.

She found him in the bedroom. Black lace panties cupped his tight, round ass and bulged in the front, not nearly big enough to cover his thick cock. Through the lace, the metal of his chastity cage glinted. He was on his knees, back straight but head bowed. Arms behind him, wrists crossed. He'd been waiting for her.

"Hello, love," she said, which was his permission to look at her.

"Ma'am." Damian's grin lit up his whole face. "How was your day?"

Bette gestured with a flick of her fingers, encouraging him to rise as she went to the dresser to place her glass. "It was all right. Nothing exciting. Glad to be home. Dinner smells delicious, sweetheart, how did you know I was in the mood for pasta?"

Damian came up behind her to nuzzle the back of her neck. "Lucky guess?"

Bette turned in the circle of his arms to take his face in her hands. Damian stood only a few inches taller than her. His height had been one of the reasons she'd been so attracted to him at first. She'd always preferred tall men, but funny how you could get imprinted on something that changed how you felt. She studied his smile and the light in his pale blue eyes, the color of a cloudless summer sky. Soft blond hair peaked above a high hairline, and he wore it close-cropped, much shorter than she preferred. He would never have turned her head if they'd passed on the street, but he'd become beautiful to her because he was hers.

Her melancholy had been triggered by the walk home under fall-turning leaves, the far-off hint of an old, familiar song and a hint of cologne on a passing stranger. The sadness had hit her with a relentless ferocity, but standing in front of her lover, Bette pushed away the memories of that other man. Why should she spend her time dwelling on the past when she had something precious right here in front of her?

She kissed Damian lightly, letting the caress linger but without pressure. She pushed her face into the curve of his shoulder so he could hold her. He smelled of soap and flesh, never cologne. She'd told him she didn't like it, which was a lie but one she didn't feel bad about telling him.

They rocked slowly together for a few moments. She nibbled at his neck and laughed at the sharp hiss of his breath. Then again when she slid a hand up his naked torso to pinch his nipple. Then his hiss became a groan, and when she pulled away to look at his face, his eyes had gone heavy lidded. His lips parted, wet from the swipe of his tongue.

It had been four weeks since she'd last permitted him an orgasm. When she cupped his cock through the lace, the metal of his chastity cage felt warm on her palm. Bette let her fingertips tickle downward over his balls, which were not contained by the device. They tightened delightfully at her exploration.

"So pretty," she murmured as she slipped down the panties, freeing him to her grasp.

Damian shivered but moved to put his feet shoulder-width apart, giving her ample access to every part of him. "Thank you, Ma'am."

"I always think I prefer you in lace, until I see you naked," Bette told him.

He grinned. "I like being naked for you."

They'd been together for almost a year. He'd moved into her apartment after six months because everything had been working so perfectly. It still did. Maybe one day, Bette thought as she circled around him, a finger tracing a line from his belly to the small of his back, maybe one day she would stop expecting it all to end.

"I'm hungry," she whispered against his back. She let her lips move over his shoulder blades. Her tongue flickered at the knobs of his spine. Her fingertips pressed the twin dimples above his ass.

"I made a salad." Damian's voice rasped. His skin had

humped into gooseflesh under her caresses. "We can start with that while the pasta cooks…"

"Perfect." Bette finished her circle to face him again. "Actually, I'm going to jump in the shower before we eat. It's been a long day."

"Are you all right?" He knew her moods the way he'd known she'd be hungry for pasta.

"Fine," Bette said. Another lie, but also one she didn't feel guilty about. "Tired. Chilly. Hungry. That's all."

Damian knew better, she could tell, but he nodded and didn't press her for more information. "I'll go start the water boiling. Everything will be ready by the time you're finished."

She assessed him. "First, I want you to go to the drawer and bring me the emerald plug."

Three inches wide, surgical-grade steel, capped with a pretty cut glass emerald that provided a wide base for the toy and kept it safe. It was one of her favorites. Serviceable, but also pretty. He could wear it for hours without discomfort—well, other than the arousal that would become painful because of the chastity device. Bette grinned at the thought.

"Ma'am…" Damian hesitated.

Her eyebrow lifted, daring him to protest. "Yes?"

"Yes, Ma'am. Whatever you want." He brought it to her at once, holding it on his palm. She hadn't told him to bring the lube, but he had, her good boy.

She brought him close again to kiss him, then to whisper in his ear, "It makes me happy to make you pretty for me."

Damian nodded and swallowed hard. "Then you know it makes me happy."

"Turn around."

He did, putting his hands on the dresser top. He bent at the waist while she took a generous amount of lube on her fingers and slipped them between his ass cheeks to press against his puckered hole. His moan sent a wave of chills through her, straight to her clit. When she breached him, slowly, Damian opened for her with another low, shaking moan.

"Good boy," Bette breathed.

He took two fingers easily enough. She went deep, curling them to press his prostate. Already, a thick, clear stream of precome was dripping from the hole in the tip of his cage. He might orgasm this way, if she kept it up, but that wasn't what she had in mind.

No, Bette had plans for more than that.

Damian groaned, long and deep, when she pushed the plug into his ass. Bette admired it for a moment, especially the glint of the jeweled top. She wiggled it a bit to make him moan again, then stepped back to look over his cock, straining at the cage. More precome stretched in a thick strand nearly to the floor where a small spot glistened.

"You've made a mess."

"I'm sorry, Ma'am."

"Clean it up. Have dinner finished and ready for me when I'm out of the shower." She pinched one of his nipples to hear him moan again, pulling him closer with her grip, but denying him her mouth at the very last second. She laughed when he made a muffled noise of complaint and flicked his earlobe with her tongue. "Go."

She took her time in the shower, shaving her legs and underarms. Though she hadn't planned it, she ended up shaving her cunt, too. Not completely bare—Bette never much liked how she looked without any pubic hair at all. But she trimmed it close around her clit and shaved it clean underneath, then slicked her skin with aftershave to prevent irritation. Stepping out of the shower, she pressed the towel between her legs. She was always so much more sensitive after she shaved. She looked at her full-length reflection, naked except for the small silver key on the matching thin chain around her neck. She cupped her breasts, watching the key disappear between them. She ran her hands down her body, turning from side to side to assess herself in the way most women had—all of her curves and bulges and dips. Her clit had plumped out from the neatly trimmed thatch of hair, and she circled it gently with her finger, then dipped inside to slick herself with her arousal.

Pulling on a silk kimono, her damp hair combed through and tumbling around her shoulders, Bette went into the dining room. Damian had set their places with her good china, which amused her even as it touched her someplace inside that she didn't want to admit to. Her boy often told her he didn't see the point in saving pretty things only for special occasions. Pretty things should be used. Appreciated. Loved.

She'd forgotten the glass of wine in the bedroom, but he had poured another for her, which he handed over with a small flourish. Bette laughed at the frilly apron tied around Damian's waist, the giggle easing into a sigh when he turned around to show off his bare ass from behind. He looked at her over his shoulder, then, deliberately and with a small, secret smile, bent forward to allow the emerald glass to shine at her.

"Bad boy," she told him, but fondly. "Come here."

He did.

"Kiss me," she said.

He did that, too.

She let her hands slide down his sides to anchor on his hips, just above the apron's lacy ties. "Where did you find this?"

"I bought it when I was out last week. I thought you might like it."

"I do, very much."

"Sit," he whispered against her cheek. "Let me bring in the pasta. Would you like me to serve, or...?"

"No, love, not tonight." She had him do that, sometimes. Be formal. Tonight she wanted to enjoy him. "Tell me about your day."

He told her all about it as he brought the pasta and sauce to the table. He waited until she'd dished herself a plate of salad before helping himself, a consideration she'd never asked of him, but one she noticed. She watched him squirm a little in his chair as he spoke. The pressure of the toy must be working on him.

"Damian." She said his name quietly, interrupting his story about what had gone on at his job this morning.

He stopped at once. "Yes, Ma'am."

Bette sipped wine, both to make him wait for whatever it was she meant to say, and also to give herself time to find the right words. "You make me very happy. Do you know that?"

Damian's pleased grin made her glad that she'd told him. "Thank you, Ma'am. You make me very happy too."

She hadn't eaten very much, but her appetite right now was not for food. Finishing her wine, she set the empty glass on the table. She stood. Without a word, only a quirk of her fingers in his direction, she left the dining room and walked back toward the bedroom. She left the kimono in a puddle of silk on the floor. She didn't look over her shoulder to see if he was following. She didn't have to.

Naked, she waited for the soft fall of his footsteps behind her. Without turning, she drew in a breath. Closed her eyes.

There'd been men before this one. There would be men after

him, she thought, once this pretty interlude had ended. But there would never be another man exactly like him.

She didn't open her eyes, not even when she felt his breath on her bare shoulder. "How long has it been?"

"Four weeks, Ma'am. Today."

She adored that she never had to spell out what she meant. "I'd like your orgasm tonight."

Damian sighed. "Yes, Ma'am."

She turned to look at him and slipped the thin chain of her necklace through her fingers. She held up the key that unlocked the cage, watching his face as she did. He looked relieved. A little embarrassed.

"My beautiful boy," she said.

He laughed, ducking his head. "I'm not sure you can be a *boy* when you're just past forty."

She moved closer. "You're *my* boy, that's what matters."

"I want to always be your boy," Damian told her.

She should have kissed him then, but didn't. Instead, she unlocked him, freeing him from the confines of the metal and taking his cock in her hands. He was hard in seconds, growing thick in her fist. Bette stroked him, her eyes on his. She loved the way his pupils dilated and the way he let his head fall back as his hips bumped forward into her caress.

"Tell me how it feels to be locked up for me," she said.

Bette had asked him this before and listened when he answered, but every time there was something new to learn from him. She watched Damian focus on her face. She eased the stroking, holding him behind the head of his cock with a firm but gentle pressure. He dripped over the back of her hand.

"It feels different ways at different times. When you're gone at work and I'm here, or out, or at work, I feel comforted. Being locked for you, knowing that you own my pleasure...that you own me...I feel very peaceful."

"And other times?" She cupped his balls with her other hand, pressing the seam leading to his asshole with her thumb.

"Other times, like when I'm trying to sleep and I haven't come in more than a few days, it's torture. Ahh..." He lifted himself on his toes the smallest bit, pushing himself into her fist. "Oh, Ma'am..."

She smiled. "But it's a sweet torture, huh?"

"Oh, yes. Definitely yes."

She'd never relished humiliation as part of her sexual power, but there was a part of being put in chastity that embarrassed Damian even though he'd been the one to ask if she would lock him up. Before him, Bette had played with tease and denial, and what was this but an extension of that? Complete control over his orgasms. He'd brought it to her as a gift, one she hadn't expected but was determined to appreciate.

"Do you remember when you asked me if I would consider having you wear a cage for me?"

"Yes, Ma'am. You said you'd never thought about it, and you weren't sure you'd like it, but you were willing to try it out for me."

"It's something I cherish about you," she told him.

He looked at her, tilting his head, surprised and aroused, but doing his best to pay attention to her. "What is?"

"That you've led me to learn new things."

Another stroke. Another squeeze. He moaned. Bette swallowed a sigh. Watching Damian's arousal was an exquisite aphrodisiac. Knowing it was all hers to do with as she pleased, even better. There were times when she couldn't quite believe any of this was real. His submission. His desire for her, and hers for him, discovered and explored in ways she'd never even thought about until they got together.

"Get on the bed," she said. "Hands and knees. Face down, ass up."

He did, ever-obedient. Prevented by the metal chastity device, Damian hadn't had an erection in a month, but now his cock rose, thick and long and hard, the tip of it barely brushing the sheets. It had already gone that gorgeous shade of dark red she loved so much. The head glistened with more clear precome. His balls were tight and swollen, perfectly placed for the tickling trace of her fingertips. He cried out when she stroked him there, and she laughed.

She admired him for a few minutes. He'd turned his head to the side so he could see her, and she took her time to tease him with her gaze. She made sure to let him see her looking at every secret part of him. It made him blush to have her inspecting him that way—particularly when she admired his ass and the anal toy adorning it. He squirmed a little, closing his legs, but at her warning mutter, Damian splayed them open again so she had a nice, clear view.

"You need a good fucking," she murmured.

"Yes, Ma'am...."

She pretended to consider her options, though of course she'd already decided what was going to happen. She'd been thinking of it, off and on, for the past few days. How to make this last, but more than that, how to make him come.

Chastity play had never appealed to her before Damian, because Bette liked cock too much to deny herself. What she'd long known about herself, though, was how much she got off by providing pleasure. To her, orgasms were a tribute, an obeisance. They were the physical proof of the worship she expected, and from Damian, received. So, as far as Bette was concerned, if locking up his dick in a metal cage and keeping the key around her neck gave her boy pleasure, she was willing to play with it. Besides, it wasn't like she didn't get her own orgasms whenever she wanted them—from his mouth. His hands. If she wanted his cock, she took it and locked him back up, afterwards, sometimes without letting him finish. It had become fascinating to her, this long-term denial. Still, nothing was as sweet to her as making him explode, and she needed that worship and adoration tonight, to chase away the lingering melancholy.

Getting on the bed behind him, she bumped her cunt gently against his ass. She dug her nails into the meat of his hips, then smoothed her fingertips over the crescents she'd left behind. "Tell me how that plug feels."

"Good. Really good."

She reached between their bodies to grip the emerald base of the toy, rocking it gently inside him. She didn't fuck him with it—they had other toys for that. But she did pull it out the tiniest bit before seating deep inside him again. He pushed back against it when she did, and when she reached around to stroke his cock at the same time, Damian cried out. A plea. A prayer. She eased back, teasing him but also herself. After four weeks without climax for him, it could be over in a minute or so. She needed it to last longer than that.

She ran both her hands over his ass cheeks, feeling the firm muscles. Smooth skin. She let her tongue follow the path she'd made with her fingers, nipping and nibbling his sensitive skin. He cried out again when she bit at the backs of his thighs. His hips thrust. His cock leaped.

"Please!"

"Please, what? Please let you come? Or please keep teasing

you?" Bette laughed and tugged at his hips. "Turn around."

He did with a rueful laugh of his own. Both kneeling, they faced each other. She put her arms over his shoulders, linking her hands behind his neck.

"Ma'am, I'm not going to last very long if you keep doing all of that."

She kissed him and took his lower lip between her teeth to tug until he winced. She licked the spot she'd bitten. "You'll last as long as I want you to."

"Yes," Damian said. "Yes, I'll try."

"On your back."

Bette crawled up his body with a trail of kisses and bites and licks and reveled in Damian's symphony of sighs and moans. She made her way up to straddle his face and brushed her cunt against his open, eager mouth. She gripped the headboard, looking down at his face between her thighs. His eyes were closed. He palmed her ass, pressing her closer so he could feast. She thought about holding back. Making him work for it...but she wanted this orgasm. She needed it to chase away the lingering memories that had plagued her all day without reason. Lost in this pleasure, here and now, what was real would have to replace what had ended. It had to, she thought, and then let the pleasure push away anything else.

Bette slipped her hand down to tangle her fingers in the softness of Damian's blond hair. Guiding him. It was too short to really pull, but she did her best to hurt him a little. Just enough to make him squirm. His hands moved over her body, and behind her, she could feel him thrusting upward, into empty air. She laughed, knowing how frustrating it must be for him. How much he wanted to climax, but couldn't...quite...manage.

His tongue flicked against her clit, light pressure. Tantalizing her. He switched to a steady rhythm with the flat of his tongue, and that was it. She couldn't hold back, she didn't want to, the building ecstasy flooded through her, overwhelming, and she came hard, shaking and crying out a name she bit in half before it could make its way past her lips.

In one smooth motion, she shifted to move down Damian's body so she could slide him inside her still-clenching cunt. She cried out again, wordless this time. No matter how many times they fucked, she'd never gotten used to the size of him.

Riding him, she kissed his mouth. Softly at first, then hard enough to bruise. She fucked him faster, grinding herself onto him so that her clit rubbed his taut belly. He filled her so deep it was almost painful, but the pleasure outweighed the discomfort.

She came again, slower this time. Ripples of pleasure washed over her, and she arched. She pulled him close to kiss him again, stroking tongues. A gasp for breath. A moan.

Damian kissed her, slowing the pace. He rocked inside her with shallow strokes, teasing her and himself with the tip of his cock before pushing back deep inside her. He closed his eyes, mouth thinning in concentration. Bette gave herself up to this moment and to this man. She opened her body to him. What had been fierce and fast became gentle. Making love, not just fucking.

"Come for me, love."

He opened his eyes at the command. Damian came, shuddering and murmuring not Ma'am, which was how they'd both agreed he should address her whenever they were alone, but her name. The sound of it was foreign in his voice and caught her by surprise, enough to send another rippling aftershock of desire through her. She bent to kiss him again, then collapsed onto him with a long, contented sigh.

They stayed that way for a moment or so, his arms around

her. He stroked her hair, down her back. Her face pressed to the side of his neck, Bette closed her eyes and breathed him in. Wishing, wishing that he could be enough.

She moved off him to curl at his side. Damian pressed his lips to her shoulder and rested one hand on her belly for a moment before he moved it down to cup her pussy. She smiled at the protective gesture. She might own him, but there was no doubt that Damian thought of her as his.

They lay in silence, dozing. She'd begun to slip into a dream when she roused herself to look at him. She watched him smile with his eyes closed.

"I didn't think you'd..." he murmured without opening his eyes.

Bette waited a second or two, wondering if he was sleep-talking. "What, love?"

"I didn't think you'd let me inside you." Damian looked at her.

She wasn't sure what to say about that at first. She stroked his cheek, her heart leaping when he turned his face to press a kiss to her palm. "After four weeks, I needed you inside me."

His smile lit him slowly from the inside, like watching a pile of tinder catch fire, but there was an edge of sadness in it. "That's not what I meant."

She didn't answer him.

"I should take a shower," Damian said after a moment. "And...do you want me locked up again?"

He sounded hopeful. Bette reached between them to stroke his cock. "Can you make it to five weeks, this time? What do you think?"

Damian shivered, pupils dilating. He wet his lips with his tongue. "For you, Ma'am, for you, I'll try."

Chapter 3

*T*HE SECOND TIME *he kissed her was in a shadow-dark hallway, both of them edging forward and away from each other, until finally she let him pull her close.*

They danced, the way they'd done the first night they met. His mouth found the curve of her neck, and he nibbled there, making her sigh. Then, moan. His hands on her, moving, restless.

And she, oh, she could not get enough of him. Up against the wall. Her hands on his belt, tugging. Unzipping. She needed him in her hand, her mouth, she needed him inside her. His fingers slipped beneath her dress, under her panties, finding her slick and wet and ready for him, and he fucked into her.

It was not enough.

With him, she would learn, it could never be enough.

Chapter 4

THE EMAIL PINGED through to her inbox stealthily, no warning, one amongst a half dozen others that she was also not expecting but that would not take her so disgustingly unawares. Bette glanced at the screen through the glasses she'd started wearing to work at the computer, and paused. She traced her fingers over the track pad, hovering the cursor over the familiar name.

It couldn't be, she thought, but knew it was.

After all this time, of course it would be him. No warning. Nothing to prepare her for whatever it was that he'd at last decided to say.

She did consider deleting it unread. For a time, she'd had her email program set up so that if he did send her a message, an automatic reply shot back to him. It said, "Your message has been received, but will not be read." She'd even, in a fit of strong self-discipline, created a filter to send him straight to the spam folder—but after a time, a year or so, she'd switched email programs and hadn't bothered with that setup. It had been so long since she'd heard from him, after all, that it had seemed she was never going to.

Yet here he was, the bold, black text of his name like a squatting spider in the list of all the other messages. Bette's fingers traced circles again on the track pad, every other second sending the cursor to hover over that message. Finally, she clicked it. She drew in a breath, steeling herself.

Saw this. Congratulations. I knew you were going to make it.

Attached was a link to the interview in **Agile Technologies Today** that had come out a few months ago, just after she'd been promoted to VP of Programming for Syntec Industries. Lots of people had read it, of course. **Agile Technologies Today** was the definitive trade magazine in the business, and he'd been the sort of man who kept up with things like that. She'd thought about that when she was answering the questions, formulating her answers in a sort of half-code that would mean something only to him.

This is my new phone number. Give me a call if you'd like to catch up.

A laugh forced its way out of her throat, closing with the swell of emotions she was tired of fighting. She closed her eyes to lean back in her chair. Thinking. Remembering. She pressed her fingertips to her lips at the bitter-salt taste of the tears that slipped free, and then she swiped away the wetness roughly. Angry with herself at letting him affect her, even now.

Call him to catch up? She shook her head, opening her eyes. As though it were that simple. Like they could meet for coffee and swap gossip, two casual friends who'd part ways at the end of the hour with a press of cheek-on-cheek and the promise to get together again soon.

Her fingers danced on the keyboard, replying.

I have lots of words, but no voice to say them with. I've thought a lot about what I want to say and how to say it, and mostly, my pride has kept me from it. Because I'll be honest – I've given you a lot of me, and I don't really want you to have any more.

No matter what path my life takes, I would've been willing to find a place for you, but there is never going to be a place for me in yours. I listen to you when you say you can't go all in with anyone. I listen to you when you say how you can't make it work with anyone. I pay attention to your busy, busy life and I know that you make the things that are important to you important. I told you more than once, I should never have to doubt my importance to you. Not as a friend or anything else. Well, I don't have any doubts about how important I am to you. Not anymore.

Bette sat back, her fingers curled. She closed her eyes and drew in a breath. Then another. She deleted the message and began again.

We used to talk to each other, every single day.

And then…not.

So, you know, there's that thing where I said you lead, and if you lead by not talking to me, the only thing I can do is let you.

It's really hard.

It's for the best.

And I just pretend it doesn't matter that I never really got to say everything I wanted to that night in Las Vegas or at your house or on the phone or in person. I pretend it doesn't matter, but it does.

Sometimes, the thing that's for the best is the one that feels the worst.

Practically, I know none of what we had was "real." It was bright and shiny and based on air; it was not meant for permanence. Made of sand, not brick. I know it wasn't real, and it wasn't right, but all along I guess I never cared because…because I needed something, and I didn't know what it was until I met you.

More words. Another pause. She stared at what she had written, and again, she deleted it. Again, she typed, this time faster, a little mermaid walking with steps like knives, though it was her fingers on the keys that stung and burned with every word.

You can't just skip in and out of my life when it suits you. You might have forgotten, but I remember that you dismissed my feelings and made me feel stupid for trying to tell you how I felt; I remember that I don't feel like I can talk to you because of that.

I remember that I don't trust you, anymore.

There was more to be said, but then, there always would be. She, however, didn't have to be the one to say them. She deleted everything she'd written, one last time.

Then, she erased his message.

Chapter 5

*T*HE THIRD TIME *he kissed her was on the dance floor in the place where they'd first met. She'd gone suddenly shy, but he pulled her close and eased her into it, mouth on mouth, the sweet slip of tongue, the grip of his hands on her hips. She blushed. He kissed her, and they danced, and later still in that same place, she fell in love with him.*

Chapter 6

THERE WAS NO dinner waiting for her when she got home, but it was unfair of Bette to be annoyed by this, as it was Damian's night to go to the gym after work and it had all been agreed upon ahead of time. Usually on these nights she liked being able to prepare a meal for him, one of his favorites, and to have it ready for him when he got back smelling of soap and water and the slightest hint of sweat. She liked caring for him in that way, as he did for her so often.

Tonight, however, she couldn't face defrosting, measuring, chopping, cooking. She ordered pizza instead and set the table with paper plates and plastic cups. She poured herself a glass of wine and went onto the balcony to smoke a cigarette, a habit she'd never quite acquired and therefore could indulge in every now and then without later having to break again. Neither the wine nor the smoke soothed her.

Damian was late from the gym. The pizza was cold by the time he got there. Bette had lost her appetite. Too many glasses of wine. Too much thinking.

She turned her face slightly when he bent to kiss her. "You're supposed to text me if you're not going to be on time."

"I was driving," he said. "I don't text and drive. But I'm sorry, you're right. I should've let you know."

She snagged his wrist as he moved away. Offered her mouth for a proper kiss. It wasn't Damian's fault the past had hit her in the face with a shovel this morning.

He stroked a hand over her hair. "What's wrong?"

"Nothing. Eat," she told him. "It's already cold."

Damian, sweetly tempered as usual, didn't complain, but helped himself to a slice. "We haven't had pizza in a long time. This is perfect, Ma'am, how did you know I was in the mood for pizza?"

"Lucky guess." She picked at her own slice but put it down without taking more than a bite. She studied him while he ate. His pale hair was still damp, slicked back from his high forehead. "How was the gym?"

"Crowded. Lots of people there I don't usually see. I might like to change my routine a little." He wiped his mouth and sipped from the wine she'd poured him. He hesitated, looking as though he meant to say more, but didn't.

"Why?"

"It's just that...well, it was more crowded. I had to wait for the equipment longer. And the locker room..." He paused again.

She watched his throat work. "What about it?"

"Not as private."

"Someone saw you locked up." She smiled, thinking of it. "You were embarrassed."

"A little. Yeah."

"So don't wear it to the gym," Bette said without sympathy.

Damian tilted his head to look at her. "But...Ma'am..."

"It's not like I think you're going to stop in the middle of your workout to jack off," she continued, watching his face. Damian wore his emotions all over his expression. Easy to read. It was one of the things she liked so much about him, how different he'd been than that past lover who'd made a habit of inscrutability. "If you're uncomfortable wearing it where someone might see it, then take it off."

"But..." He put both hands flat on the table, one on either side of his plate. "Yes, Ma'am."

They finished the meal in silence. Bette got up from the table and left him to the cleanup. In the shower, she bent her head beneath the spray and succumbed to the exquisite agony of grief. She stifled her sobs into a curled fist, not wanting Damian to hear her weeping for the loss of someone else.

He somehow knew, though. When she came into the bedroom, her hair wrapped in a towel and wearing her terrycloth robe, he'd already turned down the bed. He'd changed the sheets, replacing the cool cotton with soft and comforting flannel. He'd lit the gas fireplace, too. He waited for her, on his knees, facing away from the bathroom doorway.

He'd laid out one of her favorite toys.

If she hadn't already cried herself almost sick Bette would've wept again, not in sorrow this time but in that complicated tangle of lust and love and guilt because Damian had managed to figure out exactly what she wanted and was giving it to her, even though she did not, at the moment, deserve the gift of his service.

She took off the towel and finger combed her hair, then twisted it on top of her head to keep it out of the way. She shrugged out of the robe and went naked to the bed to look over what her boy had put out for her. It surprised her, a little, though it was in fact, perfect. The flogger had a hefty but comfortable rubber handle and multicolored rubber strands that could be used to tickle and caress...but that also fiercely stung. Lightweight enough for her to wield almost tirelessly, it was the one implement in her carefully curated collection that was guaranteed to break him into using his safe word. Bette shook the flogger to untangle the rubber strands and let them slide across her palm.

She wanted to hurt him.

She wanted to make her boy whimper and cry and writhe; she wanted to make him beg her to keep going, and she wanted him to beg her, finally, to stop. He'd chosen this for her so she could do just that, because he knew her and wanted to please her. Because he loved her, Bette thought as her fist clutched at the dangling rubber strands, crushing them against her palm.

She watched the muscles in his back tense and release at the sound of the rubber smacking against her fingers. She was teasing him with the anticipation. The desire to hit him rose inside her with an almost physical force, making her shiver. Bette closed her eyes.

She breathed.

Damian would not mind if she beat him to make herself feel better, to forget the things inside her mind that were causing her pain. Once, in the beginning, he'd told her that he'd rather she lose herself in hurting him than dwell on whatever it was that was hurting her. He would not care, Bette thought, but she would.

She put the flogger back on the bed and went to him, kneeling to curl around his back. Her face pressed between his shoulder blades. Her weight against him pushed Damian a little forward, but he was strong enough not to topple over. Her arms slipped around his waist, and she hugged him. Tight. She closed her eyes and took in his scent, grounding herself to his smell, his warmth, the distinctive feeling of his body. She anchored herself to him.

"I need you," she whispered.

He twisted to settle on the carpet and pulled her into his lap. "What's wrong? I thought you'd want to."

Bette buried her face into his neck. Beneath her thigh, the metal of his chastity cage bit into her skin. She shifted, but it was still there. She closed her fist around the key to it, dangling from the thin silver chain between her breasts. With a tug, she snapped the chain and pressed the key into his hand.

"Take it off," she said.

"It's only been two days," he began.

She didn't slap his face, though the urge was there, same as the desire to beat him had been there. This time also for the wrong reason, and worse, because she was mad. She had never struck him in anger, and the fact she had almost done it now twisted her stomach.

"Take it off," she repeated. "I need you, Damian."

He didn't answer with a *Yes, Ma'am*, but carefully slid her off his lap so he could use the key on the device. He unlocked it and held it out to her in the palm of his hand. Silent.

Bette looked into his eyes, both of them kneeling on the carpet in front of the bed. "I want your cock inside me. I need you to fuck me, Damian."

"Yes…" he began and stopped, looking at the curved metal device in his hand. "I just thought…"

"It's not your place to think," she snapped, standing. "It's your place to obey."

He couldn't hide the flash of irritation in his gaze. Maybe he didn't even try. His lips thinned, pressing together, but he nodded stiffly and looked away from her.

"Yes, Ma'am."

She might've said those exact words to him in a different tone, or a different time, and they would've turned him on. She had hurt him, and not in the way they both liked. She couldn't bear it, suddenly.

"I cannot be in charge right now," Bette said slowly. Carefully. She won the battle to keep her voice from breaking, but only barely. "I can't do this right now, Damian, do you understand me? I just…need…you. I need you."

Uncertainty warred in his expression with a flurry of other emotions, not all of which she could discern, but he nodded anyway. He got to his feet to meet her eye-to-eye. He kissed her softly on the corner of her mouth, letting her turn toward him instead of away.

"Yes, Bette. Okay. Whatever you need."

She gasped when he slid a hand up the back of her neck to twist in her hair, tipping her head back. Again, when his hand pushed between her thighs so the heel of his palm pressed her clit. With his mouth locked to hers, he walked them both to the bed. It hit the back of her knees, but his grip on her kept her from tumbling backwards—at least until he let her go. Then she fell with a low cry onto the mattress and the softness of the flannel sheets. Damian was on top of her before she had time to do more than let out that one sound. His hand moved beneath her to lift and pull her at the same time he shifted, moving them both upward on the bed.

She never forgot how strong he was, or that the only reason she was ever able to control him was because he was so willing to submit, but she was rarely reminded so forcefully. Desire ripped through her. Harder when he bent to nip at her throat, moving his mouth lower to suck at her nipples, one at a time. Bette writhed beneath Damian's touch. His other hand moved back to her cunt, sliding two fingers inside her. Not gently. She cried out again, louder this time, adding a curse.

He cut off her words with his kiss. He took her breath with his own as his fingers moved inside her, then out to circle on her clit before pushing back inside. His cock, thick and heavy, stroked her thigh as he moved, but she didn't touch him.

"Fuck," he muttered into her mouth. "You're so wet. I have to fuck you, Bette."

It was what she wanted. Needed. "Yes. Now."

In a smooth motion Damian settled between her legs. His cock nudged her entrance, and just as he'd done moments before with his fingers, he filled her in one thrust that sent another bolt of desire igniting her. He filled her so fully there was a hint of pain, but she embraced it with a tilt of her hips to drive him in even deeper. He pushed up on his hands to look down at her, his lower lip pulled between his teeth and his brow furrowed in concentration.

"That thick, hard cock," Bette said on a gasp. "Fuck, you've got such a nice fucking cock…"

He fucked into her harder. She ran her hands up his forearms, loving the veins there. Up over his biceps and the bulging muscles. Her nails dug into his shoulders, then raked his back. She gripped his ass cheeks, urging him to fuck her harder. Faster. Deeper. She wasn't going to come this way—not enough stimulation on her clit, despite the way his pelvis pounded hers, but the frenzy of it, oh, shit, yes…that was good. It was good enough.

Not for Damian, apparently. He eased and slowed, holding himself off her with one arm while he slid his other hand between them to press his knuckles to her clit. It felt good, but it wasn't going to get her off. She didn't want this. She wanted to be pounded. Fucked. She wanted him crying out her name as he came.

When she tried to push his hand away, though, Damian shook his head, stubborn. Before she could stop him, he'd pulled out of her. He rolled them both, graceful and coordinated the way he always was. He slid down the bed until his mouth could tease her cunt. Wriggling, she tried to get away, but his grip trapped her. At the swipe of his tongue against her clit, Bette shuddered.

She fought him, but he was stronger. He gripped her wrists, pinning them to her sides. With a strangled cry, Bette tried to free herself, but could not.

She did not tell him to let her go.

She wasn't calm, but she stopped struggling. Damian bent to her, using light flicks of his tongue. Maddening. Tantalizing. His breath, hot, gusted over her. At last she could hold back no longer. With a long, muttered groan, Bette ground herself against his mouth. Pleasure overtook her until there was nothing else but this. Nothing but him.

Tightly coiled springs of desire exploded inside her. She bore down on it. Muscles tensing. The whoosh-whoosh of her heartbeat drowned out the sound of her cries. Bette gave herself up to mindless ecstasy that lasted forever and ended too soon.

Breathing hard, blinking, she realized she was crying. He wasn't holding her down any longer, and she realized she couldn't remember when Damian had released her. Her fingers had cramped so much that it hurt to loosen them from the fists she'd made. She swiped at her face before moving to pull him upward. She kissed him, tasting herself along with the salt of her tears.

His hands came up to push her hair away from her face. He rolled them again, cupping her against him to keep from crushing her—it was a movement that might've been intimidating, but in his arms she felt only cherished. Protected.

Safe.

Damian tucked her back along his front, spooning her. His cock, still hard, slid between her thighs. She was so wet there was no resistance. They shifted; he slid inside her from behind. Slow, slow, he rocked inside her as his hand moved between her legs. At the press of his mouth on her shoulder, Bette arched at the gradual, building rise of another orgasm.

They moved that way for a long time, her pleasure moving more slowly this time. Bette lost track of time. She moved to push her arm over her head, finding his hand with hers. Linking their fingers. When his thrusts became erratic, his moans louder, she pushed against him. She was coming again when Damian cried her name and buried himself inside her with a shudder.

Quietly, Bette pressed their linked fingers to her lips and snuggled closer to him. She wanted to sleep. She did not want to dream.

She woke, though, in a few minutes when Damian slipped from the bed and the chilly air caressed her. With a murmur, she pulled the sheets up over herself and thought about getting up, too, but though she was sticky, she couldn't manage to make herself move. He was back a moment later with a damp, warm cloth that he used to clean her gently, hardly moving her. Then he was in bed with her again, his warmth enveloping her.

"Bette," he said right before she eased into sleep again.

She blinked, thinking she should pretend she didn't hear him. "Yes, love."

"Don't you want me to be locked up for you, anymore?"

She didn't turn to face him. His breath tickled the back of her neck. She wiggled her ass against his softness, enjoying the flesh-on-flesh that wasn't sexual. The cage would've been in the way of that.

"I like controlling your orgasms, Damian. I like being in

charge of your pleasure. But sometimes, it's just…too much. All of this," she told him with a defeated sigh.

"What is?"

"This," Bette said, hating herself. "Us."

She felt his withdrawal, the sudden and aching space between them even though he hadn't moved. "Is it something I did? Or didn't do?"

"No, love. It's not you."

Damian's bitter laugh stabbed her in the heart, but she deserved it, didn't she? Bette let their fingers unlink. She let his hand slip from hers.

"It's not me, it's you," Damian said. "Is that it?"

"Yes."

He did move, then. The bed dipped as he sat up. She heard the thump of his feet on the floor. She waited for him to leave, and she wouldn't have blamed him. After a moment, though, Damian sighed. He lay beside her again, pulling her close. He kissed the spot between her shoulders.

"What happened, today, Bette? What went wrong?"

That he knew her well enough to ask also stabbed her. Bette sat. She pulled her knees close to her chest and put her chin on them. The room had fallen into darkness while they fucked, but the glow from the fireplace was more than enough to see by. She let herself look at him, this man who'd been hers for a little over a year.

"He emailed me. He asked to see me."

Damian sat up, too. "When?"

"This morning."

"No," he said quietly. "I mean, when are you going to see him?"

Surprised, she twisted to face him. "I'm not."

"No?" He asked, this time a question. "Why?"

"Because…because…I don't want to." She hadn't known it before she said so, but once the words were out there was no question they were a lie.

Damian didn't say anything for a few seconds. When he did speak, it was in the same calm, neutral tone. "Do you remember what you told me the first time we met?"

"I can remember a lot of things I said the first time we were together, love."

"I'd brought you a glass of wine, and you said, 'good boy.' You had one of those smiles. It knocked my feet right out from under me," Damian said. "I wanted to get on my knees for you right there, I wanted to do anything for you, so long as you would say that to me again."

"I remember." Bette's voice scratched, rough and raw with emotion.

"You saw me right away for who I am. You'd never met me, but you knew me. That's how it felt. We spent the entire night talking. We ignored the people we'd come with to the party—"

"We were very rude," she interrupted mildly, with a teary laugh.

"Yeah. I guess we were." He smiled at her, though it didn't quite reach his eyes. "But later that night, when I asked you for your number?"

"I said, if I wanted you to have my number, I'd have given it to you already."

He nodded. "And what else?"

"I told you I wasn't in the market for a lover because…" she couldn't go on, not at first.

Damian finished for her. "You said it was because you'd just ended a relationship with someone who'd broken you."

"I said it that way?" she asked, surprised.

"Yes. I remember, because I thought it was interesting. Not that he broke your heart. That he broke you."

She frowned. "I was stupid. He didn't break...me."

"Nothing could break you, Bette. You're the strongest woman I've ever met. It's why I love you." Damian dragged a fingertip up her arm and along her shoulder, then cupped his hand at the back of her neck. As before, the gesture could've been overbearing, but from him felt only like a comfort.

It was not the first time he'd said he loved her. There was no pressure for her to say it in reply. Especially not now.

She did lean to put her head on his shoulder, letting the hand that had been behind her neck shift so he could put his arm around her shoulders. "I don't want to see him, Damian. Sometimes, even when you love someone, you stop believing in them. And once that happens, there really is nothing to say to each other, is there?"

"You never talk about him. You don't have pictures. There's nothing. Everyone has bad breakups, Bette, but you've never even said his name to me. The only time you ever spoke of him at all was that first night. It's like you're trying so hard to make him disappear...but you still love him. I know you do."

Bette bit her lower lip hard enough to sting. She wanted to deny it, but there was no point. It would be a lie as much as saying she didn't want to see that other man. "I don't know if it's love anymore, but it still hurts like love."

They sat in silence, then. The sift of their breathing, in and out, aligned. When the position finally became cramped, Bette moved. Damian's eyes were closed. In the shifting gold and black shadows from the fireplace, he was more beautiful to her than he had ever been. She kissed his shoulder, watching his eyelids flutter but not open.

She got out of bed without waking him. Turned off the fireplace. Fixed the blankets and pillows, urged Damian to lie down, and curled up next to him. Sleep seemed too far away from her now, but in the dark with the soft music of his breathing beside her, she could at least be content.

"You should see him." Damian's whisper twisted through the darkness.

"How could you want that?"

"Because," he said, "if you come back, I'll know you want to be here."

"And if I don't?" The words were bitter, tinged with acid edges that burned her tongue.

Damian rolled onto his side, away from her. His voice was muffled when he answered her, but she had no trouble hearing every word. "Then I won't have to wait anymore for you to leave me."

Chapter 7

THE FOURTH TIME he kissed her was in the back seat of his car, when she thought he meant to finally let her leave him, but instead he kept her even closer. When she told him that she loved him, and he said he loved her, too.

Chapter 8

T HEY DIDN'T MEET in a coffee shop.

Bette reserved a room at a hotel off the highway exit ramp an hour or so from her house. Two hours from his, but she thought, if he really wanted to see her, he'd make the drive. The last time she'd asked him to meet her, so they could talk, he couldn't be bothered. Too far to drive, he'd said. She would've have met him anywhere, driven any distance, for the chance to see him one last time, but instead she'd hung up the phone and hadn't heard a word from him. Nearly two years had passed since then.

She had waited for him many times. Waited for him to call. To text. Waited for him in parking lots and darkened clubs and in rooms like this. She'd waited for him to love her the way she loved him, but he never had.

Bette had left a key at the front desk for him. Though he knocked first, he came through the door without waiting for her to open it. Eager, she thought. Hoped. Too excited to see her that he couldn't wait.

She'd always thought, every time they met, that she was ready to see him. Yet every time that first sight of his face, his smile, set her heart to thumping. Pulse racing. She was not the timid sort, but he had always made her blush and falter. Time hadn't changed any of that, because yes now, that first sight of him made everything inside her shake.

"Hi," he said.

One word, so simple but weighted with so much meaning. It pleased her to see that he looked hesitant. Eager, but uncertain. Bette had brought a bottle of champagne, chilling on ice, and had opened it before he got there. She lifted the flute toward him without taking a step.

"Drink?" she asked him, already pouring.

"Sure. Is this...a celebration?" He took the champagne flute from her.

Their fingers touched.

This man had once been able to get her nipples hard with no more than a look and a few murmured words. The brush of his skin on hers, even after all this time, sent an electric ripple through her. Bette didn't bother to hide it. There was no point in pretending, not for his sake. If he believed anything had changed between them, it was only because he'd been lying to himself. Of course, he'd always been good at that.

Bette smiled. "I just like champagne."

He looked around the room as he sipped, then at her. He set the glass down on the desk. "So. Here we are."

"Yes," she said. "Here we are."

"I was surprised you asked me to meet you here. I didn't think you'd want to see me."

"I didn't," Bette told him and took another sip.

His smile faded. He was tentative again. She liked it, keeping him on edge the way he'd kept her so many times.

"...Oh. So then why did you agree to meet me here?"

"Because I didn't want to regret not taking the chance." She put down her own glass and moved toward him. "Because I sometimes wake up with the taste of you still lingering in my mouth. Because I miss you with a fathomless and abiding ache that is marrow deep inside me."

She had never been the one to kiss him first. In that, she'd always waited the way she had so often with everything else. Bette was done waiting when it came to him. She stepped up to him, pushing up on her toes to get at his mouth. Her fingers curled in the front of his shirt to pull him close to her.

There was an unsteady moment where she thought he was going to push her away, but it lasted only a second or so before he groaned into her kiss. His hands moved over her body. One slid up to twist in her hair and pull it in the way he knew would make her boneless and greedy with desire.

That hadn't changed.

"I missed you, too," he said into her ear as his fingers inched up the hem of her skirt, seeking the tops of her stockings.

Bette pulled away from the heat of his mouth on her throat. "Of course you did."

It wasn't what she'd have said, before. He looked surprised. His fingertips found the bare expanse of her thighs, sliding higher to the lace of her panties. He stopped before he touched her there.

It was awkward, this position, unless they were both moving. He kept still. His gaze searched hers.

"You," he said, "are so beautiful."

He'd never said such a thing to her before. Hearing him actually say it aloud set her back a step. She almost faltered. Fled, before he could break her again. But it was too late, because he was kissing her and he tasted the same as he always had, of sweetness and fire and desire and the flavor filled up all her senses until her head spun.

"I don't need you to tell me that, but you can go ahead and say it again," Bette said. She'd taken that step back, but the desk was behind her and she had no more room to move.

He moved between her legs, nudging them open with his knee. His eyes blazed. His smile grew a little wicked in that charming way. "You. Are. So. Beautiful."

"I know," she whispered against his lips when he kissed her.

Chapter 9

THE FIFTH TIME he kissed her was in a parking lot, summer heat shimmering the air around them, his mouth chilled from icy water. "Touch me," he told her, and she did. Of course she did.

The sixth time he kissed her was in a hotel hallway, two knuckles deep inside her, when he said "we could do this forever," but instead she watched him walk away.

The seventh time he kissed her was in a dream of long hallways and red doors, and a fox, running. She opened all the doors in the corridor before she found him. It was only a dream, but she had it more than once.

Chapter 10

Bette didn't wait for him to pull her toward the bed. She walked there on her own, tugging open the tie at the waist of her dress and letting it open all the way up the front. She turned at the foot of the bed with a smile and shrugged off the material to let it fall onto the floor. She kicked the dress aside and put a hand on her hip. She wore a pair of silky purple panties and a matching demi-cup bra. Black thigh-high stockings, but no garter belt—those were sexy but complicated, and she wanted easy access with maximum impact. She waited for him to say something, but to her smug delight, she seemed to have knocked the words right out of him. Was there any greater satisfaction than facing a former lover after so long a time and seeing him made speechless at the sight? Bette didn't think so, not in that moment, anyway.

When he came closer to her, though, she put out a hand flat on his chest, her arm stiff to keep him from touching her. "Not yet."

He paused, still reaching. His fingertips skimmed her bare skin. "No?"

"No."

At her tone, he stopped. Brow furrowed. "What's up?"

"Earn it," Bette told him.

He frowned. "So it's going to be like that?"

"Yes," she breathed and curled her fingers in the front of his shirt, bending her arm to at last allow him to move up next to her. She turned her face from his kiss, though, giving her neck instead. "It's going to be like that."

"What do I have to do to earn it?" His mouth brushed the spot just below her ear, making her shiver. His tongue flickered. "Something like this?"

At the nip of his teeth, her nipples peaked to an aching hardness that begged for his touch. Bette turned to press her ass against his groin and swept her hair to the side so he could feast further on her neck. His hands slid over her belly, one teasing downward to stroke a fingertip between her legs before he moved them both up to cup her tits.

"Like this?" he continued, freeing her breasts from the confines of the bra and tweaking her pebble-hard nipples. One of his hands moved over her belly again, between her legs, this time beneath the lacy edge of her panties to her bare, hot flesh. He stroked her, both his hands moving in sync.

Bette arched, letting her head fall back to his shoulder. She pushed her ass harder against his cock, thick and hard through his khakis. She ground against him, rocking her hips to let the hand between her legs shift and slide. She'd meant to tease him longer. Maybe even make him beg, but oh, fuck, this…this was too good not to give in to.

The clitoris was the devil's doorbell, and Bette was more than ready to answer its ring.

"I missed you," he said into her ear. His fingers circled her clit, then down to dip inside her slickness. Up again, pressing and stroking while the other tugged first one, then the other nipple in perfect, aching rhythm. "I couldn't stop thinking about you. It didn't matter where I was, or what I was doing, no matter how long it had been since we were together, somehow it always came back to you."

She hated him for saying that, almost as much as for telling her she was beautiful. "Shut up."

His hiss of surprise turned her to face him.

"I don't believe a word that comes out of your fucking mouth," Bette told him, even as she kissed him. Even as their tongues stroked and tangled and she let him bruise her lips from the force of his desire. With his fingers still fucking into her, his other hand now digging into her hair, she said, "So shut up and fuck me. That's all this is. Nothing else."

She pushed him back a step, fiercely enough to make him stumble. Both of them breathing hard, they squared off. When he reached for her again, she knocked his hand aside.

"Take off your clothes." Bette stepped backwards, finding the chair by the window. She sat, her back straight. Ankles crossed. Regal. A queen ready to be worshipped. She let her fingers flick in his direction. "I want you naked."

He was already tugging at the buttons of his shirt, opening them with his gaze locked on hers. "Yeah? You want this?"

"Naked," she repeated coolly.

He faltered for half a second, but rallied. He took the time to hang his shirt over the edge of the desk chair. His pants, too, neat and tidy the way he'd always been. His socks, next, shucking them off to face her and then stand tall in only a pair of snug fitting boxer briefs that emphasized his erection. He turned in a circle, looking over his shoulder at her before making it all the way around to face her again. He stroked a hand over his bulging cock.

"You first," he said.

Bette laughed with real, true humor. Of all the things that had passed between them, laughter had been a lot of it. So there'd been tears too, she thought as she shook her head with a smile. But always, there'd been this—the way they'd laughed together.

"Nope," she said simply. "You. Naked. I want to see that cock ready and dripping for me."

He blinked at her words, again surprised. She understood. In their time together, she'd never been demure or shy, but she'd also never been…this.

Without a word, he hooked his thumbs into his briefs, but he hesitated before pushing them over his hips. His chin lifted. Eyes blazed. Maybe he was embarrassed. Maybe he was going to tell her to fuck off.

She loved his uncertainty and hesitation.

Slowly, he eased the soft fabric over his cock until the tip peeked out. Bette didn't move, though she wanted to crane to catch a glimpse. She sat very still. Not smiling, and definitely no longer laughing. He pushed the material down over his thighs, then stepped out of it to stand in front of her with his erection so hard it tapped his belly.

Bette hadn't forgotten the length and curve of his cock. He was smaller than her boy—not as long. Not as thick. It didn't matter, of course, she still thought it was as close to perfect as a prick could get…but she noticed the differences.

A slow, delighted sigh slipped out of her. "You have such a gorgeous cock. I always loved it. Stroke it for me."

"You think you can tell me what to do?" His hand was already gripping, but the low and angry noise easing from his throat told her he wasn't taking her commands very well.

She looked straight into his eyes. "Yes. I think I can tell you exactly what to do, and I expect you to do it. Because you want to push that hard cock deep inside me, or else you wouldn't be here in the first place. Because I decide how far this goes, do you understand? I decide when you get to touch me, and how, and how hard you get to come, if you get to come at all."

She watched the line of his throat work as he swallowed, hard. His fist gripped his cock just below the tip. He shook his head slowly, back and forth just once.

"No," he said.

Bette laughed again, the sound wicked and gleeful and clearly affecting him because his dick bobbed, even with his grip holding it still. "Your cock says otherwise. And look, sweetheart…look at how you're already leaking for me."

It was true. Clear, slick fluid had gathered in the slit at the tip of his cock and glistened in the hotel lamp's soft golden light. It dripped as she watched, sliding over the smooth skin of his cockhead and disappearing into the tightness of his fist.

"Get on the bed," Bette told him. "On your back."

He did.

Pushing the tangled weight of her hair over her shoulders and down her back, she shook it to show off. He'd always loved her hair, and it was even longer now. She hadn't cut it since the last time she'd seen him. The curls had grown thick and wild. Unruly. It was a pain to maintain, but she was glad she hadn't given in to the urge to chop it all off, not when his eyes lit up at how it cascaded in dark, rippling waves nearly to her ass.

She straddled his thighs and put her hands on his hips. Her nails dented his skin, and she carefully watched his face for the reaction. His eyes widened a little, and he jerked, lips opening on a protest though she'd barely pressed hard enough to hurt him. She moved a hand between her thighs to circle her clit, never looking away from his gaze.

"How many times did you make yourself come thinking

about me?" she asked.

He snorted softly. "What kind of question is that?"

Her nails dug harder into his warm skin. "Answer me."

"A lot," he admitted, wincing, and put a hand over hers to stop her from digging again. "I told you, Bette, I thought of you all the time. You should know that."

"I didn't know anything."

She scored her nails over his hip and across his belly, leaving faint white lines that would turn red but leave no lasting marks. She pinched his nipple. He bucked, hips rising, and she moved upward at the same time so that when he settled, his cock was pressed to the crotch of her silky panties.

"It was always you," he said, voice harsh but muted.

She gave him a brittle smile and shifted so the softness of her lingerie teased but barely touched him. "Good. And when you fucked those other women, did you think of me then, too?"

"What makes you think there were other…fuck!"

She'd leaned to grip his chin in her fingers. Then she leaned closer to flick his lips with her tongue and whisper, "Don't you lie to me. I deserve better than that."

Still holding his chin, she let her mouth hover above his, until he pushed up toward the kiss. Laughing, she kept just out of reach. When he fell back with a small, frustrated groan, she let go of him and sat up. Both hands flat on his chest, scratching lightly downward.

"You're different," he said.

"No," Bette answered. "I'm the same. I'm just not afraid to be who I am, anymore. With you, I was always afraid."

She had always loved his body. The leanness of him. Smooth skin, hard muscles. Athletic. In the beginning she'd been self-conscious about being naked in front of him—he was strong and fit and she tended more toward softness and curves. She still loved his body, which had changed in subtle ways over the past couple years, the way her own probably had, too. The difference was that she was no longer self-conscious about the lines at the corners of her eyes or the few strands of silver in her hair, not about the softness of her belly or the curves of her hips and thighs. Her boy had given her that, and never once by *telling* her she was beautiful. Everything Damian did for her made her *feel* that way.

But she was not with her boy now.

Bette moved her mouth over his throat and along his collarbone. Then his chest, pausing to sample his nipples until he writhed and she sat up, looking stern. "Don't move."

"You gonna tie me up?" He teased at first, but his smile faded a bit at her expression.

"No. I shouldn't have to tie you up in order to make you obey me." She tilted her head to look at him and wet her lower lip with the tip of her tongue.

His gaze darkened as he looked at her mouth. He pushed up on an elbow. "Maybe I'd like it."

"You'd love it," she said. "But you don't deserve that level of attention from me yet."

With a snort, he fell back onto the bed. "So have your wicked way with me. Order me around. Is that what you want?"

Again, she ran her nails down his body. This time, he arched into the touch, even when she scratched a bit more roughly. "Yes. That's what I want. Are you going to give me what I want?"

He almost didn't answer, but then came his low reply. "Yes. Anything. Just don't stop touching me."

Bette didn't say anything to that. Not with words. She answered him with the nip of her teeth in a sensitive spot. Then, moving lower, lower, she took his cock in her mouth. She didn't laugh at the startled noise he made, though she wanted to. If she laughed, she would certainly weep, and she didn't want to do that. Later, Bette knew, there'd be tears. With him, there were always tears.

For now, there was this.

She took him in deep, inch by inch, her hand following the path of her mouth so he was never without her touch. It was an adjustment for a moment, remembering that he was small enough to deepthroat without discomfort. She could never manage that with Damian.

When he tried to touch her hair, she made a warning noise and he fell back again. His hips pushed upward, though, and she allowed it because she liked the way he tried fucking into her mouth, how frustrated it made him when she refused to go any faster.

She sucked him for a long time. A hand cupped his balls, her thumb stroking backward along the seam. She pressed that secret spot just above his asshole in time to her sucking, feeling the throb of his heart beat there. Her hair fell down around her face, shielding her. She teased the head of his cock with her tongue. She slid lower, brushing his balls with her lips and then also with her tongue. His inner thighs earned the press of her teeth and heat of her breath as her hand kept up the steady stroking along his shaft, always too slow for him to come but fast enough to make him shudder.

She was so wet her thighs slid against each other, and when she squeezed them, the pressure on her clit was enough to get her spiraling toward orgasm. She didn't touch herself. Not yet. She concentrated on him. So many times she'd yearned to have him in her mouth like this, and now she was going to take her time.

Anyone who thought cocksucking was a submissive act clearly didn't understand the power of giving pleasure. Every moan, every sigh, every tense and shift of his muscles was an homage to her, and Bette accepted all of them as her due. Years had passed since the last time she'd done this with him, so she learned him all over again. How fast, how hard, when to give or when to take. When to hold back.

When to let go.

That was what this was all about, and the release of it was a rush as fierce and defining a moment as any climax could've been. Bette shook with it, a pleasure she hadn't expected. It made her light, unburdened. It made her shake.

He said her name in a low rasp. His cock throbbed on her tongue. Bette released him from her heat but moments later sheathed him again with her cunt, panties pushed to the side. She rode him with her nails digging into his chest and her head tipped back so the weight of her hair tickled his thighs as she moved.

"It's so good with you," he said. "Fuck, it was always so good..."

It was the truth. The sex had always been good. It was everything else that had gone wrong, and she hadn't forgotten any of that. Not even when the pleasure overtook her, coiling tight and tighter until it sprang free. She looked into his eyes, at last, when she came, and he followed her within seconds. Neither of them looked away.

Sweating, the bitterness of salt on her lips, Bette eased herself free and rolled onto her back beside him. Their shoulders touched. So did their hips. After a moment when he rolled to press his lips to her shoulder, she didn't move away.

"That was amazing," he said.

"It was always amazing."

She waited for him to sleep, but he didn't. He pulled her close, nuzzling against her, and she allowed it because even now, the memory of how much she had loved him was enough to keep her from being unkind. He deserved cruelty, she thought. But she did not. She'd become better than that.

"You know…you don't realize how much something hurt until it stops hurting." Bette said this to the ceiling without looking at him.

There'd been lots of times when he'd pretended he didn't understand what she was trying to say, but not this time. "I'm sorry I hurt you."

She rolled to face him, cupping his face with a tenderness she hadn't felt until just now. "You did. And more than once, but I let you do it, over and over, so who's the fool? You or me?"

"I didn't mean to. You know that."

She stroked his cheek with her thumb, then took away her hand to sit up. "You can't make someone love you, if they don't."

"I loved—"

She stopped him with a kiss that didn't linger; she looked deeply into his eyes. "I told you. No lies. I deserve better from you. Be the man I thought you were, for once, and not the man you are."

"I *wanted* to love you," he said.

It was the best answer, because it was the truth. She kissed him again. Then she got up from the bed and began to dress. Her back was still turned when he spoke.

"Did you mean what you said? About this being only fucking?"

She tied the waist of her dress and smoothed it, then turned.

"Yes. I have someone else in my life, now."

He'd pushed to sit up against the headboard, the sheet covering him, and at her words he winced. "What? You do?"

"Yes. He's very special to me." She found an elastic band in her bag on the dresser and used it to twist her hair into a messy bun on top of her head without bothering to check her reflection.

"So...why did you...with me?"

"I told you. Because I didn't want to regret not taking the chance. I've regretted enough of the choices I made about you," she said. "I didn't want this to be one more."

"I'm sorry you regret anything about me," he said.

Bette nodded, fixing her gaze on his. "So am I."

"Did you get what you wanted, then? From this? From me?"

"I never got what I wanted from you," she told him quietly. "But I've given up hoping I ever could. So...there's that, at least."

He was silent at that. She couldn't read his expression, but the way he cut his gaze from hers told her more than he probably wanted her to know. She waited for him to speak, not surprised when he did not. Also not surprised, somehow, that his voice called her back just as she reached the hotel room door.

"Do you love him?"

"He loves me," Bette said. "More than I deserve, probably. But we're good together, and I care about him enough to try to deserve him."

"I see."

It was what he'd always said when he thought she was being ridiculous. It used to drive her mad. She no longer cared.

He surprised her with more words. "I don't want you to hate me, Bette."

"I don't hate you," she told him after a second or so. "I just don't want to love you, anymore."

Chapter 11

Darkness greeted Bette when she got home. The sun would be up in an hour or so, bringing the start of a new day, but at the moment everything in her house was black. Hushed. She put her keys on the table. Her coat on the back of the chair. She slipped off her shoes and went on cat-quiet feet up the stairs to the bedroom.

She knew Damian would be waiting for her, though her heart had lodged in her throat with anticipation at how she would find him. Damian sat in the corner armchair, a book laid over the arm. The reading lamp cast a soft glow over his sleeping face.

He woke when she murmured his name. He rubbed his eyes and held back a yawn. "You're home."

"Yes." Bette sat on the edge of the bed, facing him.

For a long moment, neither of them moved.

"I wasn't sure," Damian began, but stopped himself.

He loved her, she thought. And she wanted to deserve that.

"Come here, love," was all she said.

He went to her at once, kneeling at her feet and pressing his cheek to her knee. He closed his eyes when she stroked a hand over his hair. He waited, patient and silent.

"It's late," Bette told him when she'd had her fill of the softness of his hair, the steady pulse of his breathing. She tapped his shoulder to get him to look up. Damian's gaze searched hers, and when finally he smiled at the promise she hoped he could see in her eyes, so did she. "Let's go to bed."

Chapter 12

*T*HE LAST TIME *she kissed him was in a doorway. She stepped through. He did not follow, and she left him behind.*
Finally, she left him behind.

Excerpt

Tear You Apart

At least there's video chat.

"I'm just your little lady in the box," I tease. "Your genie."

"You gonna grant me a wish?"

I wish I could. "Depends what it is."

Will laughs, and his phone shakes a little. "I'm getting ready for bed now. Come with me?"

"Do I have a choice? I'm in the box. I go wherever you take me."

I watch my laptop screen carefully as he lifts his phone. The sensation is disorienting; for a moment I can imagine I am actually in a box, being carried in his hand. That I am tiny, that I am small. That I am made of magic.

I've been in his bathroom before, of course, but the angle is different and everything is off-kilter. Will props his phone on the sink and bends to look at me.

"Hi."

"Hi," I reply.

We're both grinning like idiots, like dogs in August, as my grandmother would say. She had a lot of folksy sayings, most of which I never understood. This one, I do. We grin and grin because there are no words, because joy is manifesting itself in my face.

Will runs the water in the sink and brushes his teeth, making a show of it. Eyeing me once in a while while he makes a grand display of scrubbing. Suds foam from the corners of his mouth. I'm totally charmed, incapable of doing anything more than watch raptly as he mugs for the camera.

With an audience, I discover, Will is a showman.

He rinses. Spits delicately. Looks at the camera.

"See what you'd be in for," he says, "if you had to face that every day."

But I want to, are the first words that come to my lips, and of course they're bitten back. *I'd love to. I want you.*

I say nothing.

I smile and he smiles, and he leans again across the counter, his face immense, and then only his smiling mouth is on my laptop screen. I wait. He retreats a little, peering into the lens as though he's looking into my eyes.

"What next?" he says.

"You tell me," I say, then boldly add, "I think you need a shower."

"Do I?"

"Oh, yes." Excitement quickens in my stomach, the beat of my heart, the pulse and throb of my blood in my throat and wrists and cunt. "Definitely."

Also by Megan Hart

Perfectly Reckless
Clearwater
Castle in the Sand
Ride with the Devil
Stumble into Love
The Resurrected: Compendium
The Darkest Embrace
Reawakened Passions
Precious and Fragile Things
Crossing the Line
Lovely Wild
The Space Between Us
Hold Me Close
Dirty
Broken
Deeper
Tear You Apart

About the Author

I was born and then I lived awhile. Then I did some stuff and other things. Now, I mostly write books. Some of them use a lot of bad words, but most of the other words are okay.

I can't live without music, the internet, or the ocean, but I have kicked the Coke Zero habit. I can't stand the feeling of corduroy or velvet, and modern art leaves me cold. I write a little bit of everything from horror to romance, and I don't answer to the name "Meg."

Megan Hart is a USA Today, Publisher's Weekly and New York Times bestselling author who writes in many genres including mainstream fiction, erotic fiction, science fiction, romance, fantasy and horror. If you liked this book, please tell all of your friends to buy it. If you hated it, please tell all your enemies to buy it. If you'd like to tell the author about it, drop her a line, but remember what Thumper's mom says: if you don't have anything nice to say, it's best to say nothing at all.

Devil in the Dark

Christine d'Abo

When developer Shona needs to beta test her new app – The Devil's Doorbell *– she goes out on the prowl for a man who will fulfil her wildest fantasies – oral sex in public. What could possibly go wrong when she finds her devil in the dark?*

Chapter 1

THE CLUB WAS loud and the people were sweaty, something that should have squicked me out but didn't. Sure, I'd showered, primped and wiggled my way into my club outfit, but that didn't mean I was averse to getting dirty. Shit, that was the reason I was here tonight—to get laid.

Well, that was the *secondary* outcome.

Really what I was doing was beta-testing my new app.

The Devil's Doorbell.

As I and my co-developer, Chandra, walked deeper into the club, the scent of alcohol, cologne and perfume mixed into an odd aphrodisiac that seeped through my skin and woke my libido. The music was some random electro-dance beat that I'm sure had some lyrics, but who the hell cared as long as it let you grind up against that hot dude or chick beside you.

Okay, so maybe it *had* been a bit too long for me. But that was the whole point of our app. If we could get some financial backing then we'd secure our place at the business incubator rent-free for a year. That was huge for us. The competition was Monday, which didn't leave us much time to work out any remaining kinks. The back-end code was smooth; tonight I had to prove that, despite what the advisor at the startup incubator said, women *would* use this app for hookups. And not just any hookups, but ones that targeted their specific sexual preferences. It would work better than anything else currently on the market.

It *did* work.

If I had to have sex with a random guy to prove it, then that was what I'd do.

Being the taller of the two of us, I cut a line through the crowds toward the bar and a small area off to the side that wasn't too packed. It gave me an opportunity to survey the dancers and see if I could guess which of the club goers might be one of my anonymous testers. We had nearly a thousand people in Toronto alone downloaded the app in the three days that it had been available. Surely at least a few of them would be using it tonight.

If not, then we might have a problem.

Chandra tugged on my arm when we stopped moving and I did my best to lean close enough to hear her. "Shona? Have you found anyone yet?"

"Haven't check yet."

"Well look! Send out the devil signal. Let's get this show on the road so we can see if this thing works. I'd like to be rich before I'm thirty."

Rich. That's wishful thinking. "I'll be happy just to pay off my student loans. And you can always do this too. There's no reason why we can't run two confirmation tests at once."

She rolled her eyes. "You lost to coin toss so you're the guinea pig. Besides you're way braver than me. Do it."

My cell phone was currently tucked into my cleavage, which I'm sure wasn't very good for the screen. *No, no, no. Absolutely no practical thinking tonight.* Still, when I took it out, I made sure to wipe the sweat from my screen protector. I wanted to have sex, not suffer any technology malfunctions. No reason to go crazy. "Fine, here we go."

The grinning devilish face popped up as soon as I woke up my phone, and oh what a beautiful sight that was.

The Devil's Doorbell.

Our pride and joy.

Chandra was a good six inches shorter than me, so she pulled my arm down to see the screen. "You need to make sure you have your preference set to straight or else I'll have to step in and save you from the hordes of disappointed women."

"You'd hate that." She was right though, probably good to double-check everything. A few swipes and I had my preference page up. "Looking for men, ages...shit, I don't know."

"Does age matter? It's not like you want to date him necessarily." She tucked one of her loose curls behind her ear. "Go for a younger guy."

The bar area wasn't as busy as the dance floor, so I had space enough to look at who was out there and potentially available. The club's patrons were my age or a bit younger, professionals or at least students who knew how to dress the part. Chandra was right in that age was irrelevant.

"I'll just check *any* and see what that gets me. I don't want to make the parameters too narrow. It's not the important part for our tests."

Chandra giggled. "Now I get to see your darkest, smuttiest fantasy."

Yeah, I hadn't really thought that part through. My forefinger hovered over the *Devilish Delights* section, waiting for me to make my selections. Maybe we should add a privacy function to the app. Something a person could set up ahead of time so they wouldn't be stuck doing this in public. *Something for the first update.*

Without worrying too much about Chandra's reaction, I made my selections with a silent prayer that luck, or at the very least the devil, was on my side tonight.

Exhibitionism.
Oral sex (female).
Dirty talk.
Masturbation (male).

"Nice. That will give us a great sample. Plus it's hot." Chandra's fingers dug into my arm. "Really hot."

I hit the search button and smiled at the grinning devil's face that popped up on my screen and told me that I was a devilish girl. *Maybe we shouldn't lay the cheese factor on quite so thick. Make a note to address that tomorrow.* "Done."

Chandra laughed. "Excellent. Let's dance until you find someone."

"If I find someone. It might be a bust for all we know."

"Well, we can't worry about it. If the competition falls through then we'll have to come up with another plan for distribution and rent. Come on."

With the app set to vibrate, I shoved my phone back into my cleavage and let Chandra pull me out onto the floor. The music had changed to a song I didn't know. My eyes drifted closed and I let my body sway to the beat. Hands found their way to my hips, fingers grazed my ass. Chests bumped against me, sometimes by accident, occasionally on purpose. I'd look at the throng of people around me, felt their heat as we fell into a mutual rhythm. I lost Chandra somewhere in the crowd.

Great.

A bead of sweat dripped down my back and the few tendrils of my hair that I'd left out of my bun were damp and stuck to the side of my neck. If someone did find me on the app, I was going to be in horrible shape. Dancing as I moved, I made my way to the bar and got in line. "Hey. Water?"

The bartender, a pixie of a woman, nodded and filled a glass for me. "There's a charge unless you're a DD."

"That's fine."

The glass was already sweating when she slid it over to me. "Two dollars. You get refills though."

Thankfully, I had change. "Thanks."

As I brought the glass to my lips and had my first sweet taste of the cold heaven, my breasts vibrated. Choking on an ice cube, I stepped away from the bar and pulled my phone free.

The devil was there and he was laughing again.

Oh.

I had no reason to be nervous. We'd designed the app in such a way that the seeker had all the control. They identified their fantasy, their gender preference and could say no if the responder didn't meet their needs. The people under consideration would snap a picture of themselves and provide their location. The seeker then had the chance to say yes again and go off to find them, or no and reset the search. So it made no sense that my hand shook as I swiped to see who'd answered my request.

It was strange; I had created this mental image in my head of the type of person who would answer a request from the devil. He'd be younger, tech savvy and looking for a good time, not a commitment. I didn't think many non-millennials would be into this sort of program.

The face of the man shining up at me had to be in his thirties or forties based on the lines around his mouth and eyes. His black hair was cropped short, almost to his scalp, and his jaw and cheeks had some scruff on them. Good-looking, solid.

Wow. Okay, I guess I needed to adjust my mental parameters of our user base.

My pussy pulsed and I could tell that the moisture between my legs wasn't all sweat. There was something about him, maybe the way the serious set of his jaw contrasted with the sparkle in his brown eyes that intrigued me. The message indicated that he was willing to do everything I'd asked. It was up to me if I wanted to follow through.

The app worked. Really, really well if he was any indication. I'd proven my point about demand and use. With next to no promotion we not only had people downloading the program, but using it as well. I had no reason to go through with the sex part if I didn't want to. Though it was only being a responsible developer to see this through all the way to the end. Right?

Hell yes.

I pressed the *meet* button and waited for directions.

Left side of the bar was the response I got.

Convenient.

Without being overly obvious, I turned as I took another sip from my glass and searched the bar opposite from where I stood. The crowd had thinned out slightly, but not enough that he was immediately visible to me. In fact, I couldn't see him at all. *Time to get that refill.* The bartender gave me only the barest of smiles as she took my glass and went in search for more ice. I took the opportunity to look over my shoulder at the men who were hovering close. I nearly missed him. Pressed against the wall, he stood with his foot braced against it and his arms crossed. His gaze wasn't on me or even the bar, but on the partyers. Was he looking for me? No, that didn't seem quite right.

"Here you go." The bartender slid my glass in front of me, and I realized the man had on the same shirt she did.

Shit, he worked here at the club.

That meant this would go one of two ways: he was going to ask me to leave the moment I approached him, or he was going to show me a side of the club I bet others wouldn't normally get to see. It was risky, but anything worth doing was a little challenging. Right? Casting a quick glance in the mirror behind the bar to make sure my makeup hadn't turned me into a raccoon, I left my glass on the bar and made my way over.

He didn't acknowledge me immediately, no doubt focusing on his job. While he was fit enough, something about him didn't quite scream *bouncer*. Not that it mattered to me one way or the other. The picture on the app didn't do justice to his looks. The black T-shirt fit tightly across his chest and the short sleeves hugged his biceps. His jeans squeezed his thighs in all the right places before disappearing into the tops of a pair of worn cowboy boots. Fuck, he was hot.

"Can I help you?"

I jumped a bit when he spoke, mostly because I wasn't expecting it, but also because he hadn't looked at me yet. *I have a few things in mind, buddy.*

"I'm not sure." I moved into his field of vision, blocking his sight of the crowd. "I sincerely hope so."

His gaze snapped to mine and I couldn't help but hold my breath for a moment. I'd seen men look at me with lust before, longing. It was a nice look; it made me feel special and beautiful. His expression was more than that. There was a hunger behind his gaze, a spark that set my heart pounding from the sheer intensity of it all. When his gaze traveled down my body, catching on my breasts, my hips and legs, I felt a corresponding shiver prickle. Sex with this man would be explosive, base, primal.

I wanted it. Wanted him.

"I just want to make sure you know what you're asking for." He straightened until his head was braced against the wall. "So that we both know exactly what we're getting ourselves into."

Fair enough. I stepped closer so I was the only thing in his field of view. "I want you, specifically. I want you to go down on me someplace semipublic. I want to see you jerk off until you come. Are you up for that?"

His mouth opened and for a moment I thought he was going to kiss me. Totally wouldn't have had an issue with that. Nope. As quickly as he swayed forward, he pulled back, tearing his gaze away, and looked toward the bar. "Follow me."

It was strange; the whole time I'd been fantasizing about doing this, I hadn't pictured it being with a man like this. He was good-looking, sure, but not the sort of looks I'd normally gravitate toward. He was hard edges, lean but noticeable muscles. The tendons in his neck were visible, even as he walked away from me, his long legs eating up the floor as he crossed it. My own stride wasn't short, but I would have had to run to keep up with him, which so wasn't happening in these heels. Tonight wasn't about being at the beck and call of a man. This rendezvous was about my needs, my desires. I took my time trailing behind him, enjoying the beat of the music. *Oh, Mackelmore, I like this song.*

Dude was already at the base of a set of stairs that led up somewhere, looking back at me. The crowd was bouncing in rhythm to the beat and I couldn't help myself, I got into it. Who knew that a song about a moped could be so sexy? It was, especially when I locked my gaze on the dude and started dancing toward him, mouthing the words as I came closer. A small twitch to his lips softened the sternness that had initially engulfed him. There we go. This was supposed to be fun! I wanted to have a really fucking good time with a mostly anonymous guy and then go home. No relationships. This didn't have to be serious or life-altering. No angst or judgments.

Simply sex and fun.

The crowd was screaming out the lyrics and I knew I'd made my point when he full-on smiled at me and nodded. That was all the reassurance I needed. Bouncing my way over to the stairs, I took his outstretched hand and followed him up. "We're not going to get in trouble coming up here, are we?"

He smiled and shook his head. "Nope. I own the place."

Sure you do, buddy. "Okay."

"I know a good spot."

Oh, that sounded promising. "Lead on."

Being this close to him now, his hand engulfing mine, my brain finally caught up, recognizing exactly how big this guy was. I'd never been with a man like him before, so this would be interesting. The top floor of the club was still open to the main area below, but the lights were off, giving it the illusion of privacy where there was none. The metal rail was the only barrier between the row of closed office doors and the dance floor below. If anyone looked up and squinted, they'd probably be able to see us, though probably not our faces. He guided me a bit farther down the hallway toward a corner that led to a more secluded area. That wasn't what I had in—

Spinning me around in the smoothest dance move I'd ever been a part of, my back was against the rail and he was standing in front of me, looking down into my eyes. My vision hadn't exactly adjusted to the dim light on this floor, but I was hyper-aware of every twitch of his muscles. He looked at me for several heartbeats before shaking his head. "I don't know if I want to thank or kill the person who wrote this app."

I blinked. "What?"

"I'm going to have to cordon off all the hiding spots." He shook his head. "Not important."

I hadn't even considered that our little devil would be such a pain in the ass for some people.

That thought vaporized from my brain when he leaned in and pressed his lips beside my ear. "It doesn't matter. Tell me what you want me to do."

Breath caught in my throat and I shivered from the raw need I heard. His voice was raspy and full of something I could only say was longing. His fingers flexed as he held my forearms, as though he wanted to do something and somehow was holding back. *Tell me.* My body responded immediately. My breasts ached to be captured by his massive hands; my pussy grew heavy and wet from want. Maybe I should rethink the whole penetration thing...

No.

Turning my head, I latched onto his earlobe with my teeth, biting down until he sucked in a breath. I let go and soothed the assaulted skin with my tongue. "You know what I want."

"Yes." He groaned. "But I *need* to hear you say it. I'm tired of being in charge all the time. Just—"

The music changed again, but I was only vaguely aware. Something else was in play here, something I hadn't considered. He wanted me in charge, and that was new. Never let it be said that I couldn't roll with the punches with the best of them. "Fine. You want me to be in control, I can do that. I'm not wearing any panties."

"Jesus fuck."

"Should I let you feel? To see if I'm telling the truth?" His body quivered and I chuckled from the sheer pleasure of having this giant of a man under my control. "Want to see how wet my pussy is? To run your fingers around my clit to tease me?"

"Yes. May I?"

Something in the way he asked—a plea for sure—contained a note of something I hadn't heard from any of my lovers before. "I'm not sure if I should give you permission. Maybe I should tease you more. Make you wonder if I'm telling the truth. I bet you can picture me, my naked skin all flushed and swollen. Can you picture me like that?"

I hadn't realized how tense he was, not until he slumped forward a few inches. "Yes."

His voice practically dripped with longing, desire. Fuck, this was hot. "I want you to take your hand and slide it slowly down my thigh until you reach the hem of my skirt. Do it. Now."

He swallowed as he moved to comply. His fingers flexed, cupping my curves as he inched forward to his goal. The caress was electric, wild and a little bit dangerous. We weren't hidden from sight; anyone in the club below could look up and see us if they were paying attention. Not that there was much of a show for them to see. Not yet.

His fingers slipped past my skirt and brushed along the skin of my bare thigh. When he curled his fingers, his nails scraped lightly across my skin, sending a shiver through me. "Not yet."

"Please." He slid his forefinger toward my inner thigh. "I want to feel you. How wet you are."

"Well, since you asked nicely, yes you may. But slowly. I want to enjoy myself."

I was thrilled that he followed my commands so exquisitely, because the teasing was turning me on with a force I'd never felt before. He tugged the hem of my skirt up just enough to get his hand beneath, caressing and teasing the skin. "You're wet here." He rubbed my moisture into the sensitive spot before continuing his torturous path up, up and *oh right there.*

The first brush of his fingertips through my pubic curls

pushed a rush of lust through me. Every nerve in my body grew electric, sparking at the barest of touches from his body. His breathing came out in stuttered huffs against my ear. "You're hot. I can smell your arousal."

"You're turning me on. Being here in the open. Anyone can see us. It's fucking amazing."

He shifted his weight so I could feel his hardened cock press against my hip. "What can I do?"

Things had gotten hot and heavy very quickly. Now that I was finally living my fantasy, I wanted to make sure that I milked every second of my time. The last thing I wanted was to rush through the moment and come too fast. I wanted to savor this, him.

I took a deep breath and mentally braced myself. "Don't touch my clit. Explore, feel me and how ready I am."

He cupped my mound, pressing the heel of his hand just above where I told him not to touch me. His fingers were positioned perfectly to press against my vagina, circling my opening and smearing my moisture along my pubic hair. The act of being caressed in such an intimate manner while avoiding the most sensitive of spots created a fissure of frustration alongside my building desire. My breasts ached and my nipples burned from neglect. The soft lace that normally acted as a tease for me became an irritant. I needed more.

Leaning back just enough to break contact with his face, I licked up the side of his cheek. "Touch my breasts. Pinch my nipples."

His fingers curled up as soon as I spoke, and he pressed one into my pussy. "Please." Bringing his free hand up, he shoved it into the front opening of my shirt and did what I asked, what my body needed him to do. I didn't bother to hold back my groan as he captured my nipple between his finger and thumb and pinched hard, as he latched onto the side of my throat with his mouth and began to kiss my skin. "Salty."

"Shut up."

He pinched my nipple again. That was better.

The metal railing was digging into my back, but the pain helped to distract from the onslaught of pleasure that tore through my body. I leaned back a bit more and tightened my grip on his shoulders as I widened my stance to give him better access. Thankfully, he didn't need any further instructions and lowered his mouth to my cleavage. The wet swipe of his tongue between my breasts felt at once strange and exciting. Voices shot through the din of music and for half a second I thought someone saw us, saw what he was doing to me. My pussy clenched around the finger that fucked me as my awareness of our surroundings grew tenfold.

He pulled my breast free of my shirt, exposing my nipple to the air for only a moment before he sucked it hard into his mouth. The earlier teasing of his tongue was nothing compared to the devilish flicks he unleashed on my sensitive tip. Teeth scraped along my skin as his mouth increased my torture. As much as I wanted this, appreciated his ability to arouse and entice, there was only so much teasing a woman could take. I needed more.

I bracketed his head with my hands and pulled his face up from my breast. "I want you to lick me. Make me come." Then I kissed him. Hard.

Any pretense that we might have had about what was happening was long gone. This was about sex, very public and primal. I didn't want safe, not like the rest of my life. For one night I was going to take what I wanted in the way that I wanted it.

When he pulled back, his lips were wet and swollen. "What's your name?"

"Shona. You?"

"Kevin."

"Nice to meet you. Get on your knees, Kevin."

His earlier smirk surfaced briefly. "With pleasure."

It's strange that when you've had a particular fantasy stuck in your head for a while, that when the reality eventually comes, it rarely lives up to your hopes. That had always been my experience in the past.

Tonight was all about firsts.

I couldn't tell you how the look of lust on Kevin's face was better than anything I could have imagined. He held eye contact as he slowly dropped to one then the other knee, until his face was parallel with my stomach. He ran his hands down my sides, caressing the sides of my breasts, my waist and hips, down along the outside of my thighs.

"You're beautiful." He shifted so that his hands slid beneath my shirt and up until he cupped my breasts. "I wish we had more time. I would stretch you out on my bed and lick every inch of your body. I'd suck your toes. Lick your ass. Fuck you until you begged me to make you come."

Shit. "Consider this a job interview then."

"Challenge accepted." He pinched my nipples.

That was the last bit of rational thinking I could manage. Kevin pressed his mouth to my bare stomach and licked around my belly button as he continued rolling my nipples. I was so wet now from his teasing, the dampness between my legs now coated the insides of my thighs as well. I did my best to keep my legs open, not wanting to accidentally push myself over the edge by increasing the pressure. Kevin must have sensed how close to the edge I really was, because he finally released my breasts and dropped his hands to my knees. From there he slowly slid his fingers up once more, only this time he didn't stop and pushed my skirt up until my pussy was fully exposed to him.

"Fuck me. You're so wet." With one hand holding my skirt in place, he used a thumb to part my slick hair and expose my clit to him. "There she is."

I had to fight to keep my eyes open. The urge to close them and simply enjoy the sensations was strong, but I didn't want to look away. The expression on his face was one of wonder, admiration. It was something I hadn't had directed my way in a long time. *Please. Do it.* Kevin finally leaned forward and licked a long, slow swipe around my clit before sucking it into his mouth.

The moan escaped me and I had to tighten my grip on the railing to keep from squirming away. The air was moist and did little to dry the beads of sweat that rose on my skin, making me even more aware of my body.

With my clit in his mouth, he teased my swollen flesh with his tongue. Once, twice flicking me before making another lazy circle around the nub. He repeated that two more times, and with each pass increased the suction. On the third go 'round, he pressed two fingers into my pussy and began to slowly fuck me with his hand.

The music changed to a beat that electrified the crowd below. It was becoming harder to ignore the fact that we were out in the open, visible to anyone who might come up the stairs or look up from the bar. Nerves battled with arousal; my chest tightened, making it necessary to gasp in order to pull air into my lungs. God, this was insane. *I* was insane for initiating public sex with a complete stranger. We could get caught; the police could be called…

Kevin turned his head and nipped at my inner thigh. "Relax."

And just like that, the tension bled from my body. "Too much."

"Want me to stop?"

"God no."

He gave my leg a squeeze before he lowered his face once more. I wasn't going to last, not with him doing…whatever the hell he was doing with his tongue. *Shit!*

Kevin must have sensed that our time was going to come to a close soon. Rather than continue with his teasing, he focused his touches, maximizing my arousal. One hand continued to fuck my pussy, while he released my skirt and returned the other beneath my shirt to my nipple. Each flick of his tongue across my clit was timed with a hard pinch to my nipple and a thrust of his fingers inside me. The sounds of his actions were nearly drowned out by the other sounds of the club. But I could hear them.

I could hear him.

Kevin moaned. The muscles of his arms shook against me, though I had no clue if it was from exertion or desire. I didn't care, couldn't care at that point. My orgasm, which had somehow been held at bay to this point, began to threaten. My pussy was oversensitive, the slightest brush of him against me a shock, a pleasure. My release was so close and building quickly. I needed to reach the end.

On impulse, I turned my head and opened my eyes. With my eyes fully adjusted now, it was easy for me to see everyone dancing below. No one appeared to be aware of what was going on a few feet above where they danced and writhed together. My breath caught in my throat when I noticed a few faces were turned up, but they didn't seem to see me. Or if they did, they didn't mind the show. Kevin took that opportunity to increase the pace of his thrusting fingers in and out of my body. I'm sure my eyes rolled back into my head as every nerve in my body fired and my muscles twitched. One moment I was hyperaware of everything—the smell of alcohol and sweat, the pounding of the music through the speakers, the feel of Kevin's body working against mine—and the next everything vanished.

Pleasure had always been something that exploded quickly when I had sex. It was more like fireworks than anything else, a burst of momentary joy that fell away nearly as quickly as it erupted. Not this time. The initial burst of release rolled through me, a crashing wave that left my skin burning and body shaking from the onslaught. If I'd been able to form a rational thought, I would have been all *well, that was good while it lasted*. I wasn't given that opportunity. Kevin continued to work my body, fucking me with his fingers as he increased the suction. My body vibrated as my muscles seized. I couldn't breathe, couldn't move or think as another, more powerful wave of pleasure tore through me. And again.

It was too big. Too strong. Too everything.

I fell forward, thrusting my fingers into his hair and pulling back on his head. "Stop. Please stop."

He listened, but only after a final lap of his tongue around my clit. "So fucking good."

I don't know what I was expecting, but having Kevin get to his feet and pull me into a hug certainly wasn't it. Being held by a stranger was weird, but given what we'd just done, I wasn't about to push him away. Hell, I could barely keep my balance. Having a solid body to lean against was a blessing.

"Wow." I patted his chest. "You're good."

"Was just doing what the lady asked me to do."

Pressed against him, I had no trouble feeling his still hard cock against my body. "I need a second to catch my breath, but then I want to make sure we do that last item on my list." Without preamble, I reached down and squeezed his shaft through his jeans. "I wouldn't want to shortchange you after the stellar job you've done."

While I might have been the one to start everything tonight, I wasn't about to walk away without making sure my entire dream was fulfilled. He could say no, and I wouldn't do anything to stop him from leaving if that's what he wanted, but I had to admit I wanted to see if his cock was as impressive as it felt.

Kevin's eyes were closed and his breath came out in pants that tickled my heated skin. His first nod was barely a movement of his head. The second was far more definite, certain. This was a thing he wanted as much as I did. Still, he didn't move.

I smiled at him. "Want me to get you started?"

He chuckled, his eyes still closed. "Sure."

His jeans were well fitted, but not so tight that it looked as though I would have any problems. I moved my hands to his belt buckle. The leather was warm from his body heat, the denim just below the belt stretched tight from his straining cock. The brushed-metal buckle was easy enough to undo and fell open, framing his fly. The button was harder to pull, and I had to tug more than once to accomplish my goal. "Stubborn fella."

"He's under duress." Kevin opened his eyes but didn't meet my gaze. "So hard."

"I can tell." I took my time with his zipper, pulling it down far slower than I could tell Kevin wanted me to. The last thing I wanted was to ruin the evening by catching his cock between the metal and…yeah, that wouldn't be fun. It had the added bonus of letting me tease him, so there was that as well. Black cotton was revealed, keeping his cock still hidden from my sight. "Now I get to see what my prize looks like."

Rather than looking down at his groin, I lifted my gaze to his face as I slid my hand into his briefs. The pained expression was there until I wrapped my fingers around his shaft and squeezed hard. Kevin shuddered. Pain and pleasure, the same feelings that had torn through me a short time ago, were now reflected on his face.

Leaning in, I sucked on his ear lobe. "You like that?"

"Yes."

"I like it too. You're so big, thick. I bet you're good in bed. You're a stud. Aren't you?"

"I like to fuck."

"Yeah, I can see why. You're good to your girls, aren't you?"

"Yes. I make them come."

"You lick their pussies the way you licked mine."

"Fuck yeah."

"Then you take your big cock and you slide it into them. Into their cunts."

"Yeah."

"Have you ever jerked off on one of them? Ever stroked this nice cock of yours until you blew your load all over their skin?"

Kevin groaned as I began to stroke his cock. "No."

"No, you haven't. What was the part of my request that you liked the most? Licking my cunt or jerking off on me?"

"Yes." A small bubble of laugher escaped him. "Both."

"Dirty boy." My body still buzzed from my orgasm. My breasts and nipples still ached, oversensitive from everything he'd done to them. As aroused as I'd been, it wasn't the same as the burning that currently consumed me. Having this strong man, a physically dominant man, at my mercy was a heady mixture of pride and power. I licked the side of his neck, enjoying the taste of his sweat. "Show me. I want to see you take your cock in your hand. I want you to come on me. On my skin. I want to wear your come home, feel it on me when I'm in the shower tonight. A reminder of what we'd done."

Kevin grabbed my wrist, stopping my stroking. "You're going to make me blow talking like that."

"Poor baby. Dirty talk was part of the deal. Remember?" I let him pull my hand out of his briefs. "Fine. I hope you'll be able to finish this on your own."

"Not going to be a problem." He looked up and around, as though he'd forgotten where we were. "Don't move."

It was cute how nervous he suddenly looked. It was perfectly fine for him to drop to his knees and go down on me in public, but taking his cock out...well, that might be a step too far. "I think we're past the point of no return. However, how about we do this." I stepped away from the railing, thankful to have the metal no longer pressing into my skin. "It will help with your balance."

We did a little dance, repositioning ourselves so he took my place and I was able to slide beside him, using my body to block the view of anyone who might come up stairs. Now where we needed to be, Kevin didn't hold back any longer. It took both his hands to pull the opening of his jeans wide enough and his briefs down far enough to withdraw his cock and balls. *Oh, that's a lovely sight.* The feel of his shaft didn't do him justice. He was longer than I realized; his foreskin pulled down to reveal a pink head coated in precome.

He wrapped one hand around his cock while he tugged his balls with the other. I fought the urge to reach out and help, to lean in and lick the tip, tease him with my tongue the way he'd done so to me only a short time earlier.

There were other ways I could get to him though.

"Stroke it nice and slow. I want you to draw this out for yourself. The same way you wouldn't let me come immediately. That's it. Slow."

His hand obeyed, moving up and down in a shaking motion. Each time he reached the top of his shaft, he swiped his thumb across the tip, teasing the head. His skin was dry, making the act of stoking difficult. Gathering as much saliva as I could, I pulled his hand from his cock and spit into his palm. "There. Should help."

Kevin groaned and quickly resumed his stroking. That was hot. More so than I ever dreamed it would be. Colored lights exploded on the wall behind us in a dancing pattern, flashing briefly before sliding away. A reminder that anyone could see us, see him. I shifted closer and pulled my shirt up to my bra. "I'm getting horny again watching you do this. I can't help but wish we had lube, a condom, a bed where we could fuck. I'd love to feel you press down on me. You make me feel small. You're so solid, strong. But you like when I tell you what to do. Don't you."

"Yeah."

"It turns you on, doesn't it?"

"Yeah."

"Are you getting close? Your cock is weeping."

"Close."

"And you're going to come all over me? My stomach?"

He groaned. "Yes."

The speed of his strokes increased, meeting the rhythm of the music pounding around us. The beat drove him, whether he realized it or not. I didn't know where to look, what to watch.

His face was contorted with pleasure and another emotion I couldn't ascertain. I was fascinated and aroused from the sight. But it was hard to compete with the real-life porn movie playing out before me. It was a visual feast that I was growing addicted to. Not to mention the noises that slipped from him. The moans and gasps that were swallowed by the music and voices of the throng of people below.

"Gonna come." His eyes were squeezed closed. "Closer."

I didn't know if he meant that his orgasm was closer or that he wanted me closer. Either way, I wanted to make sure I was in the perfect position. I tucked my shirt into the top of my bra and leaned awkwardly at an angle that gave him the most surface area possible to aim for. "Do it."

Kevin groaned loud and long as his hips bucked forward to meet his fist. The first spurt of come was hot and shot high across my side. The droplets shone in the colored light of the club, making my skin glisten. Another spurt and a large glob pooled above my belly button, making me shiver. The rest never made it to me, staying stubbornly on Kevin's fingers and cock. His orgasm seemed to last forever, but couldn't have been more than a few seconds. When I was certain he was done, I shifted so that I leaned back against the rail beside him.

I waited until he opened his eyes before I reached down and smeared his come across my skin. It dried far faster than I imagined it would, leaving my skin itchy and tight where it was stuck. "Wow."

Kevin wiped his come on the inside of his briefs before tucking himself away. "That's an understatement."

I anticipated feeling a little awkward, considering what we'd just done, and yet there was none of that. We were two consenting adults who'd just had a really fucking awesome experience. I righted my clothing and fixed my hair. If anyone were to come across us now, they'd be none the wiser as to what had happened. "Thank you for that. It had been a fantasy of mine for a long time now."

"Don't thank me." Kevin picked my phone up from the floor and handed it to me. I didn't even remember dropping it. "The devil brought us together." He looked around, his gaze quickly crossing over the crowd. "Can I buy you a drink?"

And that was exactly where I wanted my fantasy to end. "I'm going to say no to that. It's not that I don't appreciate you or what we've done here tonight. But—"

"But no thanks." He smiled and nodded. "That's fine. It was fun. I'm glad I took a chance on an unknown app." Something must have cross my face because he frowned. "What?"

There was no reason to tell him, but given what we just did, I figured I owed him the truth. "Remember earlier when you said you didn't know if you wanted to kill or thank the app designer?"

"Yes." His eyes widened. "You?"

"I was doing a final system check before we make a bid for some funding. An app competition thing. You were my final test." My lips twitched as I smiled. "Don't tell management, okay?"

He looked at me, blinking and a little confused. "A bit late for that."

"Do you need to get back downstairs? I wouldn't want you to get in trouble with your boss." I laughed at his cute expression. "Right, sorry. You *are* the boss."

He opened his mouth to speak but closed it again. He moved away from me a few inches and tried again. "You've never been to this club before?"

"No, my first time. We picked it at random, mostly because

it's close to our office. It's pretty awesome though."

His gaze drifted to the office door across the hall. Maybe he was hoping to make some sort of statement by having sex in front of the managers....

I followed his gaze to the name plate beside the door. Kevin Harridan.

Kevin.

"Shit." I pushed away from the rail. "You really *are* the owner."

He burst into laughter. "I am."

"That's why you weren't worried about…shit." Thankfully it was too dark for him to see the massive blush I'm sure covered my face.

"Hey, it's no problem. I'd heard from the staff that some people were using that app and that our place was a destination. I got curious as to the type of women who used it. Now I know. As one entrepreneur to another, I get it." For a moment I wasn't sure what he was going to do, but he leaned in and kissed my cheek. "If you're ever looking for more fun, come back anytime and ask for me."

"I will." Having a hookup with the owner of a dance bar was certainly a new experience. "Though I'm sure you'll have lots of options if you want. You have my app, after all."

"I don't do this a lot. I don't normally have time." He tucked my hair behind my ear. "But maybe I'll have to open myself up to more possibilities."

There was the awkwardness that I'd been anticipating earlier. Sex was easy. It was all the other stuff I had trouble with. "I better get back. My friend will be looking for me."

"Sure. I have some things to do in my office. Maybe I'll see you again?"

"Maybe." With a smile and a little wave, I sauntered toward the stairs. My pussy was pleasantly sore from where his fingers had worked me over. My skin tingled from the dry come. I was content and ready to dance. With each step I took back down to the dance floor, the more I relaxed. Things had gone far better than I'd hoped. The devil hadn't led me astray.

I'd no sooner hit the main floor than Chandra raced to my side. "Where the hell have you been? I saw you go up to a guy and then I didn't see where you went. Are you okay? Did you do something? Oh my God, you totally did. You're grinning. Was it good? Did he do what you wanted? Where is he now?"

I flung my arm around her shoulders and directed her toward the bar. "I need a drink."

"Details and I'll buy you as many as you want."

I couldn't hold back my laughter. "Let's just say I have a good feeling about the competition Monday."

As we walked I looked up, and while I couldn't see if Kevin was still there watching, I could still feel the weight of his stare. My devil in the dark.

Maybe I'd come back and see him again, see if there was something to that spark between us.

Maybe I would.

Chandra gave me a squeeze. "Are you okay?"

Light from his office lit up the hall, letting me see his wave. I couldn't stop from grinning. "I'm perfect."

Also By Christine d'Abo

30 Days
30 Night
Submissive Seductions
Long Shots (Double Shot, A Shot in the Dark, Pulled Long)
Calling the Shots
Choose Your Shot
Sexcapades
Wonderland
Naughty Nicks
Nailed
Snapped

M/M Erotic Romance:
Rebound Remedy
Dom Around the Corner
No Quarter
No Remedy
No Master

About the Author

A romance novelist and short story writer, Christine has over thirty publications to her name. She loves to exercise and stops writing just long enough to keep her body in motion too. When she's not pretending to be a ninja in her basement, she's most likely spending time with her family and two dogs.

- Instagram (christine.dabo)

London Calling

Megan Mulry

"Face-sitter wanted, in exchange for free accommodation in Mayfair."

—Craigslist

She hadn't planned on being quite so adventurous when she decided to spend the year in London, but when she read the ad, she couldn't resist.

Chapter 1

LONDON WASN'T JUST pricey—it was obscenely expensive. And not to be crass or anything, but I grew up with money. Big money. But that's why I'd always been so ridiculously frugal. It had never been *my* money. Not really. And relying on that level of luxury to just keep flowing in my direction was...a totally messed-up way to live. I was never going to fall prey to the fearful greed—the golden handcuffs—that imprisoned my parents and generations of Mercers before that. I could wait tables; I could be a barista; I knew how to take care of myself. Of course I did.

But, *holy hell*. Working for minimum wage in London would mean spending hours a day on the Tube and buses just to get to some shitty bedsit on the outskirts of town. And the whole point of coming to London was, well, to be *in* London. London proper.

When I left New York with all that can-do spirit, everything seemed possible. I'd finally rid myself of the bastard husband—even though it meant selling him my half of our design business so I could get out of the relationship at all. Whatever. Water under the bridge.

I wanted to do something exciting! Something just for me. Something I probably should've done when I was twenty-one, but life didn't always go in order. Or at least my life didn't. So now I was an almost-thirty-year-old woman having some sort of gap year.

I'd been in London almost two weeks and my Airbnb was draining my resources faster than I could say bob's your uncle—can-do didn't seem quite so exhilarating. A whole year was probably way too long. Maybe Maddy was right with all her disapproving scowls (and kisses) the night before I left. "Think, Lana! You need to think! You can't just up and go."

I'd been so giddy to just-up-and-go (and to finally be kissing Maddy after so many years of flirting) that I was in one of those near-manic I-am-all-powerful moods. I got all sassy and told her I was sick of thinking.

I've been thinking—hard—for the past...dozen years. Graduating at the top of my class in high school, Ivy League college, starting my own business, marrying the "right guy" from the "right family." And look where all that got me: divorced and unemployed.

No, I told Maddy. Fuck it. I'd done everything to live up to parental (and societal) expectations and I was simply done.

Over it.

So there I was in a little coffee shop off Marylebone High Street, weighing my options. I took a sip of coffee and scribbled some more notes in my blank book. I also sketched the couple in the corner, trying to be casual about looking at them, then letting my gaze slide to the street outside the plate glass window. They'd obviously rolled out of bed moments before, and they looked incredibly sexy in that rumpled-sheets way. His hair was sticking up on one side and she kept running her fingers through to tame it, then she'd sort of mess it up again and smile. And he kissed her. They were both reading—sort of, I guess—I didn't know how much they were retaining with all that touching.

Anyway. Sigh. Right. My future. Or at least my temporary future. If I stayed in the Airbnb in Southwark, my savings would only float me for about three months. The ideal situation would be housing in exchange for...something else. I could be a housekeeper or a cook. I could be a nanny. How hard could that be?

Hard. I didn't know the first thing about kids.

Of course I could call some of my professional colleagues and get a job at a design firm in about five seconds. But goddamnit, I just didn't want to be that person anymore. I didn't want to be the old me.

Did everything have to be some path to...something better?

Fuck it.

I opened my laptop and went back to the Craigslist page. First I went to the personals because, well, duh. Because it was fun to read about all the pervs and their...perversions. It was also fun to realize that I was actually the girl of someone's dreams. In theory. I was the unicorn. I was the bisexual woman who wanted to lick a woman's pussy while her husband fucked me (hard) from behind. Or go down on him while he went down on her. Or, well, you get the picture. The win-win-win possibilities were endless.

But yeah. I'd never acted on any of that because who-knows-why. Getting from point A to point B in the world of sexual fantasy had never been my strong point. I never had any problem telling my husband what I wanted, how I wanted it. Sometimes I enjoyed being downright bossy. But old habits were a bitch, and I could still hear my Waspy grandmother's voice telling me it was *beyond the pale, dahling* to...want to lick pussy and get fucked in the ass all at the same time. I doubt she would have said it just like that—to be honest I doubt she ever said *fuck* or *ass* out loud.

And yet.

Despite the lingering disapproval of long-dead grandmothers

and the probably legitimate concern of best friends back in Brooklyn, I'd started thinking seriously about answering a few really perverted Craigslist adverts.

(I was living in London so I got to say *advert*. Leave me alone.)

There were a few that were starting to sound just fucked-up enough to be hilarious. All the ones that said they were in exchange for housekeeping "or whatever we decide" with a little awkward smiley face...those I simply ignored. But there were a couple that were more, well, direct.

And one in particular was gloriously bold: *Facesitter Wanted*. I stared at that subject line in stunned disbelief, not to mention a little squirmy lust. When I clicked on it, the description was straightforward, and strangely formal. "Seeking gentlewoman to live in my house in central London (rent-free) in exchange for facesitting when I am in town."

Gentlewoman? *Facesitting*? I burst out laughing and tried to ignore the fact that my clit was throbbing despite the absurdity of the whole situation. Who had a *house* in central London anyway? This guy was probably living in a caravan in Barking.

And yet.

I started to see it as some grand adventure. *Lana does London*. I'd wanted to create a graphic novel or comic strip or something, forever, but ex-husband had always told me it was a ridiculous, non-moneymaking waste of time. Maybe if I turned into a sort of temporary sex worker I could tie that into some professional future project. In my mind. Because that would make it all kosher. Right, Lana.

Still.

Meeting wacky Brits was great fodder for anything. I'd signed up for a free trial membership at a nice gym the day after I arrived, intending to cancel it as soon as I was expected to join and cough up the full membership. I had managed to become fast friends with a couple of guys there.

They loved my American accent and my daily tales of woe about how I really didn't want to get another "real" job in an office, because that would defeat the whole purpose of being a gal about town in London. On the other hand, time was running out. I needed a plan.

THE NEXT MORNING at the gym I blurted, trying to sound casual, "So, I'm thinking about answering an ad for some guy who wants a facesitter."

Tommy laughed so hard he had to bend over. He was sweating and his dark skin was rippling with exertion and mirth and the whole giggling muscleman thing made me laugh too. By the time we finally settled down, Sam, his boyfriend, had come over and Tommy told him the story, and then the two of them started giggling all over again.

We went out for a few pints that night, and I couldn't help bringing it up again. "I'm not kidding, you guys. I've been so, I don't know, normal, my whole life and I'm ready to do something crazy like this."

"Crazy like get your throat cut in the middle of the night by some fecking facesitting freak, ya mean?" Sam asked. "You're asking for trouble, Lana, ringing the devil's doorbell if you ask me."

I laughed at his description, and then turned somber. "No." I toyed with the condensation on the side of my beer. "I don't want to be unsafe about it. I was thinking maybe one of you guys could come with me, you know, as like a bodyguard or something—"

"What? And watch you get…licked?"

"No!" I laughed uncontrollably. "No. Just when I go to meet him the first time. If he's totally messed up, we'll know. It'll be obvious, right?"

Tommy shook his head. "Lana. Seriously? You're this gorgeous American chick with your hippie blond hair and military chic fashion and all that wild eagerness in your eyes, and you think *you'll* be able to tell if someone's crazy?"

I smiled at all the compliments and care he'd managed to weave in. Sweet Tommy. I patted his biceps. "You think I'm gorgeous?"

Rolling his eyes, Tommy finished taking a sip of his beer. "Yeah. And if that's all you took from what I said, you need more than a bodyguard."

"I want to do it. I'm going to do it. I'll meet him someplace safe and neutral. Like a pub or something. He's got to be just as worried that I'm some psycho who will rob him or kill him, too. Maybe he's like some billionaire sugar daddy or something. Maybe it will be love at first sight!"

"Yeah, right. Love at first sight always starts with a Craigslist post about facesitting."

"He said 'gentlewoman,'" I tried.

The two of them were laughing. Again.

I kept a straight face and they finally got serious.

"Fine. I'll go with you," Sam said a few minutes later.

"You will?" Tommy and I replied in unison.

"If you're both going, I'm going," Tommy said. "This is too much."

"I'm so excited!" I yelped. The second pint always set me to yelping. "I knew you guys would come around."

They finished their beers and I sent a reply to the Craigslist encrypted email. Within five minutes there was a response.

Does 6 pm tomorrow at The Connaught bar suit?

I nearly choked on my beer. "You guys, he replied right away!"

"I don't believe you!" Tommy pulled my cell phone out of my hand and read the message. "The Connaught's swanky bar?"

Sam grabbed the phone next. "He's a snake. Anyone can meet in a posh hotel bar. Doesn't mean they can afford to *stay* at a posh hotel."

"So will you guys still come with me and sit at a different table or something?"

"I wouldn't miss it for the world," Tommy replied.

Chapter 2

I DIDN'T KNOW if I should get all dolled up for my face-sitting interview or just show up in my camo cargo pants. Seeing as I was going to one of the most elegant hotels in all of London, I opted for dolled up. I wore the one little black dress I'd brought with me and I even put on a bit of makeup. The September temperatures were starting to cool down, so I threw a black scarf around my neck and pulled on my high-heeled boots.

I was a unicorn, damn it!

I went back and forth on the whole *underwear* issue. It wasn't like the guy was going to ask me to sit on his face right then and there in the hotel bar, but something about wearing utilitarian opaque black tights felt like I was not keeping myself open to…the possibilities. Or something. I ended up not wearing any tights. I ended up not wearing any underwear at all.

Tommy and Sam met me outside Green Park Station and we walked through Mayfair, across Berkeley Square, until we came to the charming hotel.

"You sure about this, Lana?" Sam asked one last time. I nodded. I was sure. Sort of.

We walked up the few steps to the revolving door, but I paused and turned to see the small square in front of the hotel. After looking around at the autumn leaves in the park across the street and then up at the sparkling entrance to the hotel, I turned and said, "Why the hell not? If nothing else, it will be a great story I can tell someday, right?"

The three of us walked through the lobby, then I turned left, by myself, into the exquisitely furnished bar. Sam and Tommy had finally agreed that it was safe enough if they stayed in the main part of the hotel, while I checked out Mr. Facesitter on my own nearby.

As soon as I entered the bar, soft gray velvet curtains and silvery wallpaper created a hushed luxurious feel. Two couples were nestled in two of the intimate banquettes, one to the right and one to the left. Another man, dark-haired and angular looking, was leaning casually against the bar. There were no barstools. It was an old-fashioned, walk-up-and-drink situation. The bartender looked like the guy from the nightmare in *The Shining*: cleaning a glass with slow, turning motions—a consummate professional.

I was suddenly intimidated as fuck. By the goddamned bartender. This was such a bad idea. The dark billionaire bad-boy type at the bar turned and looked at me, giving me a shameless head-to-toe-perusal. He lifted his lowball slightly in salute and took a sip, as if he were toasting my arrival, then he turned back and said something to the bartender.

Overwhelmed by my own immature foolishness, I spun on my heel, ready to turn back toward the lobby and my friends.

"Are you Lana?" It was a woman's voice, with a thick, seductive French accent.

My head swiveled to a darker corner of the bar, right near where I was standing. A stunningly attractive couple sat at a glossy-black round table, with two flutes of champagne and a standing ice bucket holding the rest of the expensive bottle.

"Sorry?" For a split second, I thought they were friends of my parents, posh people I'd met at some corporate cocktail party or charity event in New York, and then I realized...Mr. Facesitter might actually be...Madame et Monsieur Facesitter.

In a comic double take, I actually looked over my own shoulder—as if there could be *another* Lana in the tiny bar. Another Lana who'd answered a Craigslist post to get her pussy licked in exchange for free accommodation in Mayfair.

The woman smiled, looking both relieved and sexy as hell. She shifted in her seat to make more room on the banquette, putting herself closer to the handsome man next to her, and then patting the crushed gray velvet, indicating I should take a seat.

The man looked at the woman and smiled, then looked at me with a more assessing gaze, narrowing his eyes slightly.

"Will you join us?" he asked. It was suddenly clear that the woman was in charge of this operation and he was deferring to her wishes.

I licked my lips nervously. I couldn't place his accent or his ethnicity. He could have been French or Middle Eastern or Peruvian, or just tan for all I could tell. He had the look of a man who could go anywhere, do anything, and be anyone he chose to be. He was the type of man who could offer his wife the freedom to keep a flat in Mayfair where she could keep a bit of pussy.

"Sure." I felt distinctly American, my voice sounding too loud or crass or something. As I sat down, I answered again, more politely, "Thank you."

Barely making a move, lifting his chin a millimeter, the man somehow let the waiter know he was needed.

"A glass of champagne?" the man asked me.

"That would be awesome." Again, I felt like I was an extra on an episode of *Hee Haw* while they were starring in some noirish French art house film.

The waiter brought another glass and poured the champagne

for me, then topped off the other two. After he'd walked away, the woman reached out and introduced herself. "I'm Cybelle de la Vergne. And this is my husband, David."

I looked at her elegant hand and for a second it reminded me of Maddy's—delicate and strong all at once. The recognition emboldened me.

We shook hands.

Yeah, it was one of those once-in-a-lifetime moments, all right. The air stopped moving around us. Electricity shot through me—first where our hands were connected, and then like a hot whipping wire, up my arm, down my spine, and then between my legs, where I was suddenly hyperaware of my non-underpants situation.

Cybelle's dark violet eyes caught mine and I stopped breathing. "Nice to meet you," I finally exhaled.

David leaned toward his wife. "Shall I leave you two to become better acquainted?"

Cybelle was still holding my hand and holding my gaze when she answered, "Yes, darling. I'll see you upstairs in a little while." David kissed Cybelle briefly on the cheek. He gave me a quick (encouraging?) smile, then stood up and left.

After he'd gone, she brought both of our hands to her lap under the table.

"Why would you answer such a silly advertisement, Lana?" Her hand was caressing the back of mine, where she pressed it gently against her thigh. I'm pretty sure I'd never been more turned on in my life. Just from her hand. And her thigh.

Then everything went cold and my brain told me it was all a trick, some sort of intricate practical joke being played on me. The lush gray curtains would be pulled back and someone would leap into the bar, or the walls would retract altogether and the whole thing would be a movie set, and I would be a laughingstock, a paragon of foolishness.

I realized, despite all of that, some part of me really wanted this to be real. I breathed and tried to collect my wits enough to speak.

"I want to live in central London in relative comfort, and this seemed like as good a way as any."

Cybelle set her champagne glass down and narrowed her eyes. "How old are you?"

"Thirty."

"Have you ever done this sort of thing before?" Cybelle's French accent was sublime. And her eyes. And her lips. And her long dark hair that tumbled over her far shoulder.

I laughed nervously and started caressing her hidden hand in return. "Is this a *sort of thing*? I've never even sold an old Ikea table on Craigslist, much less answered a personal ad, if that's what you mean. You're my first." My cheeks heated and I just tried to roll with it.

Cybelle smiled and it was charming and mysterious and encouraging all at once. I felt my body heating up and used my free hand to take off the black scarf that suddenly felt too warm around my neck.

"So why then?" Cybelle pressed. Her fingers danced lightly over mine beneath the table. It was incredibly distracting. And delicious.

Shrugging off the scarf, I breathed deep. "I thought it would be a funny story. I thought you would be some nasty old man, or a kinky millionaire—"

Something about the way she raised an eyebrow caught me by surprise. "*Are* you a kinky millionaire?" I asked, only half-joking.

"I am kinky. And I am a millionaire." Cybelle took another sip of her champagne and almost smiled. "But I've never thought of myself as a *kinky millionaire*. That sounds rather...unimaginative, somehow."

My breath halted. "I could be some crazy person." I almost felt like I should be the one protecting Cybelle, rather than the other way around.

"David's security firm ran a full search on you last night. A shame about Lowell + Mercer, by the way. I suspect Ned will run it into the ground."

I pulled my hand away abruptly. Creepy red flags were snapping everywhere. "I think I should probably go. This is starting to feel like *The Comfort of Strangers*."

"Would you like to meet Helen Mirren?" Cybelle asked, totally nonplussed by my alarm.

"Who wouldn't?"

She reached into her Hermès bag for her cell phone. When she took it out and began to scroll through, I gradually realized this woman was actually about to call Helen Mirren right then.

"Cybelle—"

She shut her eyes and inhaled deeply. "Say my name again."

"Cybelle," I said, softer. Sexier, I guess. I wasn't exactly *trying* to be sexy or anything, but this gorgeous woman was confusing the hell out of me and I was turned on and baffled and paranoid and, weirdly, I really wanted her to like me. Basically, I wanted Cybelle regardless, free accommodation in exchange for facesitting...or not.

Slowly opening her eyes, she looked at my mouth and then into my eyes again. "I want you for one year."

My heart leapt into a furious gallop. Fear? Joy? Excitement? Only one year? I shook my head to cast off the insanity of that last bit. "Like a love slave or something?"

Cybelle laughed and it was throaty and so fucking sexy, I wanted to be able to make her laugh like that all the time. "No, lovely Lana. Not like a slave. But we will have a formal contract, if that's all right with you. I think it protects both of us from any future unpleasantness."

Taking an unladylike gulp of champagne, I tried to collect myself. "So I just…what?"

"Let me seduce you, I suppose." Cybelle looked at my face and let the heated silence build between us. "Of course, I want control of the situation; I want the privacy and discretion my life demands." She shrugged. "To tell the truth, the Craigslist posting started as a joke. My husband—David is my husband, in case I hadn't made that clear. Yes, he has known of my desires for many years. In fact he's quite accommodating. As I am with him and his…forays."

I took another sip of champagne and continued to feel like a bumpkin. Why wasn't I born a freethinking Frenchwoman, damn it? So many wasted years! "Mmm-hmm," I mumbled noncommittally.

"So," she continued. "The two of us were laughing the other night and I told him what I really wanted. I told him I didn't want the complete detachment of paying a stranger each time, nor the emotional investment of finding a girlfriend or mistress or anything like that. Nor did I want to be with anyone from our circle of friends. I'm forty years old and set in my ways—I realized I wanted an old-fashioned *arrangement*." Cybelle glanced down toward my chest, inhaled through her nose, and then pressed on. "Here is the situation. I'm in London about ten days of every month and I told David I wanted to go home to my little place here and have some sweet, eager kitten there waiting for me. *Was that so impossible*, I asked him?"

I shook my head and licked my lips again. I kept feeling like my mouth was dry. "I guess I'm living proof that it's not so impossible."

Twisting the stem of the champagne glass, Cybelle was quiet for a few minutes before she said anything more. "We can do whatever we like." She looked at me and there was something soft yet incredibly powerful in her look. "What would you *like*, Lana?"

I hesitated—because holy hell—but then I let the truth flow out in a quiet, hopeful voice. "I think I'd like very much to be the one waiting for you when you come home to your little place in London."

Chapter 3

"*A*LORS. THIS IS a very pleasant turn of events." She pressed her fingertips together for a moment, then reached out and grazed the pulse along my neck. "Would you like to go to dinner with me? And then I can show you where I live?" Her finger came away from my neck and I leaned forward slightly, already craving her touch.

"Yes," I answered.

She smiled. "You make me think of Michelangelo's rough marbles, the slaves—all the tension and muscle and beauty there in its natural form, but raw and unfinished. Is that insulting?"

I shook my head. "Not at all."

Cybelle smiled at the irony, then let her eyes roam over me, along my neck, gliding down the turn of my upper arms, which were feeling powerful and feminine all at once since I hadn't been doing anything but going to the gym for the past two weeks.

I cleared my throat. "I'd love to have dinner with you and then…" I got my courage up and put my right hand back on her thigh, "…to see your place."

Cybelle made the slightest moan, almost a coo, when I moved my hand along her leg. I reached for her hand and put it on my leg. I wanted her to know I wanted her. I drew her hand up my thigh slowly.

Something switched and her face went deadly cool. She

pulled her hand away and took a ladylike sip of champagne. Without looking at me she said, "You don't ever need to guide me to your pussy. I know where it is."

For a few seconds, I thought I might actually cry. "I'm sorry. I thought—"

"You don't *think* when you're with me, Lana," Cybelle interrupted. The hardness was still there in her expression, but her voice softened as she continued. "You feel, darling. That is your job. That is your rent. That is your *part* in all of this. *Comprends?* You let me drive. You give yourself over to it."

She looked into my eyes then, to see if she'd pushed me too far, maybe. And my heart stumbled. I had the incredibly clear, incredibly liberating realization that there was no such thing as *too far* when it came to how I felt about this woman and what I would let her do or say to me. She must have seen the moment the thought crystalized—that I was a woman in search of experience, in search of understanding my own cravings—and how Cybelle was the one who would feed them.

"So...you will be my mistress or something?" I asked nervously.

She crossed her legs and I could practically smell her desire. I swear to God if she had asked me to slip to the floor and put my face between her legs I would have done it. I would have burrowed into her and begged her to rake her beautiful red fingernails against my scalp in front of everyone in the goddamned bar while I did anything to bring her pleasure. I'm pretty sure I was panting.

She smiled at my obvious eagerness. "Yes. I will be your *maîtresse*. I will take care of you, in every way. Sexually, physically, emotionally."

"And...I mean...I just...feel?"

Cybelle laughed quietly. "Oh, my lovely Lana. There is no *just* about it. If you are truly willing, as you say, to *feel*, to immerse yourself one hundred percent into this agreement between us, you will discover things about yourself, about your desires and the depth of your passions that you could never have dreamt possible."

"But it feels so passive, like I'm not really doing anything."

Cybelle smiled again. "Think of it this way. There can be no *us* without you. I cannot dominate in a vacuum. I need you as much as you need me. I can see it in your eyes, how much the idea pleases you."

"It does," I whispered. "It totally does," I said more clearly, as the truth of it settled around me. So. Damn. Much. "But will it be some 24/7 thing where I'm sleeping in a cage in the kitchen—"

Cybelle burst out laughing and the waiter looked over to make sure everything was fine. She waved him off and smiled at me. "I've always found there's no reason to be so doctrinaire, darling." Yeah. She called me *darling*. Unironically. "I want your warm body in my bed, Lana. You wouldn't do me any good in the kitchen. I will also want you to accompany me to some openings or out to dinner or to dinner parties when David is not in town. I shan't be holding you hostage. You will be all right to go out in public with me, yes?"

Well, that was unexpected. But sure. Why not. "Oh, okay." I figured we could deal with my wardrobe (or lack thereof) at some future time.

We both took the last sips of our champagne and Cybelle said, "Let's go to dinner and you can ask me anything. Details. All that. Then after tonight, you do not ask me anything. Ça va?"

"I do speak a little French, so, yes, ça va."

"You will be fluent in French by the end of the month. I will hire a tutor as soon as you move in." Cybelle looked into her champagne glass. "I suspect you will also want to fuck him, which is fine, if you like."

I crossed my legs and Cybelle looked her fill as my breasts swelled and my nipples hardened against the knit fabric of my black dress.

"You would like that, Lana?"

"Yes...I mean. If you think he's attractive, I probably will, too."

"Would you like it even more if I watched?"

I inhaled sharply. *Holy fuck.* The playful part of me had been so completely shut down while I was married—my ex had hated when I even looked at other guys—so I'd just sort of turned off my flirtation channel. Now, here was Cybelle both suggestive and encouraging; my insides rippled with excitement. "Yes..." My voice was more like a hiss.

"This is going to work out very well for all of us." Cybelle stood up from the booth and reached out to help me up. When our hands met again, the pulse of awareness flared, the pulse of recognition that we were about to embark on something spectacular.

Once I was standing, Cybelle kept hold of my hand and the two of us stayed where we were, only a few inches apart, almost the same height. We were perfectly suited. Cybelle leaned in and kissed me lightly on the lips, and she shivered when my small gasp and slight forward-leaning motion told her everything she needed to know about how *I* felt about everything.

"I believe we're going to make each other very happy," Cybelle said quietly, tracing her finger along my jaw and watching the shiver of pleasure that followed. "Very happy."

Cybelle let go of my hand but kept her palm against the small of my back as we walked out into the lobby. She headed straight for Tom and Sam. *Oh shit.*

Cybelle went right up to them and introduced herself.

"Hello, gentleman." They both rose to greet her. "I'm Cybelle de la Vergne. It's a pleasure to meet you both. You must be Tom," she said politely. "And you must be Sam." She turned and let him give her his shrewdest glare.

"This all seems a bit off, if you ask me," said Sam skeptically.

Cybelle looked from Sam to me, genuinely concerned. "Does any of this seem *off* to you, Lana?"

I smiled and I could see how much it pleased her and fuck-fuck-fuck I wanted this woman to be pleased. Like crazy. Like in my heart. *No!* Fuck no-fuck-no-fuck-no! I felt it like a slow coil in my chest, unraveling to lure me in and then snap violently at some point in the future. This woman could so easily work her way into my heart, and that was best avoided. Hearts were very tricky beasts.

Turning from Cybelle to my friends, I said, "Sam, Tom, you're both the sweetest, to be looking out for me, but I promise I'm good. Cybelle and I are just going for dinner to get better acquainted. I'll text you later tonight and I'll see you at the gym tomorrow. Promise."

Sam looked as though that didn't quite satisfy his worry, but he huffed out a little sigh and finally gave in. "Very well. We're all adults I suppose. A text tonight and your ass at the gym tomorrow morning at nine—yeah?"

I looked to Cybelle. *Already slipping into my role of obedience*, I thought with a tremor of pleasure. With that look I was silently asking if it was all right to go to the gym in the morning.

Cybelle smiled wickedly, ignoring the men completely. "Yes, darling, we should be done by then."

Blushing just for her, I turned back to Sam. "See? All good. So I'll see you at the gym tomorrow."

"And you'll text tonight," he prodded, without concealing his irritation about Cybelle's burgeoning control over me.

"And I'll text tonight," I agreed like an echo. I leaned in and kissed him on the cheek, then took a step toward Tom and kissed him on his cheek as well. "Thanks so much for everything, you guys. It's all good."

Chapter 4

WE WALKED A few blocks to a private supper club I'd vaguely heard of. The doorman greeted Cybelle with a respectful smile and a low, "Welcome, Mme de la Vergne."

I was on fire. Even walking down the street with Cybelle was like some form of intense foreplay. We hadn't said anything since we'd left The Connaught, but I felt myself connecting with her even in our silence. I was glad I'd dressed up—relatively speaking—when we were led into a small dining room with pastoral oil paintings and leather banquettes and about twenty people speaking in hushed tones and all of them posh and dressed beautifully. We were seated in a corner booth that allowed us to sit next to each other instead of across the table. Her nearness was its own form of exquisite torture.

"So," Cybelle began, unfolding her napkin and placing it on her lap. "Ask away."

I put my napkin on my lap and took a deep breath. "May I see other people?"

"Other than the French tutor?"

I nodded.

Cybelle narrowed her eyes and took a sip of water before replying. "Do you want to?"

"I may." I shrugged. At the moment I didn't care if I laid eyes on another human being for the next year, turned on as I was by this dark, mysterious woman who was obviously going to fulfill more fantasies than I even knew I had. But it helped to be...realistic. There were twenty days a month that she was *not* going to be here. So. There was that. "I kind of wanted to give myself this year to explore and just *live*, you know?"

Cybelle nodded. "I know, darling."

And *God* when she called me *darling* like that, in that offhand but totally intimate way, I felt my insides curl up with desire. I tried to breathe, and then whispered, "I like when you call me *darling.*"

"And I like when you tell me what you like," Cybelle replied softly.

My heart was pounding again. I took off my scarf and watched Cybelle's eyes as she gazed at the plunging vee of my neckline. "And I like when you look at me like that," I said quietly.

"Imagine how much you will like it when I..." Cybelle's voice died out as she tucked a strand of my hair behind my ear.

The waiter had arrived. "Good evening, Mme de la Vergne. Ms. Mercer. Would you like to begin with a cocktail or are you ready to order?"

I inhaled sharply, from a combination of the waiter calling me by name and from the unexpected thrill of Cybelle resting her hand on my thigh beneath the pale blue tablecloth. Very. High. On. My. Thigh.

"We're ready to order, Stephen. We'd like to begin with the Caesar salad and then the quail. And we'll split the soufflé for dessert."

He nodded politely, never taking out pad or pencil. "And to drink?"

"The 2000 Latour Pauillac, please."

"Excellent." He nodded politely and walked away.

"Do you mind me ordering for you?" Cybelle asked.

"Not in the least. I love every kind of food and you've saved me the hassle of having to decide."

"Good. So where were we? Ah, yes. You *seeing other people.*" The way Cybelle said it, as if the phrase were rather feeble, made me smile. "Tell me more about what you have in mind," she prompted.

"I guess I want to feel like I'm open to new experiences, you know, to meeting new people while I'm here." Her hand was roaming lightly up my thigh and concentration was…hard. "Not like I want to be on the prowl or anything, but there's that open-and-closed feeling—" She skirted the edge of my pussy and I shut my mouth rather than gasp aloud. "And you know, I guess I just want to be open." There. A full sentence, I congratulated myself.

The waiter returned with the wine and made quick work of uncorking it and pouring a splash for Cybelle to approve—which she did with the hottest moan of pleasure I had ever heard. The way her violet eyes darkened when she smelled the wine, and then the flush of pleasure when she had the first taste. Holy hell this women was a sensual master. Mistress, I corrected myself, with a little smile.

"Perfect." Cybelle squeezed my inner thigh, her pinkie touching my wet pussy. She smiled her approval at the waiter. For the wine. Or me. Or both.

The waiter filled our glasses and left again.

She turned to look at me and I melted. Totally melted. "I like the idea of you being very *open.*" Cybelle looked at me over the edge of her wineglass.

An image of being spread out on some huge decadent bed with my legs wide and Cybelle devouring my pussy flashed into my mind's eye.

"Mmm," Cybelle continued. "The idea pleases you as well, I see."

"Yes, it does." I had never felt anything like this zero-to-sex-in-sixty-seconds thing with anyone before, but Cybelle made me want to rip away every inhibition. With Maddy, it had been friendship, and flirting, and then kissing and some great sex. But it had all been, well, friendly somehow. This was like fire.

"Okay. So how about this?" Cybelle's voice turned professional. "I will let you be *open* to men, but I am the only woman in your life for the next year. That would please me very much."

I was pretty sure I would agree to anything Cybelle de la Vergne suggested, as long as it ended with her saying *that would please me very much* in that sultry way of hers.

"That sounds great. I mean, I don't even know if I'll meet anyone while I'm here but—"

"Oh, you'll meet people." Cybelle smiled and lifted her chin suggestively. "You're quite beautiful and you're going to be a bit of a celebrity when we start to be seen together. Can you handle that?"

I felt the heat creep up my neck. "Like, the papers are going to call me your girlfriend?" I had a vision of my father opening the *New York Post* and seeing me at some James Bond movie opening with my *girlfriend*. A smile might have passed my lips.

Cybelle shrugged one shoulder, a gesture that made me desperate to touch the diaphanous silk of her blouse. Again, she reminded me of Maddy, which reminded me... "I had sex with my best friend, Maddy, the night before I left New York," I blurted.

One side of Cybelle's lush mouth quirked up. "And?"

"And...she is probably going to come visit me...and she is a *she* and I may want to, you know, fool around with her while she's here…and I just realized that would go against that part of our agreement—of you being the only girl—but I'd like to, you know, touch her, when she's here."

"Do you love her?" Cybelle asked, with an almost scientific coldness.

"Yes. I mean, as a friend, as a person, definitely yes. But I certainly don't feel tingly and hot and bothered and like I'm going to explode with lust when I'm around her…" My voice petered out when I realized what I'd actually said without saying. That *Cybelle* was the one who made me tingly and hot and bothered and like I was going to explode with lust.

"My lovely Lana is tingly?" Cybelle's hand, which had remained still on my thigh for a few moments, began to move again. "Hot and bothered?" Another inch up my thigh.

"So bothered," I whispered. "You are so incredibly sexy and I can't believe you are touching me."

Another inch. "Not quite exploding yet…" Cybelle's finger extended the last little bit and traced the lightest feathery caress across the opening of my now-slick pussy. We looked into each other's eyes and I couldn't help pushing my hips to get closer to Cybelle's touch. I knew it was exactly what she told me not to do, but I couldn't help it, damn it.

Making a little disappointed moue, Cybelle pulled her fingers away. "Patience, darling. You will explode soon enough." Then she brought her fingers to her lips, as if she were thinking about some abstract idea, letting her hand play lightly near her nose and mouth. Oh fuck. I realized Cybelle was smelling my pussy on her fingertips right there in front of this roomful of aristocrats and peers of the realm. And I thought I might be able to have my first orgasm without anyone actually touching my clit. I tilted my hips slightly to see if I—

"Don't even think about it," Cybelle snapped, not even looking at me. "When you come for the first time—with me—it's going to be with my hungry mouth on that sweet pussy of yours. Now sit up straight and have a sip of wine like a good pet."

Oh God. It was so crazy wrong and delicious when she called me *pet*. I wanted to pant and wag and crawl all over Cybelle de la Vergne. I wanted to please her. Quite desperately.

Cybelle steered the conversation for the rest of the meal, obviously sensing my brain-scrambling lust. We talked about the latest exhibitions that were up at the Royal Academy and Tate Modern, then about Cybelle's work as a curator for a wealthy private collector in Geneva, and eventually we got around to my idea for manga or anima or comics. It felt great to talk to someone who was both objective and supportive. She smiled encouragingly and promised she'd have a drafting table set up in my rooms.

That's right. *Rooms.* Plural. I mean. Yeah, I was so fucking psyched.

Then, without changing her chatty tone, she spoke about her *expectations* for me, and how she wanted total access to my body and my time for the ten days or so she would be in town. For those days, I had to be *available* for Cybelle. Completely available.

Oh God. I was pretty sure there was going to be a wet stain on the banquette when I got up...from how turned on I was with all her talk of access and expectations and availability. My insides melted around the words *completely*. I must've sighed aloud because she set her fork down, dabbed at each corner of her mouth, and turned to look at me.

"Do you think you could come right now if I told you to?"

I bit my lower lip and my hips shifted slightly of their own accord. I nodded my silent reply.

She smiled and then continued talking as if I'd said nothing. Which, I suppose, I had—said nothing, that is.

She described how she was also a consultant for several museums, in addition to her main job with the Swiss collector, and how she'd spent many years working at the Louvre before deciding to go out on her own. She was forty now, and had been working as a private consultant for six years. She asked me more questions about my business in New York, and before I knew what I was saying I was telling her all sorts of shit about how—even though I didn't regret having started my own company—I knew I never wanted to get caught up in that type of office culture again. I watched how she listened: she collated and processed bits of information, eyes sparking with intelligence and awareness, lips quirking occasionally. She was incredibly beautiful and I got distracted from my train of thought when I was staring at the edge of her lip and wondering when—if ever—I would be allowed to kiss her.

She smiled when my words petered out altogether. After a rather lengthy silence of the two of us staring at each other like a pair of hungry animals—and my breasts throbbing and my nipples tightening—she finally started talking again.

Cybelle spoke plainly about her financial success, and also about her husband David's work as an international attorney. He was from a wealthy family, she explained, and without sounding crass or boastful Cybelle described a life of summers spent in the south of France and winters in Verbier, a life that was filled with love and art and sensual pleasure. And utterly free of judgment or shame.

Over coffee, Cybelle opened her leather bag and pulled out a document with a pale blue cover that lifted from the bottom. A contract. She took a heavy gold pen out of her purse, signed over her name on the last page and passed the pen to me. Her wrist grazed the side of my breast as her hand hovered over the remnants of our shared dessert. I shuddered, pulled my thighs tighter together, and took the pen carefully from her fingers.

Heart pounding wildly, I read every word. Everything was there in exquisite detail, nothing left to chance. The ten days a month for a year, the incredibly generous "allowance," the address of her place in Mayfair, the confidentiality clause—I wanted to experience every word.

The sound of the pen scratching across the expensive vellum in the quiet club might as well have been a vibrator dragging across my clit.

Between the wine and the food and the physical beauty of Cybelle sitting right there—her long brown hair tickling her cheek, her full lips smiling occasionally or pursing with mock displeasure while telling an anecdote about a particularly ill-humored client—I was a shuddering mess of desire by the time we left the supper club.

We walked through the cool, quiet streets of Mayfair and Cybelle kept her warm palm on my lower back as she led us to a narrow cobbled mews. I was pretty much consumed with wanting to kiss her neck or lips or anywhere really, so I wasn't quite paying attention to where we were going.

"Here we are," she announced as we walked up two steps and she pulled a single key out of her large bag. The *small place* she'd alluded to earlier was a four-story Georgian row house.

"Do you have a flat here?" I asked, looking up at the multiple floors.

"No, darling, I own the building." Cybelle pushed into the front hall and held the door open for me to enter. Sliding home the deadbolt after she shut the door, she led me toward the stairs without pausing to put down her bag or show me around the ground floor. Sensing my curiosity, she said, "You'll see everything tomorrow. Right now, I want you in my bed. Up you go." She pointed to the narrow stairs, indicating she wanted me to go ahead of her.

My heart raced and some of my initial nervousness started to return as we ascended the dimly lit staircase. What if Cybelle was some sort of sicko human slave trafficker or murderess or—

"Take your dress off, Lana," she ordered from a few steps behind me. We were halfway up the first flight of stairs and I panicked. My hand gripped the wooden railing; my legs felt like they were stuck in cement. I breathed through my nose and tried to control my heartbeat.

When I didn't do as I was told right away, Cybelle's voice turned cool. "When we are in this house, you do what I say, when I say. Is that clear, Lana?"

The way she said my name, with the French softness—*Lah. Nah.*—was both demanding and encouraging. If her directions were not clear enough, her tone seemed to say, she would happily do whatever was necessary to clarify my understanding.

We had talked about everything over dinner. I had asked all the questions I could think to ask. I knew I was supposed to obey her now. I wanted to, damn it.

But now, on the stairway, this shit was suddenly real. I kept breathing, my back to her and my heart hammering.

I didn't say another word. I slid into the silence somehow. My muscles softened, my breathing evened out, and I knew I could do it. I took one last deep, fortifying breath and reached for the hem of my black knit dress. I tugged at it quickly, grabbing the fabric, but before I could pull it over my hips, one of Cybelle's hands stayed my movements.

"Slowly, darling. Much slower. And keep walking as you take it off. We're going to the top floor."

I did as I was told, walking up the stairs and slowly lifting off my dress until I was walking in nothing but my lacy black bra and my knee-high boots. I held onto the inside-out dress, clutching it hard in my right hand and letting it drag on the carpeted stairs as we continued up and up.

I tried not to be hyperaware of my bare ass basically in Cybelle's face. Which was basically impossible. My ass was right at her eye level, for a start. And I could feel Cybelle's warm breath against the most sensitive skin on my body.

When we were nearly to the top, the sound of my pussy had become loud in my own ears—the slick kissing sound of my swollen lips as I walked, so close to Cybelle's mouth. So wanting.

The whole weird scenario only made me more slick and breathless. I was pretty sure I could hear Cybelle inhaling my scent.

"This way, darling."

I'd reached the top landing, and then Cybelle's hand was on my lower back, bare skin against bare skin, and I was being led into one of the most splendid rooms I had ever seen. Antiques and a small gas fire in the grate and small impressionist paintings in gold frames and luxurious fabrics and a huge four-poster bed, and it all fractured into beauty-beauty-beauty spinning all around me. I was reminded of that poem about the distant glitter of desert stars and I was quickly overwhelmed with how sparkling and *real* everything felt. I tried to turn to face Cybelle, but she prevented my movement.

"Don't turn around. I want to savor this moment, to feel the first time you enter my room, my world." She inhaled deeply— the sound close behind me, all around me—then she touched the curve of my bare shoulder with a whisper-soft caress. My body nearly exploded from that one tiny touch. The dress fell from my grip. "Do you feel it, too, Lana?"

"Yes," I answered, despite my dry throat and quivering anticipation. *God yes.*

I tried to focus on the paintings and sculptures and the huge bed and the pale turquoise silk of the walls, until my eyes slid shut and I simply moaned as Cybelle ran her elegant fingers down my spine, along the crack of my ass, between my legs—finally!—gently tracing the plump, slick swell of my pussy.

"Please," I begged shamelessly, desperate before she'd even begun.

"*Oui.* I like that very much," Cybelle whispered, hot and close to my ear. "I like to hear you say *please*. I know you are very wet and very needy—" her finger slid easily into my cunt and my knees nearly buckled, "—but you must trust me. Do you trust me, Lana?"

Cybelle was close behind me now. She pulled her finger out of me and stroked my needy folds with her wet fingertip. Her other hand started roaming over my quivering body, marking me, mapping me, staking her claim with every pass.

"Do you trust me, Lana?" Cybelle's hands were everywhere now, removing my bra, circling my clit, smoothing down the turn of my ass, skating up my inner thigh.

I bit my lip and tried not to come. I had to focus so hard because I'd been on the verge for hours. Cybelle had been *very* clear on that point: I absolutely, positively did not come without Cybelle's permission.

She bit my ear lobe and pinched my clit all at once, and I saw stars behind my eyelids and tasted blood at my lip where I was biting through the soft flesh rather than disappoint Cybelle.

"Do you trust me, Lana?" she repeated for the third time.

"Yes," I whimpered. "Yes. Yes, I trust you Cybelle." I didn't even know what I was saying or agreeing to, but it didn't matter. Whatever Cybelle was offering, my answer was yes.

Chapter 5

"THAT'S MY GOOD girl." Cybelle's fingers soothed and tormented my clit and nipples. "I will let you come in a moment, to calm you, and then I shall make you cry out in earnest."

If this wasn't *earnest*, I wasn't sure what was. "Please, yes…" I whispered again, my nipples taut and needy, my pussy pulsing already at the promise of impending release.

"Come here, you sweet thing." Cybelle led me to the edge of the four-poster and positioned me so I was sitting with my knees spread wide at the foot of the bed. "Hold onto the bed posts and don't let go."

I did as I was told and reached out for each of the bedposts, to my right and left. It was a bit of a stretch, causing my breasts to thrust forward and my shoulders to strain a bit.

"Lovely," Cybelle whispered. "I knew you would open for me like this, the moment you walked into The Connaught earlier tonight, and you turned to leave, I saw you like this."

I breathed through the wave of pleasure those words brought. I felt so wanton and exposed, naked except for my high-heeled boots, the outside of my knees pushed back hard against the edge of the bed. Cybelle kneeled down on the floor and leaned in to taste me. My mind short-circuited. Lights, colors, flares—just from that first touch of tongue, that first intimate contact.

Cybelle moaned her approval, her joy I think, and I felt my orgasm approaching hard and fast. I had never come like this, certainly not with Ned and his jackhammer subtlety, or his weird version of cunnilingus that was akin to a Labrador retriever lapping sloppily from a big bowl of water. Even with Maddy—even though there had been tenderness and excitement in the orgasms we'd shared our first and last time together—I had still felt *detached* somehow.

But this? This was fire, pure and simple, and I wanted to burn.

As I looked down at Cybelle's beautiful face, she caught my eye and kissed my clit while holding my gaze, then, barely pulling away, she said, "Now you can come, my pet." Cybelle's eyes drifted closed in pure bliss as she dipped her lips to my cunt and her tongue became the center of my entire world.

The orgasm roared through me so hard I was grateful I had the bedposts to hold onto. Normally that would be the point where I'd shove Ned away, or when Maddy had slowed down to give me some time to recover my senses.

Cybelle kept going.

Her mouth soothed and taunted and hummed and then without really understanding what was happening, I was coming again and crying out this time, loud and begging. Begging for *what* I have no idea.

When I finally caught my breath, thighs still quaking, Cybelle removed my boots then gently pried my fingers from the bedpost.

"That's a sweet girl. Now lie back darling."

I was limp and obliging. I would've done anything she asked. She pulled the silk bedspread back and I crawled up to the head of the bed and slid under the covers.

"Oh my God, these sheets..." I moaned into the tactile pleasure of cool silk that was neither slippery nor velvety, but some miraculously soft in-between texture. Then I let my head loll to the right and watched Cybelle undress.

The woman was beyond gorgeous, but there was more to it than sheer physical beauty. It was as if she adored being a woman, adored the body she inhabited, adored life. I watched, amazed at my own body's rapid recharging. After the two devastating orgasms I'd just had, normally I would have thought it would be impossible to be turned on again, at least for a few intervening hours.

But as I watched Cybelle finger the small buttons of her sheer silk blouse, the way she unclasped her watch and set it on the bedside table, how she undid her bra and stretched her shoulders back and forward, using her upper arms to press her breasts together, I felt the pulsing heat between my legs return.

"Pull the sheet off, Lana. I want to see you while I get undressed."

Gladly.

I pushed the sheet down with my hands, then used my feet to kick it the rest of the way off. Obeying Cybelle was already feeling like second nature, like what I would have done if I'd thought of it first. But I suspected Cybelle would always think of it first.

"Good?" I was lying on my side and resting my cheek on the pillow I hugged under my head.

"Mmmmmm," she hummed. "Very good."

I felt languid and dreamy as Cybelle removed her diamond earrings, tilting her beautiful dark hair over one shoulder and then the other; I felt the clink-clink of the metal as each earring hit the ceramic dish on the bedside table.

After her shirt and bra were off and Cybelle undid the back of her skirt, I bit my lower lip. I couldn't wait to see her completely naked. Her breasts were amazing, firm and high; I wanted to immerse myself in her. I also wanted to press my hand over my clit, but that was the second thing the contract had been very specific about: I was not to touch myself *at all* for the ten days each month I belonged to Cybelle. That was definitely going to be the hardest part of the bargain.

Look, I masturbate. A lot. Or maybe not a lot if everyone is lying about how little *they* do. Is three times a day a lot? It didn't seem like a lot to me. It was just a regular part of my day: when I woke up, at some point during the afternoon, and then again before I went to sleep.

Then I began to calculate...and to worry. Three orgasms a day...times ten days...that was *thirty orgasms* I wasn't going to be having. Well, that I wasn't going to be having alone. I had to admit it looked like Cybelle was going to keep up with and/or exceed that tally.

Letting my hand skim casually down to rest on my hip, as if I had a small itch, I tried to tilt slightly and press my palm into—

"Tsk-tsk darling. Are you already wanting to touch yourself?"

"Yes," I admitted. "So much."

Then her skirt was gone and my eyes skidded to the satin garters and lacy thigh highs and sheer white triangle that covered her dark pubic hair. And it was the hottest thing I'd ever seen.

I didn't realize I was staring and licking my lips, probably looking like some sort of lascivious teenager, until Cybelle whispered, "Come here, *chérie*."

I crawled across the small distance like I was in a dream, a dream where I could make love to anyone—man or woman—without any inhibitions, because it was so damned obvious how badly we both wanted it.

"May I touch you?" I asked, hesitant and impatient all at once. That don't-point-me-toward-your-pussy chastisement back at The Connaught had set me off-kilter, unsure of whether I should show her my eagerness or not.

"Of course, Lana. You may always touch me, unless I've asked you to hold on—like before—or if I have you tied up, of course."

Of course. My brain sent some weak signal that I was supposed to be suspicious of someone stating matter-of-factly that she was going to tie me up. But my body roared with desire, effectively drowning out any intellectual caution. My nipples hardened and I felt gooseflesh trail up my stomach.

"Tie me up?" I asked weakly. By that point, I was kneeling on the bed, a few inches away from Cybelle, who was still standing.

She reached for me and I held my breath. She toyed with a strand of my hair near my ear, her knuckles caressing my cheek and neck absently.

"Yes, love. Tie you up." Her hand trailed down my neck, then scraped over my sensitive nipple on her way down to the hot space between my thighs. She slid two fingers in with smooth efficiency—as if my pussy already belonged to her. There was no *as if* about it, I realized. I widened my thighs without thinking—to let her have what was already hers.

Her smile was wicked and wonderful. "That's right, pet. This is mine now."

I tried to breathe but the soft whiff of her perfume, and what must have been the scent of her desire, wafted around me and I felt drunk on all of it. My fingertips tingling with anticipation, I reached out to touch one of her smooth breasts, circling one dusky nipple while her fingers began to move inside me. The sensations were nearly overwhelming: Cybelle gasped when I hesitantly leaned in and kissed her nipple, the electricity passing hotly between us. The satiny texture of her breasts was mesmerizing: slightly tanned and soft, without a wrinkle or freckle. I leaned toward the other one, still in a dream, and took Cybelle's other nipple into my mouth.

Again, we both moaned at the same time, and her fingers began to work more furiously in and out of my cunt. Without knowing why, I bit down on Cybelle's nipple and before I realized what was happening, Cybelle had my hair in a tight hold and tugged ferociously.

"Naughty kitten..." Cybelle's blue eyes had taken on a dark violet cast and her skin was flushed with a mix of surprise and pleasure. And power. She tugged harder on my hair, straining my neck. "Are you very naughty, Lana?"

I tried to turn my head slightly so I could kiss her wrist, where the muscles and tendons were pulled taut. I couldn't quite reach her with my lips, so I extended my tongue until the tip licked lightly across her pulse.

Cybelle watched me with a strange objectivity, as if it was no longer her wrist being licked, but someone else's. "Are you are very hungry for me, Lana?"

Hungry? Bewitched! Under her spell! I no longer had words to describe what was happening inside my body, this almost animal need to taste and touch every inch of this woman. Or as much as she would allow. I nodded—really only a slight lift of my chin because of how tight her hold was in my hair.

Then she leaned in and licked from the base of my neck to the edge of my lip, with the very tip of her tongue, and I felt moist pleasure slipping down the inside of my thigh, and then— finally—Cybelle's mouth was on mine and I was hooked into her like a wild electrical cord that finally finds its current. The power that flowed between us had me grasping desperately for her, to hold-hold-hold lest I fly off into some vast dark abyss that surrounded us.

I became frantic during that kiss, fumbling with her garter and lacy underpants and pressing myself fully against the length of her warm almost-naked body, the two of us on our knees on the bed, pressed into each other with Cybelle soft and sweet one minute, and then fiercely wrenching my head back in that incredibly possessive, demanding hold the next.

"Oh, my pet, you're crying," Cybelle whispered between kisses. "You've been holding too much in." Her voice—like everything about her, I was coming to realize—was both commanding and inviting. She was utterly in charge, as if she were sitting behind some massive desk in some opulent corporate office with glass walls and priceless art, only to turn and face me with legs slightly open to reveal her glistening, waiting pussy. And all I wanted was to crawl across that imaginary room and have her shove my face between her thighs and feel that encouraging, knowing hand caressing my cheek or hair.

She positioned us so I was lying on my back, and she straddled my waist. She dipped her index finger into her pussy and then traced the moist tip around the edges of my mouth. I was on the verge of coming again, and the touch and taste of her slick juice nearly pitched me over the edge. I was ravenous.

I wrapped my lips around her single digit and sucked hard, wanting so much more.

"Oh how eager you are." Cybelle withdrew her finger from my mouth and I actually whimpered at the loss, trying to follow her finger with my tongue.

"Now, now my sweet. There's more where that came from."

Cybelle moved up my body, bringing her hips closer to my face, until her pussy was right by my mouth. "Would you like to lick me now?"

I'd never wanted anything more. I nodded dumbly and looked imploringly up at her. "Please…"

"Please what?"

"Please, *Maîtresse*."

"*Oui, ma petite.*" Even as she towered above me in that incredibly dominating position, she looked unaccountably generous and tender. I wanted to cry again. Instead, I grabbed onto her thighs for leverage, and began to lick and explore. Cybelle's answering moans of pleasure turned me on almost as much as the taste and feel of her quivering cunt against my lips. I realized that Cybelle was going easy on me—relatively speaking—reaching back to drag a finger gently across my slit, rather than attacking my clit the way she had before.

Meanwhile, I explored. God, I loved the taste of her, the mix of something citrusy sweet and something heady and dark. I twirled my tongue around her hard clit and she moaned, and swore something in French I didn't understand. I felt a bolt of pride that I was the one bringing this sophisticated, sensual, controlled woman to this place of desire and wicked, reckless pleasure.

I began to suck harder and work my lips firmly around her clit until she was crying out for more, and then she was *not* going easy on me anymore, but penetrating me with two and then three fingers and then she was toying with my asshole and I knew I was going to come again.

I stopped fucking her with my tongue long enough to ask if I had permission to come.

"*Absolument non!*" she barked. Unfortunately I had no problem understanding what *that* meant. She then proceeded to torment my pussy even more. I rededicated myself to hers, trying to lose myself in pleasing her, but she was driving me so hard—I discovered stomach muscles and pelvic floor muscles I didn't even know existed, clenching everything I could to hold off the imminent release—all while devouring her cunt. It was like holding up a feather to fend off a hurricane, but I managed somehow. The thought that she might never let me come again brought on a wave of near terror and I refocused all of that frenetic energy on her instead of on myself.

I pressed my palms into the soft skin of her inner thighs and then I was totally there. I made love to her; I fucked her with my mouth, pounding into her with tongue and teeth and lips. When I felt the anticipatory quiver of her impending orgasm, I sucked harder and harder until Cybelle screamed out her release, and somehow in the midst of her own screams of pleasure she (finally) gave me permission to do the same.

And we both exploded and flew and connected and laughed breathlessly, with a kind of ecstasy that I'd never known. A joyful, liberating, fiery pleasure.

Chapter 6

SOMETIME IN THE hours that followed, Cybelle moved out of reach and I made a pettish moue of disappointment that she was no longer in contact with me. I watched through half-open eyes as she put on an ivory silk robe and picked up her purse and sat by the fire. She retrieved her cell phone and began texting or checking email.

"Don't forget to text your friends like you promised," she said without looking up. She'd lit a cigarette and sat smoking it, one leg crossed over the other. I felt like I'd slipped into some sort of 1940s film noir. She was Ava Gardner and Rosalind Russell all rolled into one—dark, disheveled, and glorious.

I looked around until I spotted my small clutch on the floor and then got up to get it. I slid back under the covers and checked my messages. I shot off a few quick texts to Tommy and Sam, letting them know I was fine (I was tempted to say *awesome* but I didn't want to overdo it).

I slipped my phone back into my bag and watched her.

She dug into her purse for another cigarette and lit it with her gold flip lighter. As she exhaled, I could see the iron control returning. She slid her hair behind one ear and began thumbing quickly on the screen of her tablet.

"Go to sleep, Lana."

WHEN I WOKE up the next morning, the first thing I did, before opening my eyes, before thinking, was to lick the edge of my lips and taste Cybelle de la Vergne there. *God yes.* It had *not* been a dream.

I stretched my arm out, hoping to touch Cybelle across the bed, but there was nothing. I opened my eyes slowly and saw an envelope on the pillow—where Cybelle should have been, I thought with an almost childish petulance.

Looking around the room, I rubbed my eyes and pulled the silk sheet up over my chest in case anyone walked in. I picked up the envelope and pulled out the note.

Good morning, lovely. Your room is through the bathroom. Everything should be in order, but if there is anything you need, please text me at once. I will be in meetings all day, but will pick you up for drinks and dinner at six o'clock sharp. Wear the blue dress. C.

I stared at the paper and my first reaction was to reach between my legs and jack off to the smell of Cybelle's perfume that clung to the stationery. Before my fingertips reached their destination, I remembered my new lack of onanism—that I had blithely agreed to—and groaned.

Instead of languishing in the sheets—which reeked of multiple orgasms and only made me want to masturbate more—I tossed back the covers and walked naked across the room and on into the bathroom.

The white marble space was big and airy and splendid. Like everything to do with Cybelle, it was perfect. I continued through to the other room—*my room*, I thought with a shiver of delight—and I gasped at what I saw. The room was more of an artist's garret, with a sloped half roof composed of large glass panes. There was a single bed, rather military in a way, and a drafting table with a cup filled with various black ink pens and several different sketchpads. All expensive and of the highest quality. Even the chair was one of the pricey ergonomic ones I'd always promised myself but never thought I deserved.

Holy shit. Cybelle got shit done. Crossing the room, I opened the closet door and gasped again. Almost as big as the bedroom, the closet had built-in racks and shelves on three sides, all hung with what looked to be a complete wardrobe. All the tags were still on and I pulled one into my hand—all in my size. The aforementioned blue dress was hanging separately, on one of the hooks in front of the rest of the hanging clothes. It was made of some stretchy material that would make me feel incredibly self-conscious and exposed. Even though it had long sleeves and a neckline that could almost be considered modest, the narrow cut and elastic texture would show every inch of me. This was going to be hellish.

And the shoes.

The fucking shoes were amazing. Truth be told, I'm not that into shoes. I mean, I like my knee-high boots and clunky Doc Martens and the occasional pair of artsy platform shoes, but *holy fuck*. I bent down and touched kid leather ankle boots, and then brought one to my nose and inhaled. The smell was incredible—luxury, indulgence, desire. Cybelle.

There was a knock at the door and I panicked. "Who is it?" I was crouched there naked, sniffing a boot for God's sake.

"Ms. Mercer? My name is William and I'm the houseman." He spoke through the closed door. "Do you have everything you need?" His voice was trimmed with a Scottish accent, and as if I hadn't had enough orgasms grinding with Cybelle all night long, the lilt of his voice made me feel a new flutter of arousal.

"Uh, I'm just in here…looking for a robe."

"There's one on the hook on the back of the closet door," he suggested helpfully. "I have breakfast for you. And your friends are expected at nine o'clock."

I grabbed the robe that was hanging where he said and tried not to moan as the weight of the heavy Japanese silk caressed my already titillated body. I opened the door and forced myself not to drool. Of course Cybelle would have a mansion full of French tutors and Scottish housemen who made me want to drop to my knees and suck cock before I'd even had a cup of coffee.

As if he could read my mind, William's eyes sparkled and he nodded, even though I hadn't said anything. "You are quite as lovely as Mme de la Vergne led us to believe. May I come in?" He lifted the tray slightly to indicate he was holding it for me and wished to place it down.

"Oh, of course!" I stepped aside, pulling the door wider, and gestured for him to enter. "And what guests are you talking about?"

"Your friends Sam and Tom have been invited round, to work out in the private gym with us. A car and driver went to fetch them. Cybelle prefers that you stay nearby today, in case she has any unexpected cancellations during the afternoon and is able to return home for a brief…visit."

I got all worked up all over again at the mere mention of Cybelle…and preferences and cancellations and *visits*. I tried to shake off my budding desire since there was fuck all I could do about it. Instead, I watched as the tall, muscular man walked over to an antique round table in the corner, between two chairs against the wall. He set the tray there and then took off a small cloth and proceeded to set the table as if I were a queen having my private meal with linen and silver and crystal.

"Oh, you don't need to do that," I blurted. "I'll just eat it off the tray. I'm sure you have other things to do rather than fussing over me."

He looked up when he had finished adjusting the single peony in the crystal bud vase. "In fact," he said as he rose to his considerable height, "today I have no occupation other than *fussing* over you. Cybelle has asked me to see to your *every* need. She was particularly concerned that you would wake up with certain…physical requirements that I should tend to."

"She did?" I whispered. Because *fuck god* I had woken up with *physical requirements* all right, and not being able to touch myself was making me feel like a bomb about to blow.

"Yes, she did," he answered with that accommodating half-smile of his.

"Who are you?" I asked abruptly.

He smiled wider, but he didn't make any move to come closer to me. Standing with his hands clasped loosely behind his back, he appeared to be compliant and powerful all at once. His fitted black T-shirt and low-slung blue jeans were like a uniform and an invitation all rolled into one. "I used to belong to Cybelle's husband, David. I had an arrangement with him last year, much like the one I suspect you have with Cybelle now. And then when my year was over, they both asked if I wanted to stay on as…a helper, I guess you'd call it. I'm studying law and have two more years. I live downstairs and mind the house and, you know." He shrugged but there was nothing shy or coy about it. He was actually saying *you know* because I did *know*.

I sized him up, no longer caring that my gaze was hungry and blatant. "So, what you're saying is…Cybelle told you to do whatever I…whatever I want?"

His shoulders relaxed as if the idea pleased him to the marrow of his bones—to obey me, or perhaps even somehow by proxy, to obey David.

"Precisely. Your wish. My command. That sort of thing." His voice was already getting rough with desire, or compliance, or whatever it was that turned him on. I would wear any too-tight blue dress, any painful stilettos, and I would be beautiful and perfect when Cybelle came to get me at six o'clock—because this was going to be the best year of my fucking life and it was all thanks to Cybelle de la Vergne.

And I was nothing if not grateful.

Untying the knot of my robe, I felt like I was channeling another one of those 1940s femme fatales. And it felt fucking awesome.

"Come now, sweet William, and let me see your cock."

He hummed his agreement and began to undo the buttons of his jeans until his thick cock sprang free, and we both moaned.

"Do you have condoms?" I asked.

"Of course," he said easily, pulling a foil packet out of his pocket. He stood there patiently, in T-shirt and unfastened jeans, barefoot, with his cock just…there.

I walked closer to him. "Excellent." I traced the round bulk of his biceps and felt his body respond. Then I reached down and touched the soft tip of his straining cock with one finger. "I think I'd like to fuck you slow and steady, William, until I come around your cock. And then I'll be ready for breakfast. How does that sound?"

"As you wish." He put on the condom as I watched in amazement. "Would you like me clothed or naked?" he asked politely.

"Oh, I think clothed, don't you?" I nudged him gently until he sat on the edge of the narrow bed. "I think we're both very busy and don't have time for a seduction or striptease. You put on the condom; I fuck you, hard and slow. How does that sound?"

"Ideal," he nearly growled.

"Lie back William," I ordered. And I realized I had no desire to order Cybelle around—which would have been impossible in any case—but it gave me a deep thrill to command this well-built stranger to recline on that narrow bed so I could use him like my very own human sex toy.

He was perfectly put together. I admired him as I walked the few steps to where he lay obediently waiting for me. Fully clothed except for that shimmering sheathed cock sticking up luridly from his lap. I lifted one leg over his thighs and lowered my moist cunt onto his waiting shaft.

"Do you ever get to come?" I asked, as I sank down to the hilt, groaning with the satisfaction of it. Heaven.

"Very rarely," he answered.

I rested my palms on his shoulders, then shut my eyes and began to move my hips. The feel of denim and rivets and zipper pressing into my ass as I pulled up and slid down onto his cock added to my pleasure. I always came fast first thing in the morning and this was no different. What a fool I'd been to think Cybelle would deny me anything. The mere thought of Cybelle sent me flying into my orgasm, a clutching reminder of the numerous explosions I'd experienced the night before. I slowed down, eventually, my clit overly sensitized, my body limp and satisfied—for the moment.

I let my head fall back and then took a deep breath, eyes closed, lungs full. What type of rabbit hole had I fallen down? I straightened my spine and looked into William's eyes. He was passive, yet present. No guile or agenda. "Are you really here just to serve me?" I asked.

"There is no *just* about it." His smile deepened.

"I feel like it might take me a little while to…adapt." My hands roamed lazily over the muscles on his chest and stomach, through the taut fabric of his shirt.

"You'll be amazed how quickly you adapt to having me at your service." He slid his hands up and down my bare thighs, his thick fingers massaging me gently.

I shifted my hips and realized he was just as hard as when we'd started. "Is there a limit to how often you can…serve me?" I clenched my ass and pussy and watched his face twitch, ever so slightly, as I increased the pressure around his cock.

"A physical limit?" he asked.

I smiled in return. "No, I meant, do you have certain hours?"

"Technically I'm on duty from eight in the morning until four in the afternoon." He flexed and tilted his hips very slightly. But just enough.

I bit my lower lip and sighed happily. "Excellent." Then I stood up quickly, enjoying his gasp as he worked to repress his reaction to my abrupt withdrawal. Walking toward the bathroom, I said, "In that case, I'll most likely want to fuck you again after our workout."

"Yes, Ms. Mercer. Is there anything else?"

"Not for now. Thanks, William." I glanced over my right shoulder.

"My pleasure, Ms. Mercer." He was immaculately put together—no rude erections sticking out anywhere—when he bowed slightly and left the room.

Once I was alone in the bathroom, I stared at my reflection in the mirror for many minutes, wondering who I was, or more importantly, who I was becoming. Was all of this some crazy escapade? Antics I would look back upon years later, marveling wistfully about the outlandish larks of my youth?

My heartbeat started to pound wildly at the lie. Wherever this led with Cybelle, whatever it ended up becoming—everything or nothing—I would never again demean or downplay my deepest pleasure by thinking of it as some kind of *foolishness*. I'd never felt more real, more authentic, more myself, than I had in the past twenty-four hours. If that made me a fool in the eyes of others, then that was on them.

I looked into my own eyes—a little bloodshot, a little smudged, maybe—but there was a calmness there I hadn't seen in years. I recognized the brave, kind girl I'd once been in the woman I'd become.

And she deserved to thrive.

Also by Megan Mulry

A Royal Pain
Bound to be a Bride
Bound to Be a Groom
Bound with Honor
Bound with Love
Bound with Passion
Encore
If the Shoe Fits
In Love Again
R is for Rebel
Roulette
The Wallflowers

About the Author

Megan Mulry writes sexy, stylish, romantic fiction. Her first book, *A Royal Pain*, was an NPR Best Book of 2012 and *USA Today* bestseller. Before discovering her passion for romance novels, she worked in magazine publishing and finance. After many years in New York, Boston, London, and Chicago, she now lives with her family in Florida.

We Are All Found Things

M. O'Keefe

Rennie's trying to forget her past; her mysterious new tenant is trying to keep his past a secret. But when Rennie finds out the truth about Luka she discovers as much about herself as she does her innocent lover.

Chapter 1

~ SPRING ~

I HAD THE door open to the shop, and the breeze that came through smelled like rain and weed.

The guys from the garage next door were smoking outside again.

Which was completely okay with me. Not for the contact high but for the proof that I wasn't alone way out here on the edge of Camden. This industrial part of North Minneapolis could feel like the far side of the moon.

I bought this loft space because I needed the room. Shit was taking off for me—work-wise—and I needed my forge and welding equipment in a place bigger than the garage behind my house. And when I took the lease in the New Year, I knew it was a rough neighborhood, but jeez.

Four break-ins. In less than three months.

I've lost all my copper. My bits of silver. A lot of my steel. The fuckers were smart.

Thank God most of my equipment was too heavy to steal.

Anyway, hopefully all that was going to end shortly.

I was working a custom piece today. A bed frame for some wealthy *Game of Thrones* uber-fan. It was sharp and gnarly, a little dorky with a whole lot of badass thrown in. Which frankly, was my bread and butter.

"Hullo?"

Crap. Was it one already?

"Hello!" I pulled off my mask and stood up so I could see over the headboard. "Hey! I'm back here!"

I turned off my propane, shook off my gloves and shrugged out of my leather apron as I jumped around my worktables and equipment toward the front door.

Overeager? Yes. I was a little scared the dude might run.

Three other guys had come and gone once they saw the neighborhood.

A blond man stood in the doorway. Well, he kind of took up the doorway. He was big. Tall and wide. His straight blond hair fell down around his shoulders and I won't lie—for a second I thought he was that Thor actor.

But he turned toward me and the face was different. It was sharp. All nose and cheekbones, eyes the white-blue at the center of a propane flame.

"Are you Rennie Hernandez?" he asked, glancing down at a slip of paper held in his giant hand.

"I am. Are you Luka Samuelson?"

He grinned and I had no idea how old he was, but that grin was pure boy. And in contrast with the body and the face and the eyes—the whole package of Luka Samuelson was a little dorky with a whole lot of badass thrown in.

My bread and butter.

Some bell rang in the back of my head. And suddenly he seemed familiar not because of his resemblance to a movie star…but something else.

I'd seen him somewhere before.

Where?

I felt interest curl up along all my edges.

"So, you're here about the ad," I said, walking closer to the door.

I chimed a little when I moved, on account of my necklaces. He heard the noise and glanced up, his sharp eyes tracking over my body, finding the source of the sound.

His gaze was through. A bit like being pinned to a wall and frisked.

I was short but strong from my work, and I made a point of never feeling small. Of never being small. I took up all the space and all the air I could—but there was something about this guy that made me feel diminutive. I didn't like it.

But I didn't hate it either.

"I am," he said. "The ad said that rent was free as long as I was here every night and kept an eye on the place. Seems a bit too good to be true."

"That's the deal, on account of there have been a few break-ins and I've lost a lot of material."

"You're a welder?" He eyes took in all my equipment over my shoulder. The giant wings with the bronze-and-silver filigree hanging from the ceiling.

"Among other things."

The spring sunlight falling through the door behind him lit him up, gave him an aura and made the dust particles floating around his blond hair glitter.

"Have we met before?" I asked, because it was killing me.

He blinked and just...shuttered.

Just closed up. No more boyish smile. No more propane gaze. He was there...but not really. The truth of him, he buried deep under his skin.

I was familiar with the process because my dad was pretty good at that. So was I, frankly. Being here and then in the next minute…being gone. It was a skill and I respected it.

I knew what it meant.

I wouldn't press.

But it was going to keep me up at night, wondering who this guy was.

"No," he said definitively. "I've only been in Minneapolis since the first snowfall."

Kind of a weird way of putting it, but okay.

"Well, anyway," I said. "I just need someone here to call the cops if they feel like something suspicious is happening. I don't need a hero with a gun."

"I have a rifle. Licensed."

Hunters were thick on the ground in Minneapolis. Only to be outnumbered by fisherman.

"That's fine."

"I promise not to be a hero," he said, smiling again.

My gut was pretty ironclad but sometimes my pussy got invested and messed things up in terms of my people-reading skills. So, while I was ready to tell this guy to move right on in to the tiny bedroom upstairs – and perhaps at some point—my vagina, this was far too important to let my hormones weigh in.

"I work here nearly every day," I said. "I start early, usually around 5:00 a.m. It's loud and it's smelly."

"I work with a big game vet in town. My days start around that time too."

Well, that was convenient.

"Do you have references?" I asked, and he pulled a piece of paper out of his back pocket. He wore faded jeans, worn white around the seams, grommets and zipper.

I tried not to stare.

"My boss is on there as well as a police officer and one of the clients I do quite a bit of work for. All of them said you could call them."

I nodded and tucked the paper into my own back pocket. "Why do you want to live here?"

"Free rent." His eyebrows arched. "That's not enough reason?"

"Free rent in a shitty neighborhood with some implied threat of danger. You're not scared?"

He blinked and it seemed like his entire body settled into itself. God, he was big. So big. And I realized a guy that size with a rifle, who carried himself the way he did, probably wasn't scared of much.

"No," he said. "I'm not scared."

That shouldn't be hot. But it was hot.

"You want to see the room?" I asked.

He nodded, sending his blond hair swinging, and we went upstairs to the small loft. Between the door to the bathroom and the bedroom was a window that led to a fire escape. I went out there sometimes when the shop got too hot. Or when I was having a tough time with a project or…really, anytime I felt the need to be up and out of things, including my own head.

I pushed open the door to the bedroom. He ducked his head in and looked around. Futon. Desk. Tiny closet.

"Why don't you live here?" he asked.

"Because I have a house already."

"Why not rent somewhere safer?"

"I don't know, why don't I have a million dollars?"

"Fair point." Again that boyish, dorky smile and I smiled back. I was not a smiler by nature. I always felt like I was revealing something when I smiled. Some hidden part of me, a secret I didn't particularly want to share, but somehow couldn't help.

But I smiled at this guy, unsure of what I exposed, but keenly aware that I was exposing something.

For a second we just stood there grinning at each other.

But then he coughed, breaking the stupid spell I was under and I glanced away, out the window with the view of the garage on the corner and some kids playing road hockey in the alley.

"The futon and the desk come with the unit," I told him and opened the door to the bathroom.

Toilet. Sink. Tiny little shower.

"Shower might be tight." As surreptitiously as I could, I glanced over his body again.

"They usually are," he said in the manner of a man used to living in a body too big for most things.

He opened the small cabinet under the sink, saw my tampons, my giant first aid kit, the box of condoms and all the extra rolls of toilet paper. He nodded as if all that made sense and then shut the door and stepped out.

"Looks fine."

Bathroom tour complete.

I almost told him about the fire escape and the view and how on a good day the smell of the river came by on the wind. And how you could hear the neighborhood moms yelling at their kids to stay out of trouble and come in for dinner. But that was all still mine and as much as I needed someone here, I wasn't quite ready to share my fire escape.

So, instead I headed back down the stairs to the first floor. I could feel him right behind me. Taking up so much space. He smelled like spring in Minnesota—pine, ice and mud.

"We can share the stuff in the kitchen. Coffeemaker, toaster. Microwave and stuff. Everything except my booze."

"I don't drink," he said.

"I was joking," I told him.

"Oh."

"Do you have any questions for me?" I asked because all my nice buzzy attraction was getting weird.

He asked about the break-ins. The neighborhood.

I told him the total truth, because there was no point in having him move in only to move out a few days later. He seemed completely unfazed by all of it.

I showed him the kitchen. The garbage system. I had a thing about composting.

And that seemed the end of the tour.

We stood by my old beat-up leather napping couch.

He was looking up at my wings, tilting his head as if to get a better angle. "Those are amazing. Did you make them?"

"Part of them. I'll give you a call in a few days," I said instead of talking about the wings. See, I had my own *keep out* signs. "After I talk to your references."

He nodded, his hair slipping over his shoulders.

Seriously, the guy was painfully attractive. I imagined him, just briefly, as a Viking, swinging around an axe. Doing some pillaging.

"Thank you, Rennie," he said with lovely politeness. We shook hands, my calloused, blistered hand swallowed up by his calloused blistered hand and I felt myself grow shy for just a moment.

Which was not at all my style.

He left and I closed the door behind him. From my back pocket I pulled out his references and called them all.

"He stays at my house," his boss said with the kind of Minnesota accent that indicated she'd never left the state. "Well, the tiny apartment over my garage. My kids love him. Our clients love him. He's just a real good guy."

"Great to hear," I told her.

"He's quiet. A bit intense sometimes. Awkward. But I think that's just how he was raised."

"Raised?" I asked, the skin on my neck prickling.

She was silent for a moment. And all my spidey senses tingled.

"Do you—" She cut herself off.

"Do I what?" I asked, when the silence stretched on.

"Nothing." She laughed, awkwardly. "Nothing at all."

The rest of his references gave Luka glowing recommendations so I decided not to wait another day—like he was some guy I met at a bar, and I was trying to play it cool. I called him a few hours after I met him and told him he could move in next week.

All night long it bothered me, this sense that I knew Luka. And all night I told myself I was imagining things. That we'd had a little chemistry and he looked like a very famous movie star—those two things were working against me. Making me think there was a memory when there wasn't.

But at three in the morning I woke up with a gasp. I pitched forward in bed, my hand over my heart.

The Mountain Man from Minnesota.

I grabbed my phone and Google confirmed it.

Luka Samuelson was The Mountain Man From Minnesota.

Chapter 2

~ SUMMER ~

Too hot. Too freaking hot to do anything.

I'd come in after sunset, thinking the day would have cooled down enough for me to finish some work on the statue for the Walker Center Sculpture Park. That's right, I was going in with the spoon and cherry. But I looked at my forge and my welding equipment and thought fuck no.

Instead I walked to the fridge and grabbed a cold beer.

It was hot here, it was hot at home. It was hot everywhere. Except maybe the fire escape. It was high up out of the concrete and if there was a chance of finding a breeze—it would be there.

But all I did was look at the stairs.

Luka had been home when I came in; he came to stand out on the second floor landing when he heard the alarm go off.

"Hullo," he'd said when he saw me.

"Hello," I'd said. "Is it gonna bother you if I work?"

"Nope." And then he went back to his room.

The day he moved in, I almost said something. I almost said;

You're the Mountain Man From Minnesota. You saved that girl. Your dad—

But then he looked up at me, his backpack over his back, his rifle case in hand, and those blue eyes must have seen what I was about to do. Must have seen this moment I was pushing us into and he stood up straight and he…closed up.

Just like the day he applied for the job.

Just like Dad when I asked about Mom.

Just like me anytime anyone asked me…anything.

His entire body said *No. Don't.* And his eyes all but begged me to pretend I didn't know.

So, that was what I'd been doing. Pretending I didn't know who he was.

Which was cool. I respected that. He didn't owe me his pain. He was a tenant, and so far a great one. No more burglaries. He called the cops once, but that was all.

Over the past few months we'd settled into a routine, Luka and me. He was doing some night classes, and if he was home while I was working, sometimes he'd come downstairs and study at one of the stools at the bar in the kitchen. He never told me what classes he was taking and I didn't pry.

A few times he helped me bring in new materials, something that went a whole lot faster if he was around. Once or twice he just stretched out on the couch and read while I worked.

We didn't talk much.

But somehow the silence we lived in downstairs was comfortable. And intimate. He made me tea, brought it to me in my favorite mug. The one with the unicorn on it. Sometimes we'd split a pizza or pierogis from the Polish place down the street.

All without saying anything about his past. All without saying much at all.

But upstairs felt so much like his domain. If he didn't come down, I didn't go up. Like we'd drawn lines when he moved in and I didn't even use the bathroom upstairs much anymore.

But God, I wanted to drink this beer on my fire escape.

Was that so wrong?

Fuck no, I decided. It was my goddamned building. He was probably sleeping anyway—the guy worked harder than me, and that was saying something.

I mean the chances he was on the fire escape were pretty small.

Which, really, was the only reason I grabbed another beer and headed up. As soundlessly as I could, I climbed the stairs and then out the window in the hallway between his bedroom and the bathroom onto the fire escape.

The second I stood on the metal landing, the city and its neon landscape spread out in front of me, it was cooler.

Thank God. I closed my eyes and let the breeze blow my hair across my face. I let it flirt with my shirt, pressing it against my breasts. I stood there for a long time, letting the breeze do its good work.

"Hey."

I screamed and jumped.

"Sorry! I'm so sorry."

I looked back to find Luka sitting on the steps above me. He was shrouded in shadow, only revealed by the glitter of his eyes and flashing white of his teeth. When he turned his head, I saw that he'd pulled his white-blond hair up in one of those messy man-buns, that had no business looking good. Not at all.

But God, it did.

"I didn't mean to startle you," he said, his face dark, his voice quiet.

"It's all right. I thought you were sleeping." Crap. This little bubble we were in made of heat and night was somehow made smaller by mentioning him sleeping.

"Too hot," he said and I could hear in his voice that he was smiling.

"No kidding. You want a beer?" I asked and held out the icy cold bottle.

"Thanks," he said and to my surprise he took it, but instead of drinking it he pressed it to his neck. His forehead.

"Can I join you?" I played with fire for a living so I totally recognized the danger I was courting.

This was his upstairs world. And it was complicated. Loaded with night. Heat. Beer. My raging curiosity about him.

The chemistry.

"Sure."

He moved up a few steps and shifted his legs as if to make room for me, But I sat several steps beneath him and turned sideways. The metal step bit through my denim and the railing was a hard rod against my back.

"Hot," I said again, because it bore repeating.

"So hot."

I drank my beer. He didn't drink his.

I'd squashed the question for months, but it was here, again. Maybe because we were upstairs and not down.

Maybe because I could feel the heat of him all along my shoulder.

Are you the Mountain Man from Minnesota?

Don't say it. Do not say it.

"Someone new is moving in on the corner," I said, instead.

"A brewery."

"Like beer brewery?"

"That's what the guys in the shop said."

"Well, they would know."

Luka laughed a little. "They do like to gossip."

I took another sip from my beer. He held his unopened in his hands.

"Did you grow up in Minneapolis?" he asked.

"Nope." I could feel my own doors locking, my own shutters coming down over my windows. *Stop. You want him to open up to you, you have to open up to him. Maybe. Or something.*

"Oklahoma," I said. "I came here for grad school six years ago. Never left."

"Grad school?"

"Art."

He shifted on the steps and his knee pressed briefly into my shoulder, and the heat of us, the sweat between us, was not off-putting. I felt my skin was too tight and my body was too tight. I needed something to break me open.

I glanced at him; his blue eyes found mine in the moonlight and for a minute it seemed possible that he needed the same. He needed something to break him open.

His eyes took in my tank top and the pile of hair on top of my head. It was as if he traced each strand looking for the one piece he could pull and the whole thing would tumble down around me.

He wanted to touch me.

I could feel it in the air between us. Smell it. Taste it even.

Kiss me, I thought. Touch me.

But instead he said: "A dog at one of the farms I visit had puppies."

"Yeah?"

"Yeah. I was thinking of maybe taking one of them. He'd go to work with me, but he'd be here at night."

"A dog?" I smiled at the idea. I didn't want the responsibility of having a dog, but I wouldn't mind having one around if someone else was taking care of it. "I had a dog growing up. Or my dad did, I guess. He was totally my dad's dog. Paco just barely tolerated me."

"We had dogs too. Lots of them. We didn't name them."

It was the very first time he'd mentioned his past and I held my breath waiting for more. But he was silent as stone.

"Go ahead and get a dog," I said. "But you have to name him."

That made him smile at me and it wasn't unlike getting my father to smile. That serious man with so much weight on his shoulders. I felt far too clever for so small a thing.

"I've never lived in the city during the summer," he said. A car alarm went off in the distance. A woman shouted.

I exhaled slowly. Carefully.

"I spent my whole life in the woods," he said. "Cities were bad. That's what I was always told. All the bad things—corruption and crime and evil…it all happens in the city."

"Evil happens everywhere." I was feigning a kind of nonchalance. I doubted it was believable.

It happened to you, I wanted to say. *Out in the woods. It lived with you.*

He laughed and used the collar of his shirt to catch a bead of sweat rolling down his neck.

"But so far…" He sighed. "So far the city is just hotter."

I laughed.

He shifted and so did I and my shoulder touched his knee. I waited for him to shift away. To move. To keep the distance between us, but he didn't. The denim of his pants pressed into my skin and I could feel his sweat and his heat and his…intention. This wasn't an accident. He was touching me on purpose.

"It's lonely too," he said. "All these people and I'm…I'm so fucking lonely."

The swearing was a little shocking. Almost as much as the admission.

It doesn't have to be would be the cheesiest thing to say. The stupidest so I just managed to swallow it back. I took a sip of beer to make sure that the words stayed down.

"Anyplace can be lonely," I said. "I've been in relationships that were the loneliest place on earth."

He made a laughing sound in his throat and I glanced up at him, smiling myself.

Oh God, his eyes. His entire body was coiled, heated with some kind of intention. Some internal heat. Some wild instinct.

I felt the same instinct rise up in me, fierce and unguarded.

"Luka—"

"I don't...."

He swallowed, his throat wet with sweat. The shoulders of his gray shirt dark with sweat. I knew I looked the same, wet and steaming. We were evaporating in the heat between us.

Carefully, like I might spook, he touched my hair, carefully tugged it, and fuck, wouldn't you know, it all came down around my shoulders. I had no idea I was a puzzle that could be solved so easily.

"I want to kiss you," I said. He blinked, holding himself so still it had to hurt. I could see his heart beating in his throat.

"Can I? Kiss you?"

"Do it."

He said it like I was going to remove a bullet from his skin. Like I was going to hurt him with force. And I didn't know how to get around his obvious discomfort. I almost said forget it.

But then he said, "Fuck...just—" He grabbed my arms and hauled me up and across the metal steps. Into the open vee of his legs. His mouth met mine, open and wet and hungry.

I shook off his hands and wrapped my arms around his neck, better to hold onto him. Better to grip his head. And he was doing the same to me. His hands in my hair, too hard. Too wild. But it didn't matter.

My mouth was cool from the beer and his was hot. He tasted of mint and summer. Of man and coppery desire. He sucked on me like I was an ice cube he wanted to melt on his tongue. Sweat pooled and ran between us and he held me close to him in his fists. Fists in my hair and my shirt.

It was rough. So rough. Too much and not enough all at the same time.

Gleeful and on fire I cried out against him.

Loud.

The sound vibrated up through my chest, up my throat across my lips into his mouth.

Suddenly he stopped. He let go of me so fast I fell back on my heels between his legs. I would have fallen down the steps but I caught myself on his thighs, hard and round under my hands. So big I could stretch my fingers out as far as they could go and I wouldn't even cover the tops.

His face was red and running with sweat. His lips swollen from my teeth. His eyes wide with horror. With horror. Real…horror.

His hands were lifted, frozen over my shoulders, like he wasn't sure if he was going to grab me or push me away.

I dropped my hands from his thighs and fell back against the railing, the metal scraping my back. I barely felt it, stunned by his horror.

Was I hurting him? What…what happened?

"I'm sorry," he said.

"There's nothing…"

He squeezed his eyes shut. All the way shut, like a child with a nightmare, and I got to my feet, trying to catch my breath.

"Are you okay?" I asked, because he seemed so not okay.

His eyes flew open. "Are you?"

"I'm fine…" I laughed, a kind of awkward and gusting thing. Part laugh part groan.

He got to his feet and I had to step away again or risk falling down. He reached out for me but stopped when he saw I was fine.

"I'm really sorry," he said.

And then he was gone.

For a giant man he was down the steps, past me and through the window so fast and so silently it was eerie.

And then I was alone on the fire escape. With the moon and the heat and a beer and a thousand questions. And no relief in sight.

Chapter 3

~ FALL ~

THE INTERVIEW AIRED in November. On the Sunday just after Thanksgiving.

Anna, the girl Luka saved, had come of age and written a book and now she was on air with Leslie Stahl. I watched it on the exact same couch on which I'd watched his story unfold four years ago.

It was just as awful as it was four years ago. Worse even. Anna was being so brave. So careful.

I hope Luka isn't watching.

That was all I could think.

Please don't let Luka be watching.

After that I saw him even less. He didn't come downstairs anymore in the loft. There was no more tea. No more studying at the counter.

If he heard the alarm go off in the loft when I came in, he'd come to the second floor landing—see it was me and then go back to his room.

A few times I stood at the bottom of the steps and thought about going up there. Thought about asking him if he was okay.

But then I chickened out.

So, just before the holidays, I texted him.

I won't be coming in this week. But I will be having a New Year's

Eve party at the loft with some people from the neighborhood and some friends. Would you like to come? You're more than welcome. I haven't seen much of you.

He wrote back:

Thank you.

I stared down at my phone for a long time. But he didn't text anything else.

Chapter 4

~ WINTER ~

PAULO AND I sucked back the shots and then I tipped my glass upside down on the counter, letting him know he could keep the rest of his tequila to himself.

"*No mames!*" he said, his silver eyebrows lifted in surprise.

"I'm onto you, Paulo," I answered in English. Since Dad died I didn't speak Spanish much anymore. I didn't crave his posole for breakfast. I didn't go to mass. Or light candles for him and my abuela. Dad died and I immediately moved. Left everything I'd been behind. "You just want to get me drunk so you can take advantage."

He laughed and poured himself another shot. "No one takes advantage of you, Rennie. No one."

He knocked back the shot and I started dancing backward to the dance floor.

"You coming with me?" I asked. Rolling my hips, dipping my shoulders. I loved the way my brown skin looked under the Christmas lights, the way my rings gleamed. I loved everything tonight.

"I like to watch." He cocked that lean hip in those two-hundred-dollar blue jeans against the counter and I heard the sound of panties dropping all across the land.

Jesus. Paulo was so handsome it hurt. But for some reason I

couldn't do it.

Well, not some reason.

A Luka reason.

After that night on the fire escape I'd done my best to fuck him out of my head. Well, Paulo had done his best, but in the end it didn't work.

I couldn't *not* think of Luka and that kiss.

And I didn't want to think about it anymore.

Tonight was for tequila and dancing. It was New Year's and my only tradition was getting blind drunk and trying to forget.

I lifted my hands above my head and waded into the dance floor. It was my party so I could say it—this was the best damn party.

In the most fucked-up way.

The guys from the custom hot-rod shop on the corner—most of them were here. They'd been in this desolate part of Minneapolis as long as I had and we'd grown friendly. Ish.

The microbrew guys who'd just moved onto the block came with a keg. That was nice.

The beer was shit, but it was nice.

And they'd all shown up in their tight plaid shirts with their beards and smarty-pants glasses.

A little bit; I loved them.

And to round it all off there was a group of art students from the grad program at the U.

We'd met on the gallery circuit the past few years and some of them were okay. Some of them were awful. A few were fucking fantastic.

Say for instance Priya and Keesha, who'd brought the weed brownies (honestly, like it was undergrad week or something), and were grinding each other in the corner of the dance floor.

Much to the Neanderthal pleasure of the shop guys.

Scattered amid that strange assortment were some other artists and a few of my models. Like Paulo.

And tonight—everyone was young and beautiful and shit was easy.

The lightest of my welding equipment had been pushed to the side, the giant steel wings with the filigree feathers that I never seemed to have time to finish were wrapped in Christmas lights.

It was festive. It was weird. It was perfect.

The bracelets clinked and my necklaces got tangled with the hair at the back of my neck but I closed my eyes and gave into it. Gave into it all. The tequila. The music. The scent of lust and ozone in the air.

A sudden draft, the cold of Minneapolis in the winter, announced the entrance of another person, and everyone turned to the door.

A big man stood in the doorway, in a thick black coat and a black knit cap pulled down low over his ears. His face was flushed from the cold. Bright and pink.

Everyone else went back to partying.

I could only stare.

Luka.

Shit. He must have forgotten about the party.

Petey, his dog, saw me and came over to sit on my foot, nosing my hand until I patted him.

Luka's white/blue gaze took in the lights and the crowd. His whole body arrested and he dropped that aloof expression of his that made me crazy with curiosity and a lust I was growing increasingly embarrassed over.

All the people scared Luka—well, maybe *scare* wasn't the

right word. I didn't know the guy well enough to know what scared him. But he was clearly uncomfortable walking into the noise and heat of my party, and it took him a minute to hide it.

A minute, there at the doorway to gather himself.

Among the hipsters and hyper-aware models, the gearheads with the grease under their fingernails, he seemed altogether different.

Altogether…more.

More real. More awkward. More haunted and hunted. More self-contained.

More fascinating, clearly. To me anyway.

Stay? Go? Which one was it going to be?

It shouldn't matter to me. I tried to make it not matter to me. But somehow it didn't work. I wanted him to stay.

I wanted him.

He took off his knit cap, his white-blond hair falling down into his eyes.

Stay. He was staying. Slowly, I blew out the breath I'd been holding and told my hormones to give it a break. He would undoubtedly go right up to the room he lived in. Luka might not go back into the freezing cold night (because who would) but that did not mean we were going to be having tequila shots and dancing.

Though God…Luka dancing. Dancing with Luka.

My hormones were *not* giving it a break.

Petey went to examine the kitchen floor, littered with delicacies.

"Your junkyard dog is here," John, a model and former lover, muttered in my ear. That was John's strong suit. Muttering in ears. We'd been together four years ago when Luka had been all over the newspapers. Without sleeping we'd sat on my couch and followed the story day and night for a week. We were all wrapped up in the Mountain Man from Minnesota updates (never mind that there were no mountains in Minnesota—whatever, who needs journalistic integrity when you have a shot at such alliteration).

John and I watched Luka fall from hero to victim to suspect all in a week's time. And a few months ago I made the mistake of telling John that Luka was living in my loft, and now he wasn't letting that shit go.

"Did you see that interview with the girl a few weeks ago?" John said. "Jesus—"

"Her name is Anna," I said. *The girl*. Like she was a part in a play that needed casting.

"Right. Whatever. Anna. The point is that was some harrowing shit. I get you're a tough woman, Rennie. And that guy has…charms. But he's dangerous. And I worry—"

"Fuck off, John." John's jealousy stank like privilege and failure. I grabbed a glass of wine and made my way through the crowd toward the door.

And Luka, still standing in the doorway like he'd grown roots.

If I were to sculpt him I'd use earth elements. Wood and clay. Bone would be interesting. There'd been that installation at the Walker a few years back with the repurposed old classroom skeletons. That would work. So would fur. I'd made my name in metal but that was far too cold for Luka.

Luka breathed. He pulsed. He illuminated.

The dark room seemed brighter for his being in it.

I opened my mouth to yell his name over the noise but before the word was out of my mouth he looked my way. It was strange how he did that. How he found me. It wasn't just that he saw me. Or heard me. It was like he scented me before he saw me.

Felt me in the air of the room.

"You're having a party," he said in his clipped way. Observation more than question.

"I am. I told you—"

"I forgot." He smiled, that sheepish boy smile so out of context on his face. The loud heart of the party was over on the dance floor and even that was thinning into the darker corners my studio space offered.

"Wine? Beer?" I asked.

Luka surprised me by taking the wine. "Thank you." He dropped his leather work bag down by the door. "What's the party for?"

"New Year's!" I pointed up to the wings, draped in lights as proof.

"Oh, right."

"If that's not enough reason for a party, some of the art students are celebrating portfolio review."

"Art students?"

I pointed to the Priya and Keesha in the corner. Cam and his girlfriend were in the kitchen, feeding meatballs to Petey.

Luka whistled between his teeth, and Petey's head snapped up and he came trotting over with his tongue out. Luka gave him a good ear rub and then pointed to the dog bed in the corner and Petey obliged.

"They seem so young. Those kids." Luka said. Those blue eyes met mine and then glanced away as if eye contact was too personal.

"Because they are."

For all I knew Luka, Keesha and Priya were the same age.

Hell, I wasn't much older than the girls. But Luka was old as snow. As ice.

"Anyway, it's a party." I lifted my wineglass in a cheers. He paused for a moment in one of those socially awkward moments he had, as if he wasn't familiar with holidays or the act of toasting. But finally, he lifted his glass toward me and took a sip.

And then he shocked me by draining the glass dry in one long swallow.

"Luka?"

"Yes. Happy New Year." His glance struck mine again, and there…right there in those clear blue depths was this new thing he could not hide.

It was carnal. And real. And very very hot.

Lust. His own that he didn't know what to do with.

That night on the fire escape. He couldn't forget it either.

And then it was gone, his gaze moving over the party. I watched him to see if maybe he looked at other women like that, unsure if I wanted him to be spreading that look around indiscriminately or if I wanted to hoard it all for myself.

Priya and Keesha were out on the dance floor, covered in a fine sheen of sweat, giggling happily into each other's arms, exuding a kind of easygoing sexiness. They were young and nubile, but Luka looked right through them.

He looked right through everybody on his way back to me.

It was for me, that look. Only for me. And I tried—I did, because it felt slightly wrong wanting him like I did and knowing what I knew about him at the same time and never *talking* about it—but that look of his…fuck.

I mean…fuck.

It went right to my head.

"I haven't seen you around lately," I yelled over the music.

"Busy," he said. "Brucellosis outbreak at a reindeer farm."

I must have looked at him blankly. "Foot rot," he clarified.

"Lovely," I said and wrinkled my nose.

He smiled, sadly, and looked down at his glass. "Yeah, I'm not very good at parties."

"You're fine," I said. "You just need more booze."

"In that case, can I have some more of this?" He lifted his empty glass and I found an open bottle of red stuck inside a tuba someone had been in the process of dismantling. Art students, I'm not kidding.

"Here." I refilled his glass.

He took a deep breath, his chest lifting under his canvas coat. He was a giant man. Tall and wide. Everything about him seemed made for some other world. Some other time.

I'd spent my fair share of time with my hands between my legs imagining him in the role of Viking marauder.

But today there was a shadow over his bright eyes. His shoulders were curled in the manner of the world-weary, the nearly defeated.

Swear to God, he was a walking heartbreak.

And he drank the second glass of wine nearly as fast as the first.

"You all right?" I asked, because I couldn't not.

"I am...the same as I always am," he said with a sigh.

"Is that good or bad?"

"It is...not sustainable."

"Luka—"

I stepped forward, through our bubble. Past my boundary and past his. I put my hand on his arm. The muscle beneath his shirt was tight and hard. He turned his face aside.

"Please, Rennie," he breathed. "Don't."

Okay. All right. I stepped back again, but the bubble was broken. Our boundaries a mess.

"There's some food." I pointed toward the small kitchen in the corner. The countertop was full of pizza and meatballs and mostly ignored veggie trays. The weed brownies and some fudge Keesha had made. Chili in a big pot on the back of the stove. "You should eat."

"You mothering me?" He even grinned when he said it, but he didn't mean it kindly. The words were sharp. Prickly. *Mind your own business*, that was what his tone said. *Leave me the fuck alone.* And that too was surprising. He was telling me to fuck off, largely, but I liked it.

"I wouldn't dream of it," I said. "But the brownies have drugs—"

"This is you not mothering me?"

"You want to puke red wine everywhere that's your prerogative."

I walked away. Because I wanted to fuck him and I wanted to take care of him and I wanted to hear his secrets. And I kind of wanted to tell him mine. My pain was attracted to his pain. And maybe some part of me wanted to heal him with my magic vagina or the power of a blow job or some shit.

And he knew it. And it was very clear at this moment – he wanted no part of it.

MINUTES LATER, OUT of the corner of my eye I watched Luka go upstairs with a bottle of wine and some of my joy in New Year's Eve went with him. Midnight came and went. Kissing all around. I gave Paulo some tongue and let him cup my ass, trying to cheer myself up, but it didn't work. John tried but I shut him down so he left. Paulo did too, once he realized nothing more was going to happen between us. Priya and Keesha left with one of the microbrew guys, which frankly was a surprise to me and to the gearheads. All of whom, after the show was over, hugged me and left.

I woke up one of my models who'd passed out on the couch and got her bundled up for home.

I called a cab for everyone, because no one could drive and this part of town wasn't entirely safe in this part of Minneapolis this time of night. And winter was here, a bright cold wind blowing through the city.

I shut the door behind everyone and switched the stereo back over to my music. Neko Case filled the empty spaces of my studio, surrounded my welding equipment and my scrap. The wings on the ceiling, a half-finished reminder of everything I was trying to forget tonight.

I tried not to imagine Luka up in that tiny bedroom.

Really, I tried not to think of him at all.

I imagined all the women in his life lining up to try to ease his pain. Girls on the bus unable to look away from the despair he couldn't begin to hide.

Stop, Rennie, just stop.

I gathered up an armful of beer bottles and kicked a balloon out of the way. I considered the wisdom of another weed brownie. I wished I'd just taken Paulo home, because my head was a mess tonight.

That's when the screaming started.

I TOOK THE metal steps up to the second floor, two at a time. My heart in my throat.

It was a woman screaming. In my loft.

Outside the bathroom, Luka had one of the grad students—Cam—pushed against the wall, his hand around Cam's neck. Cam was screeching and thrashing against the wall.

"Luka!" I cried, charging across the small hallway to pull on his arm, trying to get him to let go of Cam.

"Rennie!" The door to the bathroom was open and inside was Cam's sometime girlfriend Daphne, pulling up her leggings.

I glanced over at Cam and saw his pants were undone.

Shit.

"Luka," I said again, in a quieter voice. Luka wasn't looking at Daphne, or at Cam, but instead his eyes were locked on a small square of scoffed wood halfway between his feet and the bathroom. His aloofness now was just scary, his bland quiet face as he slowly strangled Cam was eerie. "Let him go."

"He was hurting her. She was screaming."

"He wasn't hurting me," Daphne came forward like Luka was a lion with a taste for blood. "I swear."

Luka did nothing.

"We were fooling around," Daphne said to me. "Just fooling around. Cam…didn't lock the door, which is so fucking typical—"

Cam made a garbled sound in his throat.

"Right." She closed her dark eyes. "And this guy came in, took one look at us and grabbed Cam by the neck."

I walked over and stood in the place where Luka was staring.

"You have to let him go," I said. "Now. He wasn't hurting her."

Luke blinked, his gaze lifted to mine. "He wasn't," he said. Again. Not quite a question, not quite a statement.

"No. He wasn't."

"She was screaming."

"What the fuck is wrong with you?" Daphne asked. "You can't tell—"

I lifted my hand, shutting Daphne up.

"He wasn't hurting her," I repeated.

Luka stepped back, his hand dropping from Cam's throat. Cam fell forward, braced on his knees, sucking in air.

"I'm sorry," Luka said.

"Fuck you!" Cam took a wild swing at Luka. Unbelievably it connected, snapping Luka's head back. I took a deep breath, ready to throw myself between them but Luka just took another step away.

"I'm really sorry," he said to Daphne, his cheek now florid.

"It's...okay," she stammered.

"The fuck it is!" Cam cried.

"You want to hit me again?" Luka asked Cam.

"Sort of."

Luka smiled.

"I wasn't hurting her." Cam said. "You can't...you can't tell people I'm like some kind of rapist—"

"I wouldn't. I won't." Luka stepped back again and then again, as if repelled by the word *rapist*, until he hit the wall.

"You're the one who fucking assaulted me." Cam finally tucked his junk back in his pants. His color was coming down and his skewed glasses slipped off his nose but he caught them in his shaking hands.

"You're right. You can tell anyone you want about that," Luka said. I didn't know if he was joking or not.

But that really would be a disaster. I doubted Cam knew who Luka was. Grad students tended to live in a self-absorbed bubble of delayed adulthood. And if Luka got arrested for assaulting Cam, combined with the interview with Anna on Sunday—the whole nightmare from four years ago would get pulled out of its grave.

"Cam," I stepped into the mix with my phone pulled out. "I'll call you and Daphne an Uber. Everyone has had too much to drink and he only thought he was helping."

Cam was not quite ready to calm down, but Daphne pulled him away.

"You did forget to lock the door," she muttered, which got her a glare from Cam.

Luka turned and went into his small room. The door closed behind him with a quiet little snick that managed to seem so loud.

I watched over the landing as Cam took the weed brownies. Like he was owed something and getting away with taking it.

Fucking grad students.

I sighed, waiting until they bundled up and left. I ran down the stairs and locked the door behind them.

Now. What to do.

I didn't want to be "mothering" him. Pushing care or worry on him when he so clearly didn't want it. But that had been a serious scene and if he were a woman, I wouldn't think twice about just making sure he was okay.

It was silent behind his door, so I knocked quietly.

"Luka?" I said. Deciding I would let him tell me if it wasn't my business.

"Come in."

I pushed open the door to find him standing at the one window in the room. The lights from the Holiday Gas Station across the street fell through the window and bathed him in red and blue. Giant flakes of snow hit the pane of glass and as they melted they appeared as spots running down his face.

Like tears. Like he was crying.

I bit back the words "are you all right" because they were lame. Useless.

A sleeping bag was stretched out in the corner, next to it a lantern and a stack of books. There were small things on the desk. A bunch of rocks. A tripod looking thing made out of wood.

On the back wall hung his rifle.

He sleeps on the floor, was somehow all I could think. I'd put a futon couch in the room but he chose to sleep on the floor.

"I'm sorry," he said, not looking at me.

"There's nothing to apologize for."

"I ruined your party."

"It was over. You didn't ruin anything."

"You've been really good to me. Most people who recognize me…they're not as nice."

He knows. He knows I know. And we're going to talk about it.

And I could imagine how people treated him once they knew who he was. Even though he was innocent, the story was so ugly most people couldn't get past that.

I could barely breathe.

He looked up at the ceiling, the corner of the room. Anywhere but at me. "I've liked it here. I've liked this place, with your art and equipment. I like the way it smells different if you've had a good day or a bad day."

"I'm not asking you to leave," I said. "I don't want you to leave."

"Thank you."

"Luka, if you want to talk. I'm here. I'll listen."

He glanced my way. "I've never had a friend, so I don't know if that's… I mean…is that we are?"

"Yes."

"That night...last summer? On the fire escape?"

I nodded because apparently we were talking about ALL the things and I didn't have any words.

"I think about it," he whispered. "I think about how you felt in my arms, so hot and so sweaty and so strong all at once. And how you kissed me. I think about it all the time."

"So do I."

He turned to look at me and those ice-blue eyes of his were far from inscrutable. They burned. I was surprised my clothes didn't smoke, my skin didn't sizzle under the heat of those eyes. I could read everything in them, how badly he wanted me and how badly he wanted to not want me.

"And then tonight..."

"I know," I said, stupidly. Inanely.

"Do you know what I thought?"

I nodded, still in the doorway, still holding the cold beer I'd thought he could press against his cheek. But he didn't look like he needed first aid. He needed something else entirely.

I ached to touch him. To hug him.

My throat was suddenly dry and small. The force of this man's repressed pain sliced right through me. To the bone.

"You thought he was hurting her," I whispered. Whispering seemed in order.

"She was screaming."

"It was..." Did he really not know? "It was a good scream."

"Good scream." He lips twisted into something rueful and angry. "That's a thing. That's a thing other people have. Other people get that. Good screams."

"Luka—"

"You know what I get?"

Me, I almost said.

"I get to think normal sex is rape. I get to choke a guy who was giving his girlfriend a good time in a bathroom at a party. I get to relive—"

He cut himself off, ruthlessly.

Helpless—really and truly helpless I lifted the beer. "Would you like this?"

Lame. So lame.

Our gazes met again, tangled.

"Would I like what?" His face was wide open. He...was wide open.

Me. Would you like me? Because I would like you.

"The beer."

I lifted it toward him and he took the bottle. Our fingers brushed and if he were any other man, I'd say he did it on purpose. A high school come-on. But his entire neck turned red.

"I thought you could press it against your—"

He twisted off the top and took one long swallow.

"—eye."

Or not.

"I've never seen that," he said, still looking out the window. "I mean...not like that."

"Sex?"

He shook his head.

"Luka? Are you..." Jesus. Was this really happening? "Have you ever had sex?"

He laughed. Lifted the bottle but then lowered it. He was nearly crawling out of his skin, I could see that. "You know...about me. I know you know."

All I could do was nod. I blew a thin stream of air out my lips, waiting. It was the two of us. Just the two of us. And the winter.

And nothing else.

The tips of his ears were bright red.

"What did you see?" I asked. "In the bathroom, what was Cam doing?"

"She was up against the sink. Her hands braced—" He put out his hands just for a moment, as if to show me. "—and he was behind her. He had one hand between her legs and the other was holding onto her hip. She was holding the sink and their…knuckles were white, they were holding on so hard. I swear…I only saw them for a half second but I saw their bones under the skin of their hands. She had her head tipped back, resting against his shoulder, and she was screaming."

"It was…it was an orgasm."

"That's normal? I mean…the screaming?" He took another deep drink from the beer. So flushed. So embarrassed.

"If it's good, yes. Some women scream."

"Women scream when it's bad too," he said.

Oh, God, that was the brutal truth. My heart cracked open. And I saw how narrow and terrible his experience with sex was. So terrible he kept himself locked inside it, in fear of spreading it around. In fear of being wrong. In fear of hurting someone else.

He just lived alone with his rotten knowledge.

"How?" he asked. "How does someone make someone else feel so good, they scream? How does a man do that to a woman? How is that possible?"

I stepped inside the room.

He watched me. Like I was shifting the balance of the earth, he watched me. Like I was a wild animal he tracked me with his eyes. His body coiled for…something.

Tomorrow I could blame this on the tequila, if I had to. The wine. The weed brownies. If he rejected me I'd grab the rest of the tequila and leave. I'd get blind drunk and convince myself this never happened. I'd go back to being a landlord and Luka would go back to being Luka.

But right now, I wanted him. To my muscle fibers, to my bones, the tips of my hair, I wanted him. And it wasn't just this moment.

The truth of tonight had its roots in the moment he came to my door with the ad in his hand.

"Do you want to? Make a woman scream like that? Make a woman feel that way?"

He didn't nod. Or move. But he listened to me with his whole body.

His whole soul.

I realized what made Luka different than any other man at this party or in my world. Any other man I had ever met.

His soul was right there. Just under the surface of his skin. All it took was one tiny scratch. One tiny shift and it was revealed.

He. Was revealed.

I didn't reveal myself. I never shook off my bracelets and my necklaces. Or smoothed the rough edges of my blistered hands, my shitty attitude. Not for anyone. At any time. The world I lived in was pretenses and walls. Half-truths and half-lies that everyone told everyone else.

So this, walking into this room with him, was like walking right into a forge. Hot enough to change everything.

It was terrifying.

And thrilling.

"Luka?"

"You're asking me if I want to make someone feel so good they scream?"

I nodded, walking into the space between the heat of him and the cold of the window. "Do you?"

"Yes," he gasped, blinking as if I were a bright light. "My God. Yes."

"I don't know what to do." He was glacier-still. Like he'd never moved. Like he never could. He'd been frozen and could not imagine heat that would thaw him.

"Let's start with a kiss." I reached for him, carefully. As if asking permission. "Can I—"

"Don't..." He grabbed my hand and the heat of him was searing. Not frozen at all.

His eyes, his touch, his skin—every part of him burned.

"Don't treat me like an experiment. Like I'm some poor sad victim and you're doing a good deed. Kiss me like the fire escape."

Thank GOD.

He was so tall I got up on my toes, my hands clenched in the warm flannel shirt he wore. I pushed my body into his, my lips onto his.

And he kissed me back. He kissed me like I could save his life. Like it was now or never.

His hands were in my hair, holding my skull. Holding me still for this nonstop plundering kiss. It was nearly hard, his teeth and his desperation but I absorbed that and returned it to him, softer. Quieter. Until the kiss gentled into something sustainable. Into something that wouldn't make us both cry at the end.

He stepped forward, his big body crowding mine against the desk. He pushed me up onto it, knocking off books and the small rocks. I spread my thighs and he stepped between them, pushing them wider with his size.

His giant fucking size.

His palms were rough, the callouses on his fingers catching in the fine strands of my hair, and the small licks of pain up and down my skull were a hot counter-tease against the sweet licks of his tongue.

He smelled like winter. Like ice and damp skin under layers of clothes. It was animal—that smell. He was animal.

And he was turning me into one too.

"Touch me," I said.

"I am." He clenched his fists, as if to show me, my hair in his hands.

"Touch me more." I pulled one of his hands out of my hair and put it on my waist. He might be inexperienced and slightly damaged but he wasn't slow. That big wide palm covered almost my entire rib cage, like I was caught in the trap of him, and slowly it slid up, raking over my jersey tank top to find my breast.

I gasped.

He gasped.

He squeezed me in his giant hand, a wild compression that almost hurt but backed off at the last second. His thumb found the hard point of my nipple and worried it. Ran over its contours, tested its strength as if he were memorizing me.

A current arced between his hand, my clit and my brain.

"Take off your shirt," I said between biting kisses of his lips.

"This is…this is about you. You and some good screams."

I laughed. Sweet guy. "You without a shirt is very much for me."

He leaned back without smiling. Without flirting. More of his soul, right there in his eyes.

His blunt fingers made short work of the soft red flannel shirt he wore and it dropped off his body. He grabbed the back of the neck of the black thermal he wore underneath it and pulled it over his head and tossed it down beside the sleeping bag in the corner.

His hair was static-y and wild and I smiled at him, patting it back down. My hands fell to his wide pale shoulders and I leaned back, taking him in.

It took me a second, distracted as I was by his being ripped to shit. Abs, chest arms. He was stunning. He was human anatomy brought to life.

And he was scarred. All over.

Slashes and nicks. Long red slices. Scar tissue that stood out, pink and red against his skin.

"What—" I traced the edges of what looked like a bullet wound on his shoulder, "—happened?"

"It's nothing." He leaned down to kiss my neck, my ear. It wasn't at all nothing but he didn't want to talk about it. "Can I take off your shirt?" he asked, changing the subject.

I lifted the black jersey tank over my head. My necklaces fell back against my bare skin. Cold and a little shocking.

Beneath the tank top I wore a black bra, and my jeans and boots. My tattoos. My bracelets.

"I like these," he said touching my longest necklace with the feather and the key. "Your decorations."

I very nearly put my hand over them, but I stopped myself. This was not a moment to stay hidden.

"Thank you."

His fingers slipped over the fine muscles of my arms and back, tracing their edges like boundary lines on a map. He covered the owl on my shoulder with his palm. Touched the arrow of geese flying south on the inside of my elbow. In the reflection of the window I saw him looking at the phoenix on my back.

My body had more tattoos, birds and otherwise. Across my knuckles of one hand was the word *want* and on the other hand *need*. A reminder of the only scale that really mattered.

"You like birds."

"My name is Wren." There were other reasons for the birds, but this mood should not be spoiled by such things.

"Rennie." His eyebrows went up. "I like that."

"So do I."

"You're like a fox," he said, his thumb running under the lace edge of my bra.

"A fox?" I smiled.

He smiled back, as if realizing that might be strange. "I like foxes. They're smart and sly and sleek. Ferocious and sweet in turns."

My heart curled up in my chest. That was easily the best compliment I'd ever gotten.

I popped the buttons on my pants. "Take off my boots."

And the big strong man with the scars of a perilous life I couldn't begin to understand knelt at my feet, unlaced my boots and pulled them off. His bright hair caught the moonlight and glowed white. Like bone.

So did his skin.

It was as if he had his own luminescence.

Crouching at my feet, his jeans pulled taut over massive thighs, he glanced up at me, waiting.

I pushed my black jeans down off my hips, the lace of my underwear got caught in the current and slipped down over my hips too. I got it as far as my knees and he took over, pulling them off my body.

I expected—I wanted him to come up off the floor and cover me with that big body. But he didn't. He stayed right there, looking up at me.

"You're so strong," he said, looking at me in pieces. My legs. My stomach.

"It's the work," I said. Forging and welding. Hammering out metal against an anvil. It was the kind of work that built muscles. I liked them, too.

"Touch me," I said.

"Where."

"Wherever you want."

His fingers found the small dips at my hips. He ran his hands down over the muscles of my legs and then back up, skirting toward the inside of my thighs, inching ever closer to my pussy.

I spread my legs, because I wanted to be touched there. Because I ached for his touch there.

But he paused.

What's wrong? I almost asked, but I knew what was wrong. At least the bare bones of it. And frankly, he didn't want to talk about what was wrong. That was the whole point of this. He was tired of what was wrong.

"Do it," I said.

He swallowed and nodded in the way of a man about to jump off a high dive. Part jubilation, part fear.

His thumb slipped up the tender skin of my inner thigh. So, slowly. Agonizingly slowly. So much I had to force my muscles to relax, I had to breathe through the near pain of the anticipation.

The tip of his thumb found the seam between my legs and I sucked in a breath. Not realizing I'd been holding it.

He ran his thumb over the seam, as high as it went, down

low, low until I had to spread my legs further so he could feel everything he wanted. If I were an exploratory mission, I would give him everything, show him all my secrets. His thumb touched the puckered flesh of my asshole and I jumped.

He jerked back, eyes wide. "I'm sorry."

"You just startled me," I said. "It's good, it's all good. Keep going."

His hands went up to my inner thighs. His thumb, starting at the bottom, worked its way back up to the top, without once ever slipping inside the lips. I was wet and hot and this slow agonizing touch was torture. I sighed and curled my hips toward him a silent invitation.

"Tell me what to do."

"Inside. Touch me inside."

He whispered the word back at me and slipped his thumb though the sleek folds of my pussy. It felt like an intrusion. Wide and dry, a calloused thumb that was not mine. Deliciously foreign.

"Oh, Jesus, you're so hot."

Yeah. I was. I tilted my head back, trying to catch my breath. And that thumb of his found my clit and I jumped again.

I could feel him about to retreat and I put my hand over his. "That's good. It feels good."

"It's...it's hard to know."

I imagine it could be if your entire sexual knowledge was as fucked-up as his.

"This..." I shifted his hand a little, until he found my clit again, "...is my clit. Touch it."

His thumb ran over it like it was a stone he was polishing. Around and around. Back and forth with a featherlight touch that was awesome until it was frustrating.

"Harder."

"I don't want to hurt you."

"You won't."

He applied harder pressure. More pressure. "I want to...see it."

I nodded. Swallowed. *Yeah, sure. Look all you like.*

His thumbs spread me open and I gasped again at the twinge of the tender skin being pulled taut.

"It's pretty." His breath a gust over the exposed pink flesh of my pussy. "I can smell you."

Oh, Jesus, why did that turn me on.

His face was so close, his eyes so rapt, I could not resist.

"Lick me."

He gave me one quick look for confirmation and whatever he saw in my face must have been enough, because he dipped his head and put the flat of his tongue against me.

My breath shuddered in my throat. The tide was rising in my body.

His hand slipped around me to grab my ass, one cheek in the palm of his hand like he needed to hold me still. Ground me for what was to come. He fell from his crouch to his knees with a heavy thunk against me. His face, the point of his nose, the knob of his chin, pushing into me.

His tongue found my clit in an ecstatic lush swipe and a return for more.

My body was bright hot coils now, connecting all over my body. The bottom of my foot, the top of my head, my clit and my fingers. Everything was connected and it glowed, now. He was the spark that lit it all up.

"Suck," I said. And he sucked me into his mouth. The pressure, internal and external, was electric. The flesh captured in his mouth he tortured with his tongue without any prompting from me.

But then I groaned and he let go.

"What?" I panted. "Why did you stop."

His face was wet, his eyes wild and dilated. "Am I hurting you?"

I shook my head. "Trust me. It feels good. Really, really good." I curled my leg over his shoulder, about to press him back into me. "Do you like it?"

God. Was I somehow forcing him to do this?

"Yes," he breathed. His eyes back on my pussy, his hand gripping my ass. I bent my leg, urging him back to me and he went willingly. Fell eagerly onto my body.

He sucked. Licked. Feasted. It was messy and wet and his enthusiasm was exciting. Thrilling even. No one had ever gone down on me with half this much enthusiasm.

Paulo had sex like there was a camera crew in the room.

Luka ran his nose through the folds as if memorizing my scent. As if he was looking for a way to experience more of me.

"Use your fingers," I said. "Inside."

"Inside?"

I showed him. I dropped my death grip on his hair and slipped my finger into my pussy. I was wet and hot and the pressure felt so good. "There."

"That…that looks so good."

"Yeah?" I stroked myself a little more, turning my wrist so I felt the pressure deep in my belly. I wanted to watch him touch himself. I wanted him to sit on the futon and jack off while I fingered myself until we both came. I wanted to be bent over this desk and plowed into the wall. I wanted to suck him into my throat. And I wanted to come on his face.

I wanted a lot of Luka.

I removed my finger and it was wet so I slipped it into my mouth, tasting myself. My desire. The radical and righteous humors of my body.

He watched with wide eyes and I took my finger and wiped it across his lips, my spit and my come making them shiny. His tongue swept over the slick I'd left behind.

"You do it."

Slowly, he pushed his finger deep inside me.

We both groaned, I bent forward. My dark hair over my face.

"You are so hot, inside." His finger was wide and blunt but I was seriously turned on and I needed more.

"Use another finger. Two…two fingers."

Another stretched me and I shook on the edge of the desk. "Fuck me with them." I opened my eyes and found him staring at me. "Do it."

A long slow push inside, so deep. So full and then an equally long slow retreat.

"God, oh…God, yes," I sighed. My hair was a tickle down my back and I swung it slightly because it felt so good.

Everything felt good.

And then he licked me. He licked me and fucked me with his big wide fingers and I lost myself in the pleasure. I curved myself around it, gathering more and more like a giant snowball made of the best feeling in the world.

I clutched the back of his head, pressing him deeper and harder into me and he lost his tentativeness. He lost his hesitation, and the force of his giant body was applied to mine.

"I'm going to come," I told him. "You're going to make me come."

He made a sound in his throat, wild and encouraging, but he

did not stop. Harder and faster until I was nothing but sparks burning in a night sky.

"There! There!" I fucked myself against him, greedy and punishing. Until finally, finally, it felt like I combusted from the inside. A series of chain reactions until I was sagging on the desk.

Sweating and aching and content.

I sat back, gave him some space, but not quite able to let go of him. I petted him. His hair, the beautiful soft skin of his shoulders.

He lifted his serious face to mine. Totally unaware that he wore me like a fine sauce all over his face. I smiled at him and cleaned him up with my fingers. My thumb touched his lip, the lush corner, and he turned slightly, capturing my thumb with his mouth.

He did the same to each of my fingers. I have never in my life felt so savored. And despite that orgasm, despite the completeness of it, I grew interested again.

"You screamed," he said.

"Good scream."

He braced his hand on the desk and got to his feet, my legs fell from his body, my hands slipped from his shoulders, until he was towering over me.

"That looks uncomfortable." I pointed to the erection in his jeans.

"It's always uncomfortable." He reached down to arrange himself in the tight denim.

"It doesn't have to be," I said, not coy, just matter-of-fact. "I can do to you what you just did to me."

"A blow job."

I smiled. "A blow job."

He hesitated like he didn't want to put me out. Like he was

asking to borrow my keys or something, and I wondered at the sparseness of his experience.

I very suddenly had to give him a blow job. A great one. I had to blow the back of his head off.

"Let me," I said to him, looking up at his eyes. "I want to."

I undid the button of his jeans and revealed the damp patch of underwear over the head of his cock. I bent forward and licked that cotton, tasted the salt of him, and he jerked against me. So turned on he wasn't going to last. His fingers cupped my head, touched my ear. Such soft strokes, barely there. But totally there at the same time.

His sweetness was too much.

I jerked his pants off and slipped the fabric of his briefs down under the length of his cock. He was big. Thick. Hot against my hand as I eased him away from his belly.

He made a sort of gasping/laughing sound in his throat and I smiled up at him.

Fun. What a thing to forget, that sex could be fun.

"Has anyone ever done this to you?" I asked.

He shook his head.

"Brace yourself, buddy," I whispered and slipped him into my mouth.

"Oh God!" he cried, his soft touches at my ear and neck suddenly turning into a hard grip. "Jesus. Rennie—"

He was uncircumcised and I pushed the skin back away from the head, running my tongue over the tip, finding that salty little slit and teasing it.

His knees buckled and I smiled against him.

I spit on him, lubricating as much as I could and I jacked my hand, twisting it, while sucking him as deep as I could into my mouth.

His hips started thrusting into my mouth and I let him control the rhythm. His hands cupped my head and I imagined what we looked like, him so tall and fair, fucking into my mouth.

It was hot.

He was groaning, pushing deeper, and I eased back a bit because he was huge and I didn't want to choke. That would undoubtedly freak him out.

I found his balls with my hand, contemplated sticking my finger up his ass, but there was no time. He was groaning and jerking into me and I squeezed his sack, just a little. Just enough and he cried out—roared, really.

Totally Viking.

And he came in thick spurts down my throat. Across the top of my mouth.

When he stilled, I slipped back away from him, my lips slightly sore from being stretched and I suddenly wanted to fuck him. I wanted the pleasure/pain of that girth inside me.

He reeled back, away from me, totally unsteady on his feet.

Wide-eyed he stared at me and I wiped my lips. He groaned and reached for me, pulling me up off the desk so he could kiss me.

He was cleaning me up again, like we were animals. Softly and sweetly he stroked my back, my hair. I stepped forward and he was so agreeable he moved backward, and I walked us to the futon, where we collapsed in a messy heap.

Sweat was cooling on my body and the loft was impossible to keep warm in the Minneapolis winter, so the chill coming from the cold window behind me made me shiver.

"You're cold," he said.

"I am."

Not cold enough to get my clothes. Or to leave. I was cold

enough to drape myself against him and let his body heat against the front of me do battle against the cold at my back.

"Here." He shifted and I shifted with him, like a baby possum or something. He grabbed the sleeping bag on the floor and unzipped it, snapping it out around us so it covered us like a cape.

"Better?" he asked.

I nodded. Tequila. Weed brownies. A shattering orgasm. The weight and depth of the conversation our bodies had been having while our mouths could not talk at all—it all suddenly piled on top of me.

"I should go," I said with a yawn.

"I don't want you to."

"If I stay I'll fall asleep."

He shifted us sideways on the futon, arranging us face to face, the sleeping bag over us. A warm flannel cocoon that smelled like campfire and Luka.

"What are these?" he asked, his fingers sifting through my necklaces. The feather. The key. The shell. The bead. The tiny little silver skulls. The six quarters. All bronzed.

"Found things," I said, my eyes drifting shut. "Just…found things."

"You found quarters, bronzed them and made necklaces out of them?"

"They were in my father's pocket when he died."

He stilled. I stilled. I had never told anyone that before and he took the words like he knew that.

Gently he untangled the chain from my hair, straightened them all around my neck and put his big hand over them. Like they were a secret both of us were keeping.

I WOKE UP to a room so cold, when I exhaled I could see my breath. The snow blanketed the window, making it impossible to tell what time it was. It seemed dawn-ish. Murky and half-lit. But thanks to all the snow it could be noon.

I was also alone on the futon.

Downstairs there was a thunk and a clink and I finally registered the smell of coffee being made.

Shivering, I pulled on my pants and my tank top, but still freezing I grabbed Luka's flannel shirt from the floor and put it on.

It was a dress on me. No amount of sleeve rolling could make it fit, but it was warm. So it stayed.

Luka was cleaning up the mess from the party. Walking around the fringes of my shop with a garbage bag, gathering red plastic cups. He wore the jeans from last night and the black Henley that fit him like another skin.

Petey snuffled through the corners, licking up chips and meatballs that had fallen on the floor.

My mouth went dry at the sight of Luka. My entire body responded with a pulse of heat that made me blush and sweat. Uneasy and unsure. I felt impossibly young in this moment. Younger than I had in ages. Maybe ever.

My equilibrium was all off and I didn't know how to put it right.

"You don't have to do that," I said from the staircase.

He started at the sound of my voice and looked up at me. Inscrutable again. There was no sign of the man from last night, holding my head still as he fucked my mouth. No sign of the man who licked my fingers clean. Who ate me out with such life-changing enthusiasm.

He was aloof Luka again. Careful and wary.

Hmm, I thought. This was not going to be a familiar morning after.

"I'm happy to do it," he said. "There's coffee."

On the edge of the small kitchen's counter was the wooden tripod thing with a suspended linen pouch. There was a jar of coffee beneath it.

"That's a coffeemaker?" I asked.

"It is."

I took the jar and poured some into a clean red plastic up. "Is it from a museum?"

His lip curled slightly. "It makes very good coffee."

After a sip I had to agree.

The silence was broken by the soft thunks of red plastic cups hitting each other in his bag and the howl of the wind around the building.

We were very alone.

"Why haven't you finished those wings?" he asked, pointing up at the huge wings hanging from the ceiling. The Christmas lights were off and they looked sad up there, unfinished.

"Too many other paying projects," I said, but it was hardly the truth.

Luka watched me for a long time as if waiting for me to elaborate, and I realized with a start that he knew I was lying. And that he was hurt by that.

And disappointed.

He went back to cleaning up, the tips of his ears red. His signal—that he was feeling something huge.

Fuck.

"My dad and I were working on them when he died," I said. "My dad was a welder by trade and while he was real proud of me and my art, he never worked with me. But I'd finally convinced him to do the wings with me. He did the frame and I was doing the detail work and that's...that's as far as we got."

I took another sip of my coffee. People asked about the wings all the time. Every model, every other artist. The guys from the shop down the street—but I never told anyone the truth.

Except Luka.

"How did he die?" he asked.

Jesus, he was really asking for everything, wasn't he?

"New Year's Eve six years ago. We went to a corner store in our neighborhood to get some chips for me and some cigarettes for him, and some meth-head held the place up. Dad got shot."

"You were there?"

I nodded.

"I'm sorry."

"Thank you."

"And your mother?"

"I had no mother. She...left when I was a kid. It was just me and Dad."

"I'm sorry for that too," he said.

"Me too," I said. "It would have been nice if she'd stuck around."

He tossed another cup in the bag. And then another. They made a hollow, wet sound.

"You really don't have to do that," I said.

"My father took us into town a few times a year," he said as if I hadn't spoken. As if he had to say this now, right now, or it would never be said. The words ran from his mouth as if escaping a fire. "Different towns for different supplies. He rarely went to the same place twice in one year. He was obsessed with us being found. In making sure it never happened."

I held my breath and he was holding his. The moment strung

like a filament about to break between us.

"But we always went to this town just outside an Indian reserve in Canada. There was a woman there and when he decided I was old enough, he paid her to have sex with me."

"I'm sorry," I said, because it sounded awful.

"He told me before I went in that the woman—I didn't even know her name—she shouldn't enjoy it. That I had to make *sure* she didn't enjoy it. He told me the clitoris was the devil's doorbell and I nodded, like I understood such a thing. Like I even knew what a clitoris was. We lived out in the bush, I barely knew what a goddamn doorbell was. He told me that if she moaned, if she asked me to do something I should hit her until she shut up."

"Oh my God."

"And then he just…shoved me into this room with this woman. And I was so freaked out. Like…" He stared up at my wings. "So freaked out. I couldn't do it. I couldn't even look at her. But she took his money and I pretended like I did it and we went back every year. Her name was Cindy. She had two kids. A granddaughter."

There was literally nothing I could say. So I was silent.

"Then a few years ago he told me I wasn't going on that supply run and I was…" He tossed another cup in the bag. "I was so relieved. He was gone for a long time. Two weeks. And fuck…it was the best two weeks of my life. It was just me and the work and…it was perfect. I even started to think he was dead. And that I could leave this house we'd made. I could go anywhere. Do anything. But…then I just kept remembering how he told me that if we were found it would be bad. And suddenly being found seemed scary. It seemed impossible. I had no idea how to act in those towns we went to. How to live or work. I hated the way people stared at us and whispered about us. I hated the way I looked compared to them. Like some hairy, wild animal. That's how I felt, like he'd made me the perfect wild animal. And the only thing I was good for was this life of ours. This weird, fucked-up off-the-grid life that was so hard. And so grim. And so lonely."

I remember interviewers asking him why he didn't just leave and he'd said that he didn't know he could. I saw the truth of that now, the terrible invisible prison he lived in.

"One day I was checking the traps and I came back and I could tell, even before I went into the house, that something was different. It smelled…all wrong. Like blood. And other things. I went in and the girl was there. Anna. A lump on the bed, bloody and naked."

I was breathing hard. I wanted to tell him to stop. That I knew. That I'd watched the news, but this wasn't about me needing to know these things, it was about him needing to say them. Out loud. To me. To someone.

"She moaned and Dad hit her—his knuckles were already bruised and bloody like he'd been hitting her for days. And then he said he brought her for me. Because he knew I didn't like the old lady outside the reservation. I…" He shook his head, sagging a little. "He kidnapped that poor girl for me."

"No, he did it for himself. And that was just part of his shitty justification."

He seemed to run out of steam, like the clockwork mechanism that had been wound up and kept him moving just stopped and he was mired in guilt and grief all over again.

"You fought your dad," I said, remembering the news reports in detail. "You knocked him out and you grabbed Anna and walked sixty miles to Elk Falls." A town of less than 80 people. He walked into a liquor store with a Canadian Girl Guide in his arms who'd been kidnaped from a campground five days earlier.

"I didn't understand what was happening," he said. "At the hospital and then at the police station. I didn't realize that people thought I'd taken her. I didn't understand why I was being handcuffed and why the police were yelling at me. And then I realized they wanted my father. So, I took them to my father. They arrested him. Anna's family got me a lawyer. I couldn't believe it. They said I was a victim too and they fought for me. For months. And then after the trial, the police and all those people…they just let me go."

"Just…like that?"

"Just like that. There was a social worker who gave me her card, who told me I could contact her at any time. That she would do what she could to help me, and I took her up on that. Ended up in Minneapolis with the big game vet. And here." He glanced over at me, shy with his blue propane eyes.

To me.

"I'm glad you're here," I said.

"Me too."

He threw a few more cups into the bag and I shifted off the stool and walked toward him. I knew he was watching me, even as he threw more garbage in the bag. I knew he was aware of me, just like I was aware of him.

Closer I crept, waiting to see if he would tell me to stop. Tell me no. But he didn't. He set the bag down and turned to face me. So big and wide and beautiful and hurt.

I put my arms around him, his thick waist. And he slipped his arms over my shoulders, pulling me close until I was in the cocoon of him. I wished I was big enough to do the same for him.

"Thank you for last night," he said into my hair.

"Thank you," I said and squeezed him closer.

I felt his cock against my stomach, growing harder.

"Sorry. I'm just…attracted to you."

I shook back my hair and grinned at him. "How lucky for me. As I am attracted to you too."

He touched the hair along my face, my cheek. The corner of my lips.

"I feel like all I know how to do is be alone," he said. "It's the only real skill he gave me. And I'm so tired of it."

"You were at a party tonight," I said. "That's not alone."

He smiled at me, humoring my lame attempt at humoring him.

"You're not alone now," I told him. "I'm here."

If this were a movie I might take off my shirt. Show him how not alone he was.

But it wasn't a movie.

And this man was complicated in a way I could not take lightly. I could not diminish.

But he seemed frozen somehow. Stuck.

Fuck, maybe it was like a movie.

I took off my shirt.

His ears went red again. His eyes went wide.

I peeled off my bra, and my brown nipples got hard in the cold of the loft.

"I'm a virgin," he said.

My heart thunked, like bad plumbing when you turn on the water for the first time in a long time. Like it wasn't quite sure it could handle what was expected of it.

"Okay. Take off your shirt."

His eyes flared and then he grabbed his shirt at the neck and all but tore it off his body.

"Your pants," I said.

And those came off just as fast. He stood there naked but for a pair of socks. His cock growing harder as I watched. Suddenly Petey came sniffing around, his nose going right for Luka's junk, and we both laughed.

"Uh-oh," Luka said, covering himself with his hand and shifting sideways. "Go lie down, Petey."

Petey whined once and did what he was told.

I met Luka's eyes and we were both smiling. Our hearts light despite the darkness we came with. And I was almost grateful to Petey for showing us that we had both inside us.

"Let's go upstairs," I said.

"Race you."

He won because I took a detour to the bathroom and my big box of condoms. With one in my hand, I charged into the room, and he pulled me onto the futon, into the blankets. Our skin was chilled and we ran our hands over each other, warming ourselves with our breath and our own heat.

I cupped his cock in my hand and he sucked in a breath, just as I did when his fingers found my sleek folds. He was dry and I was wet so I shifted forward and slipped my leg over his hips, so his cock was pressed up against my pussy. He ran through my folds, not inside me, but against me.

"Oh my God." His head rested against my shoulder, his breath along my breast. "You're so hot. So wet."

I hummed something in my throat, some nonsense, because the head of his cock nudged my clit and my brain was buzzing with this pleasure. I held him against me with my hand, sliding myself along the hard ridge of his cock, and slowly he found the rhythm, moving in a little tiny thrusts against me. We were both slippery and hot, our fingers tangled. He licked my breast. Sucked the nipple into his mouth.

"That feels so good."

"Yes," he hissed.

He was a virgin and I was clean and on the pill but still I put the condom on him, watching him watch my hands as if I was performing some mysterious ritual. And then I slid him down so on the push up, he slipped inside me.

"Oh God!" he cried. His eyes wide.

For a second I couldn't move. He was big and wide and I was not totally ready, but the stretch and pull of him felt good. Felt real.

In years of feeling as little as possible, it felt good to feel all this pleasure and the laughter and the grief and yes, a little of the pain.

"Are you…okay?" he asked. Those ears of his almost neon.

"Yes," I said. "Yes."

"I'm going to… I want—"

I knew what he wanted. I pushed him over so he lay flat on his back and I got up astride him so he was buried all the way inside me. And now I was ready. Now I was wet and swollen and still it took me a second to get used to him inside my body.

His hands on my hips were so careful, so gentle. And his eyes on my face were completely reverent.

"You ready?" I asked, smiling at him, my heart somehow too full and not full enough.

He nodded, his neck flushed, his eyes hot.

Slowly, I lifted up and then down. I rocked forward and then back. I watched his face and saw what he liked. I moved his hand to my clit to show him what I liked.

We were hushed and not at all hurried. I leaned forward, pressed my chest to his and he wrapped his arms around me, so tight I could barely move. He thrust forward and I thrust back and we found our way.

"Yes," he moaned. "Yes. Oh, God…yes!" His hips lifted up into mine hard and fast and I braced myself on my knees, letting him fuck me the way he needed. And when he was done I fucked him the way I needed. I pushed his thumb against my clit and braced myself against his shoulders.

When I came it was with a sob.

I could feel him pushing my hair back, petting it over my shoulders. Touching me in such a complete and casual way.

And then he stopped.

"You're crying."

"Because it felt…really good." I shook out my hair and smiled at him, a tear falling across my lips and onto my tongue, where its salty-sweet taste dissipated.

"You're not hurt?" he asked.

"I'm not hurt. I'm…happy."

"I am too." I knew how deeply new that was to the both of us.

I fell forward and wrapped my arms around him. And he wrapped his arms around me. He was still inside me. Not as hard, but not at all soft either.

I wanted to put him in my mouth to find out what the two of us tasted like on his cock. I wanted to climb up his body, so he could taste us on me.

I wanted to lie on my stomach and feel him cover me like a living, breathing blanket. I wanted to take a shower and hear the story behind every scar on his body.

I wanted to draw him and make castings of his legs and arms.

I wanted a great deal of Luka Samuelson.

But what I said was "It's New Year's Day."

"I guess so."

"Have you ever had posole?"

"I don't know what that is?"

"It's a soup. My dad made it for me for breakfast on special occasions. How about you and Petey come over to my house—it's warmer. And I'll make you some posole."

"I don't know how to do this," he said.

"Well, so far we're doing sex and posole. And I think you're pretty amazing at that. Unless you don't like soup—"

"I like soup."

"Then we're rock stars."

"I feel...you know so much about me. I don't know anything about you."

"That's funny. I feel you know so much about me and I know so little about you."

I crossed the ruins of all those walls that usually surrounded me. I crossed the pain and horror of his past and I put my arms around his thick stomach. I laid my head against his strong chest.

This is how it begins, I thought.

He lifted my chin and kissed me. Like the end shot in some cheesy movie I watched as a kid. I should scorn such care. I should make some joke. But those walls were in ruins and so I sighed into his mouth. My cold body melting into the heat of him.

His hand landed on my shoulder, a finger tangling in the thin chains and cords of my necklaces.

"I want to hear about these things," he said, running his fingers over the quarters my father had in his pocket when he died. The feather from my mother's coat, hidden in the back of the closet like a secret we didn't talk about. The pearl I found here in the shop when I first bought it, wedged in a crack in the cement.

His calloused fingers stroked the sensitive skin beneath the necklaces. I felt my skin. My blood. I felt myself rise to his touch. I looked down and saw his fingers there among my memories. And I felt my soul rise to his touch.

"What did you call them? Your found things?"

I nodded, oddly moved. Unable to speak past this lump in my throat. He kissed me as if he knew. And he probably did. Luka was a man like that.

"I think," he said against my lips, "in the end, we are all found things."

Excerpt

THE HEART OF IT

O N THE OUTSIDE rich and successful Gabe Paterson has everything.

No one would guess the ghosts from his past are tearing him apart.

Desperate, he reaches out to Elena – a resilient call girl, with her own childhood scars – for help.

In their moments of honesty, the two forge the most surprising relationship of their lives.

But will they be brave enough to make it into something more?

SHE SLIPPED HER hand into his, curled the back of it against his palm like some warm trusting thing, and his body exploded into physical life. He felt his blood vessels, the blood thudding through them, the twitch of his hamstrings. The ache of his lungs. He felt all of it. All of himself. In the presence of her.

"Mike?"

He lifted his eyes to hers, a starving man, helpless under her brown gaze. No doubt he was revealing all of his desire. No doubt he was practically drooling.

Mike. Right. That's me.

Before he could say anything she leaned forward and short-circuited his brain with the warmth of her cheek inches from his. "Would you like to go downstairs?" she whispered in his ear. "To my room?"

Speechless. Shaking. He nodded, once. A quick jerk.

Yes, yes please God, yes.

The heat of his desire, the way it bordered on desperation, terrified him. Panicked him.

And that horrific miasma of fear and desire, that was where the snarling monsters of his past lived. It was the ugly stew they called home.

Last year he'd gone to this counselor to try and get help with his drinking. Well, with the drinking and the sex. And the counselor told him that the drinking gave him distance when it came to sex, and that if he wanted to have sex without getting hammered, he'd have to come up with his own way of distancing himself. Of disengaging from the fear and then managing the desire.

So what he tried to do was make a nice cold hard slice between his body and his mind. He wasn't very good at holding onto the distance, but for the moment, it allowed him to sit back, pull his wallet out, and throw a fifty dollar bill on the bar.

They stood together, and he grabbed his coat, the scarf he'd felt so stupid about.

Was that a half hour ago? Less. How had this happened? How could she seem so casual when he felt like a giant giraffe, all knees and elbows and an awkward raging hard-on that he covered with his jacket folded over his arms.

She led him out of the bar, and before he could stop them, his eyes traced the round edges of her ass, the curve—top and bottom hugged so perfectly by that dress.

I want her, he thought. I want her so bad.

And then: Please let that be enough.

Also by M. O'Keefe

Everything I Left Unsaid
The Truth About Him
Burn Down the Night

About the Author

I hope you enjoyed WE ARE ALL FOUND THINGS and the rest of this amazing anthology! If you are inclined I hope you'll consider leaving a review (good or bad) on Goodreads or Amazon! Reviews help readers find books and as an author (and a reader) I appreciate every one of them.

Please sign up for my newsletter at www.molly-okeefe.com to get release day news, free reads and other fun giveaways!

M. O'Keefe can remember the exact moment her love of romance began—in seventh grade, when Mrs. Nelson handed her a worn paperback copy of *The Thorn Birds*. Writing as Molly O'Keefe, she is a USA TODAY bestselling author of over thirty novels. She lives in Toronto, Canada, with her husband and two kids.

CPSIA information can be obtained
at www.ICGtesting.com
Printed in the USA
LVOW04s1803241016
510064LV00011B/1411/P

9 781940 078229